RESCUING LACEY

REBECCA HEFLIN

RESCUING LACEY

REBECCA HEFLIN

Cover Design by The Killion Group, Inc.

Published in the United States of America by:

Rebecca Heflin Books, LLC

Gainesville, Florida

Second Edition

ISBN: 9781735055183

www.RebeccaHeflin.com

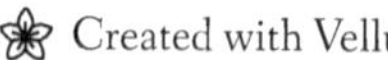 Created with Vellum

ACKNOWLEDGMENTS

To Ron.
Thank you for providing the experiences
that inspire me.

Thanks to the original ensemble of beta readers for this book back in 2011, when it was first written: Lynda, Yvonne, Susan, Suzie, and Renee. Your feedback was invaluable.

Thanks to my friend, neighbor, and small aircraft pilot, Jay, for taking the time to brainstorm over aircraft mechanics, malfunctions and flight mishaps. His knowledge and insight was greatly appreciated. Any mistakes in the depictions are mine alone. Sadly, Jay lost his battle with cancer a few years after *Rescuing Lacey* was published.

And thanks to my readers for making *Rescuing Lacey* one of my most popular books.

QUOTE

In your soul are infinitely precious things that cannot be taken from you.
— Oscar Wilde

PROLOGUE

She tried to run. One of the men grabbed her from behind by her ponytail and jerked her backward, then forced her to drop to her knees. The men circled her like a pack of wild dogs, snapping and snarling at their prey, their breath a fetid cloud as they shouted at her in their native tongue. The smell of their unwashed bodies mixed with the more sinister stench of bloodlust engulfed her.

One of her captors seized her camera, clawing at her neck and yanking the strap so hard she thought her neck might break before the strap gave way. Wrenching her head backward by her ponytail, another exposed her throat to the jagged bite of a machete. She didn't beg for her life. There'd be no point. Closing her eyes, she prayed for a quick death.

CHAPTER ONE

*F*ucking *frogs,* Lacey thought. *I can't believe I've been reduced to shooting frogs.* "I hate frogs," she muttered, drawing unwelcome attention from the man seated next to her.

The Cessna Grand Caravan banked, tipping the wings so the ground looked as if it were rising up to meet it. Lacey gazed out of the window at the lush green landscape of Costa Rica, her home for the next two months—or longer if she couldn't get the shots she needed.

The airport resembled something out of a B-movie. As the plane bumped onto the runway she expected to see a couple of aged Hummers emerge from the jungle filled with AK-47-toting drug runners. Meager though the airport was, boasting only a small terminal consisting of a row of benches covered by a tin- roofed overhang, it wasn't the worst airport she'd seen.

She stepped off the plane and into the heavy, humid air. If it was this hot in November, July must be a killer. Hitching her equipment bag up on her shoulder, she watched as a couple of men unloaded the rest of the luggage, tossing it carelessly onto the pockmarked tarmac, confirming her decision not to check her equipment bag. Spotting her army-green duffle, she walked over to pick it up.

"Lacey Sommers?"

"That's me." Lacey didn't look toward the voice as she bent to pick up the bag and toss the bulk over her other shoulder. A hand slid beneath the strap and she turned to glare at the offending appendage. The hand was large, square, and calloused. Capable. Powerful.

"I'll get that."

She was rarely caught by surprise, but this was one of those times. She gazed directly into a pair of aqua-green eyes as clear and deep as the waters off the Costa Rican coast and suppressed an unexpected frisson of desire.

"Why?" was all she could think to say, her eyes narrowing behind her sunglasses.

"Well, because I have two free hands, and because it's the polite thing to do." A half smile accentuated the dimple in the man's chin. His windblown, honey-blond locks were highlighted by nature's hand. Her sister would kill for those highlights.

"I'm Luke Hancock. I'll be your pilot, your driver, your guide, and—" He took the duffle from her as if it were packed with feathers and tossed it onto his shoulder. "—your bellmanduring your stay in Costa Rica."

He stood a good head taller than her five-foot-eight frame and had all the markings of a beach bum: tanned, sun-kissed hair, board shorts, faded Oakley T-shirt, flip-flops, diver's watch, and even the cliché ratty hemp friendship bracelet. Just another overgrown boy, like most of the men she'd encountered in her adult life. The kind of men who made a profession out of avoiding responsibility.

"I'm quite capable of carrying my own bag." She planted her feet in a belligerent stance, one hand on the strap of her equipment bag, her other lifted to her forehead blocking the sun. She didn't expect to be catered to. She'd been self-sufficient during her assignments, and she had no intention of changing that now.

"I've no doubt you are capable." Luke didn't know what he'd been expecting, but this was definitely not it. The name Lacey Sommers, and all it implied, didn't fit the woman standing in front of him. There was certainly nothing frilly about her. Tall, tanned, and muscular, she couldn't be accused of being girlie, but neither was she the care-worn, jaded photographer he'd envisioned. A knot of desire formed in his stomach.

Dressed in an army-green camisole, khaki cargo shorts, and a pair of worn hiking sandals, she appeared quite capable . . . of many things. The color of her eyes, hidden behind a pair of dark sunglasses, piqued his curiosity.

Her only adornments were a heart-shaped garnet that hung from an antique-gold chain and an enormous Breitling watch strapped to her left wrist. He recognized the expensive brand as one he often saw on his ex-father-in-law's wrist. No engagement or wedding ring, but there must be a rich boyfriend in the picture. A girl didn't buy those things on a staff photographer's salary.

"Let's get one thing straight, Mr. Hancock, I'm no helpless female. I don't need pampering."

She lifted that Breitling-adorned hand to tuck a golden strand of hair behind her ear. The simple movement caused a firm bicep to ripple beneath the smooth bronze of her skin. That's when he noticed the vicious white scar that ran across her neck; jagged at the edges, yet straight and about three inches long, very near the carotid artery.

Her wavy hair coiled tantalizingly around her throat as if to caress the scar. He swallowed hard, wondering how such a lovely neck had been so brutally desecrated.

Dragging his gaze from the scar, he said, "That's good," before striding off toward his Jeep without waiting for her.

"I'm not the pampering type."

———

After a perilous ride through the jungle in the open-air, doorless Jeep, fording flooded streams, and bouncing over muddy potholes that could have swallowed compact cars, Lacey's right side was covered in water, mud, and who knows what else. Not to mention, her neck felt like she'd been riding a bucking bronco.

She began to wonder if her editor were secretly trying to get rid of her when they finally arrived at the gates of a resort tucked among strangler figs and Kapok trees, still dripping from a recent rain. The sign, adorned with an enormous Blue Morpho butterfly, read MARIPOSA LODGE.

According to their website, the lodge had been built on a thousand acres of pristine tropical lowland rain forest three hundred fifty feet above the point where the Gulfo Dulce and the Pacific Ocean collided. The eco-resort offered visitors a peaceful retreat—something she hadn't had in she couldn't remember how long. But she wasn't there to relax. She was there to save her career. If she screwed this up, she'd be relegated to shooting screaming kids on Santa's lap.

The last conversation with her editor still rankled. When she'd gone in for her assignment, she'd been hoping for the story on gorilla poaching in the Congo. She should have known better after the previous incident in Africa, but she'd never expected this.

Not usually one to toot her own horn, she hadn't hesitated to trumpet away under the circumstances. None of her arguments had worked on him.

"Look, Lacey, you're the best photographer around, but I can't have a repeat of Tanzania." Simon shook his head, his bushy eyebrows drawn together in a unibrow.

"But frogs! Christ. It's humiliating." There was *no way* she was telling Simon about her fear of frogs, that the slimy little things gave her the willies.

"Damn sight less humiliating than a meltdown." His voice became placating. "Listen, go down to Costa Rica, get some great shots of the poison dart frogs and any other wildlife you come across and we'll see. Should be a nice, easy assignment for you. Maybe you can even squeeze in a little R & R while you're there."

"Come on, Simon, please—"

"Damn it, Lacey, this is it. You either do this, or . . . you're out. I'm sorry." He'd held his palms up in resignation.

Luke's big hand jostled her shoulder, snapping her back to the present. "Hey, Sommers, we're here."

No sense brooding over her situation anymore. *It is what it is.* She'd get the best damn pictures of frogs the magazine had ever seen and then she'd go back to the high-risk, high-reward assignments she preferred.

———

"*B*uenos dias, José. *Como estâ usted?*" Luke asked one of the resort's friendly employees as he and Lacey stepped into the lobby's relatively dim interior.

"*Pura vida,* Luke."

"*Bueno*. José, this is Lacey Sommers. She'll be staying with you for several weeks." Turning to Lacey, he said, "José will take it from here. We have an early start tomorrow so get some sleep. I'll meet you here at five-thirty a.m. And don't worry, you'll be awake." The corners of his mouth lifted in a slight smile.

She'd taken off her sunglasses, and for the first time Luke saw her eyes were an indigo blue of infinite depth, rimmed by lashes so thick they looked like they belonged in one of those cosmetic ads. He stared into her eyes longer than he'd intended. *Christ*, he thought as he dragged a hand through his hair, *like the Bahamas' great blue holes, a man could get lost in those depths.*

Lacey shifted from one foot to the other. Luke's intense stare made her uneasy. She returned his gaze with a bravado she didn't actually feel. He stood within inches of her and although he wasn't touching her, the sensation was just as disconcerting as if he had been. The heat rolled off him in waves, carrying the clean, salty scent of the beach.

"Right." She narrowed her eyes, something she did whenever it seemed like someone was trying to pull something over on her. How did he know she would be awake at that hour?

"See you." Without a backward glance, Luke strode out to his Jeep with the easy gait of an athlete.

She had to admit, he had a nice ass, even in those baggy board shorts. "Uh, José, can I have coffee in the morning?" "*Claro*, of course," José said with a bright smile, watching her watch Luke.

Busted. Damn. "Uh, thanks. At that hour it will be the only thing standing between me and unconsciousness."

———

Lacey surveyed her new living quarters. Her thatched-roof bungalow could only be described as rustically opulent. Built of bamboo and mangrove, both sustainable hardwoods, the interior gleamed as if it were polished copper. The floor-to-ceiling screened walls offered a one-eighty view of the turquoise water below.

Mosquito netting draped two queen beds, while ceiling fans whirred in the heavy air. Despite its openness, once occupants crossed over the threshold of their bungalow, they had total privacy. That same privacy extended to the wraparound deck.

Nestled in the middle of a private nature reserve, the resort could boast one of the top spots among the world's eco- resorts, but it wasn't for the faint of heart. There was no TV, telephone, radio, internet, air conditioning, or blow dryer. Electricity could be hit or miss, with the lodge depending on solar panels and a biodiesel-powered generator.

Hence, the box containing her laptop, a satellite phone for internet access, and a solar-power charging station had already been delivered to her room. All the necessary accoutrements to upload her photos and send them to her editor in New York.

She unpacked the box and set up her work station on a modest bamboo desk that faced the expansive deck. The deck boasted a private outdoor shower, hammock, and lounge chairs. She stepped outside, the cooling breeze from the water a respite from the heat. The spectacular view of the ocean could prove a little distracting if she weren't careful.

"Speaking of distractions," she mused aloud. Luke Hancock could prove more than a little distracting. He could prove to be downright dangerous, especially for her. Why did she seem to be always drawn to the sexy heartbreakers, the ones who were all form and no substance? Despite her feigned disinterest, being near him set her heart racing and scattered coherent thought.

"Keep your mind on your work, Sommers," she chided. "Get it done and get out of here."

A cool shower and dinner in her bungalow sounded like the perfect way to wind down. Unless you liked to party with iguanas, the nightlife around here looked to be nonexistent, which was probably a good thing since she had to be up at the butt-crack of dawn.

The shower, like the ocean side of the bungalow, was screened, giving the occupant a view of the rain forest.

"Jesus!" As she reached for her towel she nearly lost her footing on the slick stone floor. A squirrel monkey watched her with grave curiosity.

"What the hell?"

The tiny monkey, whose head markings resembled Eddie Munster, continued to stare at her with no sense of shame. "Pervert." Wrapping the thick towel around her, she stepped out of the shower and sighed. "This is going to be a long assignment."

———

On time as usual, Tony pulled into the narrow dirt driveway adjacent to the beachfront house, right behind the Jeep.

Luke smiled. He could always count on Tony.

Best friends since Luke's family started spending their winters in the cozy house at the tip of the Osa Peninsula, he and Tony were thick as thieves.

For years, he and Tony had spent their days swimming the uninhabited beaches of the Peninsula and running the palm swamps and virgin forests with Luke's twin sister, Lisa, tagging along.

A deep welcoming bark from Luke's new resident greeted the men as they strode toward the house.

"Hey, *amigo*." Tony wore his perpetual grin. Dark-skinned, not only from his Hispanic and Boruca heritage but also from his time spent in the tropical sun, Tony's toothy grin sparkled stark white in contrast. Hair black as pitch with eyes to match and a stocky muscular body, Tony was a hit with the women. Not that Tony noticed. He only had eyes for his wife of five years, Alejandra, or Allie, as she liked to be called.

"*Hola*." Luke clapped Tony on the back.

The two ambled toward the kitchen door, the dog's barks becoming more insistent.

"Stand back. She explodes with the power of Walter Payton off the line." Luke opened the door and eighty pounds of squirming, barking, whining, yellow fur bolted a good fifty yards, then circled back to the men.

Luke knelt down and gave the lab an affectionate tussle, allowing her time to calm down before she greeted Tony. By the time it was Tony's turn, her pent-up energy had been reduced to mere shivers of delight as her whole body wagged in opposition to her tail.

"*Hola, Señorita* Sandy."

Sandy's tongue lolled as her face split into a big doggie grin. Tony bent over to grab her silky ears and give her rump a warm pat.

Luke was already in the kitchen at the fridge. "Want a beer?"

"Sure."

After taking the first satisfyingly frosty swig, the men stepped out onto the deck to relax in the lounge chairs, Sandy by their side. At a signal from Luke, Sandy laid down, her head on her paws.

"How's our new client?" Tony asked.

Luke hesitated, then at Tony's questioning glance, a sly grin spread across his face.

"That good, huh?" Tony shot him a questioning look. "Are you going to bang every female client who hires us?"

"No, not *every* female client, just the sexy single ones," he said between pulls on his beer.

"With your track record, some could accuse us of running an escort service instead of a guiding service."

Luke shrugged. "One of the perks of the job."

"You ever going to settle down?"

"Been there, done that. Don't see any reason to do it again." His chest tightened as he thought about *her,* his rash mistake, never to be repeated. Caroline Clarkson. They'd married shortly after being college sweethearts at the University of California Santa Barbara. A cool, tall blonde who'd secretly harbored materialistic tendencies. Just one of the many reasons why Caroline was his *ex*-wife.

"So, she's sexy and single?" Tony asked, bringing him back to the present.

"Oh, she's sexy. And she appears to be single. No ring of any kind." Luke frowned, remembering the necklace and watch. He took another pull on his beer before continuing. "She's what I imagine Lisa would be like if she were still here. Tall, athletic, fresh. Nothing artificial about her."

"Yeah, I miss Lisa."

A masculine silence descended, the kind of silence that acknowledged shared emotions without the need to speak of them.

A day didn't go by that Luke didn't think about Lisa, miss her. Like with a phantom limb, he often had the sensation that she was still there, still a part of him, her body moving through the forests in tandem with his.

"But our client's got a chip on her shoulder." Luke broke the silence. "You know the type: stubborn, independent, doesn't want or need any help."

A beat passed in silence.

"Just like Lisa." The men spoke in unison and, grinning, tapped their beer bottles together in a toast.

CHAPTER TWO

The next morning as she waited in the resort's reception area gulping hot sweet coffee, Lacey understood why Luke had said she'd be awake, even if not coherent.

The howler monkeys had started warming up their vocal chords at about four-thirty that morning. They performed in full concert mode by five and, as she could attest, the Mormon Tabernacle Choir had nothing on the howlers. If this is what she had to look forward to, it was not only going to be a long stay, but a sleepless one as well.

Taking another sip of the aromatic coffee, she closed her eyes in delight. This was the best part of her stay so far–rich, Costa Rican coffee.

When Luke walked in, he noticed the look of unadulterated pleasure on Lacey's face. His heart jolted. Then he noticed her closed eyes. A wave of chagrin shot through him as he realized her expression wasn't meant for him.

He took a moment to allow his gaze to sweep up her tall frame, from those long, shapely legs, over her almost boyish figure, with slim hips and narrow waist, to the swell of her breasts, then finally to her slightly wet hair. Even dressed in a nondescript beige camisole and black cargo shorts, she was still the sexiest thing he'd seen in . . . well, he couldn't remember when. She still wore the garnet heart and watch.

"Morning."

Luke's voice startled her. Lacey opened her eyes. He leaned against the doorjamb, looking über masculine in his hiking shorts, sandals, and T-shirt. His straight hair, still damp, swept over his forehead into his eyes. She yearned to reach up and smooth the stray strands back, wondering if his hair was as silky as it looked.

"Is that what it is?" She grimaced. "I thought it was still the middle of the night."

He laughed. "You'll get used to it. Before long, you'll sleep right through the howlers."

"Right." She found that hard to believe. She'd never gotten used to the sound of artillery fire in Iraq and Afghanistan, like the soldiers said she would. Grabbing her equipment bag and backpack, she followed Luke through the dark to the Jeep, noticing he didn't offer to help this time.

"Toss your bags in the back." He hopped in and started the engine, which reverberated in the soggy air. Up to that point, the frog concerto had been the only sound. Of course, the howlers' performance had ended. Mission accomplished: everyone was awake.

They drove along the muddy road, and while the silence in the Jeep wasn't uncomfortable, Luke felt compelled to speak anyway. "How's your bungalow?"

"Oh, it's great. But I'm curious, is the Peeping Tom monkey part of the package, or do I have to pay extra for that?"

He chuckled. Lucky monkey. "Capuchin or squirrel?"
"Squirrel, I think. Eddie Munster hairdo . . ."

"Squirrel. He's part of the package. It's the capuchins that are extra."

"Thanks. I'll keep that in mind."

"You'll see all four native monkey species in Corcovado. Beware the howlers though. If they get riled, they'll throw their feces at you."

"Damn, and I left my Roncomatic shit-shield at home."

Luke laughed, a deep rich infectious laugh. "We'll be camping in Corcovado National Forest the next few days," he said, before beginning his tour guide spiel. "At only eight degrees north of the equator, the tropical rain forest, which covers most of the western portion of the Osa Peninsula, is considered the Amazon of Costa Rica."

As they retraced yesterday's bumpy route, Lacey wondered why she'd bothered with a shower. By the time they got to the airport she'd be covered in muddy splashes again. According to Luke, the best way in to Corcovado, other than an eleven-mile hike on foot, was to fly into Sirena Station, a research and visitors' station, with a grass landing strip.

"So, you're after frogs," Luke's voice interrupted her musings on the state of her cleanliness, "which we're sure to see in Corcovado. It's a good place to spot the red-eyed tree frog and the glass frog, but I think we'll have better luck in Monteverde next week with the poison dart frogs.

"And with any luck we'll catch a glimpse of the Resplendent Quetzal, Costa Rica's national bird." Luke expounded on the history of the park and the ecological diversity it boasted. As he warmed to his subject, the extent of his almost encyclopedic knowledge of the area surprised her. She shifted to look at him, eyebrows lifted in amusement. Beneath the surfer-dude exterior lurked a sharp mind.

He caught her gaze and stopped mid-sentence when he noticed her looking at him with a half-smile on her face. "What?"

"Will there be a test on this later?"

"Sorry. I get a little carried away."

He wore a chagrined expression she found unexpectedly appealing. "No, I enjoyed it."

He turned his attention back to the rutted excuse for a road. "Tony can tell you more."

"Who's Tony?" she asked, before losing her breath in a *whoof*, as they dropped into a pothole the size of the Grand Canyon. She needed to learn that when Luke slowed down, a rut was imminent.

"Antonio Rojas is my best friend, my business partner, and the best guide in Costa Rica. The forest was his playground growing up. You'll meet him when we get to Sirena Station."

Dawn painted the eastern sky with watercolor brushstrokes in shades of lavender and pink. Lacey wished she were on the beach right now with her tripod to capture the sky's ever- changing colors as they reflected off the deep blue of the water.

After forty-five minutes over teeth-jarring potholes, they arrived at the Puerto Jimenez airport. Luke parked next to a white and green Piper Cherokee. As they loaded bags, camping equipment, and some food through a large double-door in the back, he explained that the plane originally had six seats, but he'd modified it by removing two of the seats, making more room for cargo.

The plane clearly belonged to an outdoorsman, Lacey thought. No frills on her, the vinyl seat covers torn and stained. Despite the plane's worn appearance, she had great lift as Luke pulled back on the yoke before banking west.

The grid-patterned streets of the small town of Puerto Jimenez gave way to the green of dense forests and low-lying mountains as Luke pointed out various landmarks during the relatively short flight south and west to Sirena Station.

The grass landing strip came into view and before long they bumped gently across it to a smooth stop near a cluster of buildings. The sun rose well above the horizon, already radiating a heat that promised sweltering temperatures later in the day.

Tony met the plane. "*Hola*, Luke."

"Tony, this is Lacey Sommers. Lacey, this is Tony Rojas, outdoor guide extraordinaire."

"*Hola*, Tony." Lacey extended her hand.

"*Hola*." Tony visibly winced when she gripped his hand.

Turning to Luke, Tony said, "Uh, Luke, Carlos was supposed to take a researcher to Los Patos today, but his wife is ill. Do you mind if I take him?"

So that meant a day alone with Luke in the jungle. Why did that prospect make her heart take a little stutter-step?

"No problem. His wife going to be okay?" Luke asked with concern.

"Oh sure. She just needs some bed rest . . . and a break from the kids." Tony winked at Luke, who chuckled in response.

"Well, with five kids, who could blame her? You'd better get going. I can unload the supplies."

"I've got two hands." Lacey shot Luke an annoyed look.

"No, but you're the client, I'm the guide. Let me do my

job." Luke and Tony exchanged a telling glance. "See you at dinner, Tony?"

"*Sí*. Nice to meet you, Lacey. And don't let him turn your hike into the Bataan Death March," he glanced back at Luke, "although from the looks of you, you'll have no problem keeping up with him." Tony gave her a face-splitting grin and a wink before trotting back toward the research station.

"So, you drive your clients hard, but you won't let me help unload supplies?" She picked up her pack and camera bag.

"You'd be surprised what some people think of as driven hard," he said as he dragged a box toward him. "I've taken out several pretty pampered clients who needed a spritz of Evian after two miles and actually demanded transportation back to Sirena after five. I don't know what they expected . . ." He shook his head in disgust.

"Don't worry about me, I can keep up." She reached into the cargo area to retrieve a box of food, but found her attempts blocked by one of Luke's big hands. "And it's not like I'm on vacation. I'm here to work."

"I'll get that, just the same." He plucked the box out of her hands. "Go . . . take some photos if you'd like." She stood her ground. "Sommers, you don't have to prove anything to me." He gave her an appreciative glance. "One look at that body of yours and I can tell you're no lightweight." He turned back to the cargo area, effectively dismissing her.

A trail of heat traveled up her neck and into her face. She couldn't remember the last time she'd blushed. After spending a few years in the company of rough-and-tumble military men and women who'd done little to censor their behavior, there wasn't much left that embarrassed her. But the thought that he'd obviously given her body more than a passing glance produced a visceral response that was not at all unpleasant. Oh yes, Luke Hancock was dangerous.

———

They'd been hiking for hours and so far had only *heard* the dreaded howler monkeys. She was relieved she hadn't had to run a gauntlet of monkey dung. But they'd also encountered a three- toed sloth sleeping in a tree; a couple of tapirs—a mammal similar to pigs; and an inquisitive coatimundi—the raccoon of the Central Americas.

Covered in sweat, her hair matted to her neck and forehead, she wondered why she'd cut her hair off. At least when it was long, she could pull it all back—off her neck, off her face. Whoever said short hair was cooler was f—.

"Have you always been a wildlife photographer?" Luke asked, unwittingly interrupting her internal diatribe as they trudged through the dense lowland vegetation that ran parallel to the Rios Sirena.

The question surprised her, then she remembered he didn't know anything about her past. Sometimes she felt as if it were tattooed on her forehead, spelled out for everyone to see: I'm a failure. "No, up until two years ago, I was a photojournalist with the AP, Associated Press. Covered the wars in Afghanistan and Iraq." *And Darfur.*

"Those must have been dangerous assignments." Luke appraised her again. No wonder she had a layer of toughness about her.

"It was, and I was good at it. My photos told the stories in a way words never could."

He could hear the pride in her voice, and something else . . . regret perhaps? "So why did you leave the AP?"

The inevitable question. She told him what she'd told

her prospective employers. "Health problems." That phrase generally stopped people in their tracks; put up an invisible barrier most people were reluctant to cross. Apparently, Luke was no exception.

"Oh." Health problems? She looked healthy as a horse. What kind of health problems would have prevented her from covering the Middle East, but not the jungles of Central America? "Do you miss it—the excitement, I mean? Being surrounded by gunfire, terrorists with IEDs, and the threat of suicide bombers, must have been a hell of an adrenalin-producer."

"Yeah, it was, but I find other ways to get my adrenalin fix. You know . . . extreme skiing, sky-diving, rock-climbing, cave-diving . . . things like that."

His brows shot up in surprise. Health problems, my ass. Those weren't the activities of the unwell. Clearly, there was more to her story than she was willing to admit.

***

L acey knelt down, adjusting her telephoto lens to achieve the sharpest image. They'd finally stumbled across a red-eyed tree frog, one of the must-haves on her list of shots. Satisfied with the composition, she pressed the rapid-fire shutter.

Before she could adjust her angle, she shot to her feet, like toast from a toaster, camera dangling from the strap around her neck, hands fisted at her sides.

"What?" Luke asked.

"Get him off me," she ground out, her teeth gritted in revulsion. She pointed toward her leg and Luke glanced down in time to see the frog climb up her inner thigh and duck beneath her shorts.

Lacey sucked in a breath. The cold, wet suction-cup feet clung to her. She couldn't even breathe, afraid any movement would prompt the slimy thing to crawl further up under her shorts. If it got to her crotch, she would die on the spot.

Luke didn't think it was possible, but Lacey's eyes grew wider as the frog apparently made his way farther north.

Enjoying her dilemma, he explained, "You know, because water and air flows so easily in to and out of amphibian skin, amphibians are much more vulnerable to possible pollutants on our hands—"

"Just. Get. Him. Off. Me. I didn't invite his invasion of my person. He should have thought about that before he assaulted me," she hissed through gritted teeth.

Luke couldn't hold back the chuckle that escaped, or suppress his wicked thoughts as he knelt down and peered up her shorts to see where the frog was hiding. The sight of her muscular thigh and pink panties nearly made him forget his mission. He slowly slid his hand beneath her shorts and up her inner thigh.

"How do you know it's a *he*?" he asked, taking pity on her at last and hoping to distract her from her obviously uncomfortable predicament.

"Like that even deserves a response," came her sarcastic reply. His soft laugh only inflamed her ire.

"Don't you think it's rather ironic that you're afraid of the very thing you've been sent here to photograph?"

"I'm not—" Her angry denial was cut off when his warm, calloused hand closed over the sensitive skin of her inner thigh, cupping over the frog and making her flinch at the heat rocketing up her spine.

"Hold still," he instructed, "otherwise I can't promise he won't head for . . . warmer regions."

She shivered in response to his touch. She had a frog on her thigh, and astonishingly she now had sex on the brain.

Luke's hand rested on her thigh longer than she thought necessary. "You're enjoying this way too much," she said through tight lips.

Damn right I am, Luke admitted to himself. Her thigh was as hot and smooth as sun-warmed silk. His fingers itched to glide further up her leg, to hear her gasp in pleasure, rather than in disgust. Between the monkey and the frog, Costa Rica's fauna was making better time with her than he was. "No, I'm simply trying not to startle him."

"Then lose the shit-eating grin."

He struggled to assume a disinterested face, while she eyed him furiously.

His hand gently closed over the offending amphibian, grazing the apex of her thighs with his fingertips, triggering yet another wave of heat up her spine. He slowly inched his hand out from under her shorts, extending the exquisite torture. She didn't know which caused the stronger adrenalin rush: her revulsion of the wet frog, or her arousal from Luke's warm hand.

As soon as his hand cleared her shorts, she began pacing and cursing.

Good thing the forest was devoid of tourists, Luke thought, otherwise their ears would have been scorched. Her vocabulary could make a hardened criminal blush. Luke released the frog, watching it hop away without a backward glance.

"Good riddance," Lacey muttered.

"Hey, frog's no fool. Saw a warm, inviting spot and went for it."

"Spoken just like a man."

Ignoring that comment, he asked, "Want any more photos?"

"No, I don't. I'm done with that"—she shivered—"frog."

Picking up her pack and turning away, she continued to walk in the direction they were previously headed.

He hefted up his bag and followed after her, wiping his hands on his shorts. "Let me get this straight, you've covered two wars, but you're scared of a little frog?" He shook his head at the vagaries of women.

"I wasn't scared. It just—it startled me." She refused to admit to him she was ranidaphobic. "How would you like it if something wet unexpectedly landed on your thigh? Wait! Don't answer that!"

His only response was a low rumbling laugh that carried deep into the rain forest.

CHAPTER THREE

On the hike back, Luke had explained that Sirena Ranger Station, which lay in the Corcovado Basin, served as the headquarters of Corcovado National Park. With its extensive facilities for the support of academic research, park improvement and protection activities, and for camping, overnight lodging and meals preparation, it made for a rather comfortable camping experience.

By the time they arrived at the ranger station, the sun had set and the mosquitoes were out in force, with bats swooping and diving after them.

Lacey surveyed her surroundings. In addition to dorm-like accommodations, a screen-covered platform provided campers a relatively bug-free campsite. Also, an expansive lawn in front of the facility welcomed campers to pitch their tents if they preferred that to the covered camping area. Common restrooms, showers, and food preparation facilities also provided campers with modern conveniences.

Tony had set up their 'campsite' in the screened enclosure, which had a large, open floor plan; no walls or other dividers to offer any kind of privacy.

"What's with the tent?" Lacey asked, glancing at the small half-dome tent set up in a corner of the enclosure.

"I thought you'd like some privacy," Luke explained. She narrowed her eyes at him. "I don't need a tent."

"Suit yourself," he said with a shrug.

"Hi. How'd the hiking go?" Tony approached them with a warm, friendly smile.

"Fine," Lacey said before Luke could answer.

"Dinner'll be ready soon," Tony said. "I'm grilling some snook I caught this afternoon." Tony turned to Lacey. "You've time for a shower before dinner."

"Thanks. A shower sounds good." She grabbed some things out of her backpack and headed toward the shower facilities.

Luke knelt down to gather his own shower supplies from a small duffle and said to Tony, "You must have burned up the trail if you got back in time to catch dinner."

"Yeah, the researcher was anxious to get there, so we only took a short break. Nice guy, he's from California. Too bad you didn't get to meet him."

"Yeah, too bad," Luke muttered. His unruly mind kept drifting to flashing blue eyes, a silky thigh, and the almost irresistible temptation to pull Lacey into his arms and kiss her breathless.

"So, you two made it through the day without killing each other."

"Just barely. I'm going to take a shower." He strode out of the enclosure.

He passed Lacey on her way out of the women's shower. Her hair was wet and her skin was still damp and smelled of lavender and rosemary. Her thin tank top clung to her, revealing her braless state. She simply nodded at him as she strode past.

He stopped in his tracks, breathing in the scent of her. Fresh. Clean. It suited her better than the floral or fruity fragrances most women wore. Between that and her clingy shirt, his thoughts took a baser turn. *Damn.* A cold shower was definitely in order now.

———

Lacey grinned at Tony's joke. After a surprisingly good dinner of grilled snook with a papaya and jalapeño salsa, *ensalada palmito*, and warm, soft tortillas on the side, she, Luke, and Tony sat on their sleeping mats around a camp lantern while Luke and Tony shared war stories from previous camping expeditions.

So far, Tony had top honors with his story about a client who'd insisted on bringing along a portable, rechargeable coffee grinder. This client also happened to be an early riser and thought it would be nice to have freshly ground coffee for her fellow campers. Her fear of leaving the screened enclosure without an escort drove her to grind the coffee beans inside her tent.

"The noise from the coffee grinder startled everyone from their sleep, rattling nerves and nearly causing a few heart attacks as campers stampeded for the door, trying to get away from the unholy racket."

Lacey giggled in response to Tony's deep-bellied laughter.

"I've got a new one to top it," Luke said, with a sidelong glance at her.

Her laughter dried up, and much to her consternation, Luke began relating the story of her close encounter with the frog.

"Hancock! Don't you dare." She narrowed her gaze at

him. Her warning didn't affect him in the least. He continued his story, salting the narrative with a few exaggerations to make him look the hero and her, the damsel-in-distress. "She considered the frog a pervert. I considered him an opportunist."

Lacey could tell Tony tried not to laugh, but as Luke continued the story, Tony threw back his head and let out a long round of laugher.

"I swear to you, Hancock, you will pay for that. I don't know when and I don't know how, but you *will* pay." She gave him a look that would melt the polar ice cap.

Luke shot a glance at Tony, who returned it with lifted brow. Luke didn't know how much of her threat was bravado and how much of it was real, but given her time in two war zones surrounded by prototypical alpha male soldiers, he had no doubt she'd been privy to some pretty harsh practical jokes.

He'd have to sleep with one eye open from now on.

———

Distant flames from the burning village revealed the destruction drawn in stark relief against the pitch-black night. The smell of death hung heavy in the air. The cries of an infant gave way to wails of terror and grief, punctuated by angry shouts and the staccato of gunfire. The woman reached out for the screaming infant before the sound abruptly stopped. In its place came the keening moan of a mother's unspeakable anguish.

She tried, but she couldn't get to her. She couldn't stop it. She couldn't save her. Hands clawed at her neck, grabbed her hair. Menacing faces closed around her, shouting, spitting, snarling; then, the bite of a blade against her neck. She tried to scream but couldn't find the breath—

"Sommers, Sommers. Wake up. You're dreaming." Someone gave her a none-too-gentle nudge.

She awoke with a start, disoriented. By the time she figured out where she was and what had happened, Luke had already rolled over, turning his back to her.

Her breath still came in harsh pants. The damp sleeping bag tangled around her legs and her clammy tank top clung to her like cellophane. She threw off the sleeping bag and rolled onto her back, staring through the dark at the ceiling, trying to regulate her breathing and slow her galloping pulse.

It had been over two years since that night in Darfur. Would the nightmares ever go away? Their number had decreased from the almost nightly occurrences, but they continued to plague her with unpredictable frequency.

She didn't know what external manifestation her nightmares took. She'd made sure no one had ever witnessed them. Until now. Embarrassed that she'd disturbed Luke, and mortified by his observation of the episode, she wondered if Tony had heard as well.

She rolled onto her side, facing away from Luke, as if it would erase the humiliation if she couldn't see him. She closed her eyes as her pulse slowed to a canter, hoping Luke wouldn't mention the episode in the morning.

———

The sun was barely up, but of course the howlers made sure everyone else was. Stumbling to the washbasin to brush her teeth and wash her face, Lacey felt hung-over after her sleepless night.

The nightmares had returned several times, but each time she'd managed to will herself awake before she could disturb Luke or Tony again. Uncomfortable with the thought of facing Luke after last night, she nevertheless needed her morning caffeine fix.

Staggering back to the enclosure in a zombie-like trance, the robust scent of the aforementioned savior and the tantalizing aroma of food quickly made her forget her concerns.

Breakfast was delicious. Tony served the traditional Costa Rican breakfast of *gallo pinto*, fried plantains, and fried eggs with a soft tortilla, accompanied by orange juice and hot, sweet coffee.

They planned to hike to the mouth of Rio Claro, circling back to Sirena for lunch, then venturing north toward Guanacaste in the afternoon.

"Let's go. We've got a hike ahead of us if we want to be back in time for lunch."

Before she could finish her coffee, Luke bolted out the door.

Thankfully, he hadn't mentioned the nightmare. She wondered if he even remembered waking her last night. His demeanor toward her hadn't changed. He was still the same aggravating, appealing, sexy Luke.

Not up for conversation this morning, Lacey settled for listening to Luke and Tony talk about the trail they hiked.

They reached the beach around mid-morning. Lacey sat on a fallen tree and poured water from her bottle onto a bandana before mopping her face with the cool cloth, welcoming the refreshing breeze. The water looked cool and inviting but Luke and Tony had warned against swimming in the ocean or the rivers, which often contained bull sharks and crocodiles, respectively.

The beach was alive with hermit crabs of various sizes

scurrying around in their salvaged seashells, drawing Lacey's attention. She slowly approached two hermit crabs engaged in combat.

"They're fighting over the shell." Luke continued, quietly approaching the scene of the battle, clearly wearing his tour guide hat as he explained their housing preferences. "The coiled shells of sea snails are a particular favorite, but hermit crabs will inhabit any vacated gastropod shell of suitable size."

"The bigger one needs an even bigger shell, so he's going after the smaller crab who, in all likelihood, recently found that shell since it's a little large for him. With all the hermit crabs on this beach, the competition for limited resources is often fierce."

Lifting her camera to her face and adjusting the lens, she took a series of rapid-fire shots as the two crabs battled one another. She'd never seen hermit crabs fighting. They tumbled over each other like two wrestlers, trying to grasp onto one another with their claws.

The bigger crab finally faced off and got a firm grip on the smaller crab. To Lacey's astonished amusement, the bigger crab literally pulled the smaller crab from the shell, effectively evicting him (or her), before wedging himself into his new home.

Lacey laughed at their antics even as she continued to snap pictures.

Luke watched her, admiring her simple delight. Her mirthful profile revealed a dimple, making Luke wonder if she had a matching dimple on the other side of that delectable mouth.

The vanquished crab promptly took up residence in the discarded shell, causing Lacey to laugh even harder, throaty, bubbly, sexy, sounds. Doubled over, she turned to

Luke, her smile confirming the presence of a matching dimple.

"They could have avoided the whole skirmish if they'd just swapped shells."

"Yes, well, what would be the fun in that?" Her eyes twinkled with amusement, and he thought she looked beautiful despite her sweat-soaked face and hair. Even the entertaining tales of last night hadn't generated such unguarded delight. "Come on. Let's get to the mouth of the river, then we can take a break before the return trip to Sirena." He bent to pick up his backpack and met Tony, who'd just rejoined them after making a pit stop in the seclusion of the forest.

Once they reached the mouth of the river, they found a shady spot to sit. A large crocodile, at least ten feet long, dozed on the shore basking in the sun.

"Just ignore him, and he'll ignore us," Luke said matter-of-factly.

Tony produced two mangoes from his backpack. Slicing them up, he presented Luke and Lacey with wedges dripping with juice.

"These should hold us over until lunch," Tony said.

Lacey took a bite and moaned. "I can't remember anything tasting so good," Lacey exclaimed. "They're so sweet and juicy." She devoured her slices before he handed her two more.

"Thanks." She wiped the juice that ran down her chin with the back of her hand.

Luke watched as she bit into the ripe mango, causing more juice to run down her chin. He wanted to reach out and stop the trickle with his thumb before tasting her lips. They'd be sweet from the mango, and warm. *Okay. Enough.* He groaned as he rose to his feet.

"Time for a visit to the little boy's room," he said as he headed into the forest.

Lacey watched as Tony took out a bottle of water and washed the mango juice off his hands, then offered the bottle to her to do the same.

"Thanks, Tony. That was delicious." She took out her bandana again and poured water over it to clean the sticky juice off her mouth and chin.

"*De nada*. Do you like avocado? There's a wild avocado a couple of meters from here."

"I love avocado." Lacey glanced up at Tony as she stretched out her legs and reclined on her elbows.

"I make a mean guacamole. I'll just go see if there are any ripe ones and we'll have them at lunch."

"You're a genius, Tony. I don't know how you manage to serve such tasty food in the wilds of Corcovado. My mouth waters when I think about what you could do in a real kitchen."

"Thanks." Tony blushed beneath his swarthy skin. "You okay here by yourself? Luke should be right back, and I won't be gone long."

"I'm fine. I'll just doze a few minutes." She laid her head back on the sand and closed her eyes.

———

Luke did need the little boy's room, but he also needed a little solitude to get his head on straight. Lacey was tempting. Too tempting. Lying next to her last night, even separated by the camp lantern, had been torture.

Wafts of her rosemary and lavender scent invaded his slumber more than once. When she started moaning in her sleep, he'd been on the edge of an erotic dream starring her.

But her moans had quickly changed to whimpers of fear, penetrating his brain, and making him think there might be a wild animal in the enclosure. When he woke, she was thrashing in her sleep then suddenly went rigid and even appeared to have stopped breathing.

He'd nudged her, wanting only to pull her out of her nightmare, but when she recoiled, he turned his back, knowing already how she hated being perceived as soft. So much like Lisa.

It took everything he had not to reach for her, comfort her. He could hear her raspy breathing long after she woke. He hadn't drifted off again until her breathing regained the slow, steady rhythm of sleep.

He tramped through the thick vegetation back to the beach, wiping the sweat from his face and the back of his neck with a bandana.

The horrors of two wars would give anyone nightmares. Could be the health problem she referred to. He wondered if she'd gotten help. The nightmares could be a sign of post-traumatic stress disorder.

He knew first-hand what that was like. He'd had persistent nightmares for years after Lisa died. Even now, he had the occasional nightmare, never quite sure what triggered it. Before he could think any more on the subject, Luke stopped in his tracks, the scene before him a real-life nightmare.

CHAPTER FOUR

Lacey stood with her camera to her face, not ten feet from the crocodile. His enormous mouth open, vicious teeth gleaming, head turned toward her in an aggressive posture. Most people thought crocs were slow, but Luke knew the animal could cover that distance in a matter of seconds.

"Sommers." Her name escaped as a mere breath.

She continued to snap photos, seemingly oblivious to the danger. He'd never lost a client, and he'd be damned if he'd start with her. He picked up a long, sturdy stick. If he headed north and circled around, he could distract the croc with the stick long enough for her to get away. After that, he didn't know what he'd do.

He didn't want to take his eyes off the crocodile, but he didn't have much time. The animal became more hostile by the minute, now turning his upper body toward Lacey.

Luke pivoted and sprinted into the woods, coming out just north of the reptile. Lacey had finally realized the danger and started retreating slowly as the crocodile turned to face her.

"Sommers. Stop." She started to move in his direction. "No, don't turn around. Don't run. Just stand perfectly still." Luke struggled to push the commands past the knot that formed in his throat. His breath came in shallow gasps.

Muscles tensed, he cautiously stepped onto the sand, his eyes never leaving the crocodile as he slowly approached the massive reptile. Once close enough, he nudged the croc's tail with the stick. The croc swung his massive head in Luke's direction.

"Run!" Luke's strangled cry jolted Lacey to action. She turned and ran straight into Tony's arms.

Tony grabbed Lacey's shoulders to keep her from falling, steadying her. "Stay."

Tony yanked his knife from his belt and ran to help Luke, who now confronted one pissed off croc.

"Throw me the stick," Tony commanded, "then run. I'll take care of him."

"No, Tony—"

"Just do it."

Luke speared the stick to Tony, who caught it easily. Tony used the stick to prod the crocodile, redirecting his attention. Luke ran to Lacey, then watched Tony use the stick to calmly, and capably, herd the crocodile away from them and into the river.

As boys, he and Tony would often use sticks to steer small crocodiles like the hunters of legend, but Luke never thought he'd see Tony taming a ten foot croc with nothing but a stick. The hulking animal slid gracefully into the water before Tony headed back to them, wiping sweat out of his eyes.

Luke finally caught the first full breath since stepping out of the forest.

Lacey's eyes were wide and her chest heaved with each breath. "That was such a rush," she whispered.

Luke whirled to face her, incredulous. "A rush? Is that what you call it? If you want a rush, stick to your extreme sports. Don't look for a rush on my watch!" His voice became increasingly harsh, as his panic changed to anger.

He stepped closer to her. "As long as you're my client, you're my responsibility and I take that responsibility very seriously." He leaned down so that they were practically nose- to-nose. "So from now on you *will* listen to me. This isn't a democracy—it's a dictatorship, and *I* am your supreme leader."

The air between them crackled. His proximity did more to elevate Lacey's pulse than the crocodile, but she didn't let him know that. "Should I genuflect now, or wait until you've given me leave?" she asked with barely concealed sarcasm.

"You're impossible," he ground out as he pivoted on his heel and stalked off.

"Are you okay, Tony?" she asked with concern when he approached her.

"*Sí.* I'm fine." He leaned down to whisper conspiratorially, "You're right, it was a rush." He winked. "But don't do it again," he said, and his look meant business.

———

To say the hike back to Sirena was tense would have been an understatement. Lacey couldn't wait to get back. Luke made her walk between him and Tony, like a prisoner being escorted to her cell. He wouldn't even let her stop for photos along the way.

The only time Luke spoke, it was to Tony, as if she didn't exist.

When they arrived at Sirena, Tony nabbed one of the shadier picnic tables and started making lunch. Luke stalked off toward the buildings.

Damn, her bladder felt like an elephant danced a jig on it, but she didn't want Luke to think she was following him. She sat down on the bench and tightly crossed her legs, chatting with Tony while he sliced and peeled one of the avocadoes he'd picked.

"Munch on that, while I prepare the rest of lunch," Tony said, "and try not to get into any trouble while I'm gone," but his voice held no rancor as he sauntered in the direction of the common cooking facilities.

A few minutes later, Luke came out of the camping structure and stalked toward his plane.

Lacey watched as he opened the doors to the cargo area and banged around inside. When he emerged, he marched to the engine compartment, toolbox in hand. He hadn't mentioned a problem with the plane. She frowned as she watched him tighten this and lubricate that.

For all his highhandedness, he'd been something to behold, especially in his anger. She had to admit, if only to herself, she'd been unsettled when he yelled in her face like an angry drill sergeant. Unsettled and . . . aroused. He was all male and he knew it, and that self-knowledge translated into undeniable sexual attraction.

Boys, and later young men, had always been intimidated by her tough-girl attitude. She'd been unapologetically rough and tumble. She didn't take crap from people, and she gave as good as she got. It didn't help that she could out-run, out-swim, and out-do just about anything most boys her age could do.

These characteristics did little to encourage prom dates, despite her long, wavy golden blond hair, her sapphire blue eyes, and what she hoped was a lean, sexy body. But she'd rather kiss a frog than admit the lack of dates hurt, especially when she watched her younger sister flaunt her endless suitors at every society function and charity ball in Manhattan.

She'd never met men confident—or perhaps arrogant— enough to handle her until she started with the AP. David Carson had been one of those men. A free-lance journalist whose stories had received critical acclaim and more than one book deal, David was an unrepentant cigar-smoking, scotch-drinking man's man.

Brash, good-looking, and smart, he'd attracted Lacey's attention from the moment their paths crossed. He could definitely hold his own with her, a quality she found very appealing, and for the first time ever, she'd fallen hard. So hard that her heart still carried a few bruises from his stunning betrayal.

They met while covering Iraq, and when the AP sent her to Darfur to cover the genocide there, he tagged along to chronicle the story himself. Lacey thought she'd found in David the one man, besides her father, whom she could trust. She couldn't have been more wrong.

A loud bang, followed by Luke's angry curse interrupted her musings. He continued to mutter to himself as he nursed his evidently injured thumb.

Luke had resembled the quintessential hero when he'd put himself in harm's way so she could escape to safety. He had rescued her. Although not the damsel-in-distress type, she'd been oddly comforted by his protectiveness.

Of course, Luke's motive wasn't exactly selfless. Having

one's client eaten by a crocodile wasn't exactly a rousing endorsement for one's guiding skills.

Even so, she was sorry that she'd put him and Tony in unnecessary danger. That had not been her intent. She'd only wanted to get some great, up-close and personal shots of the croc, so she could prove to her editor she was capable of handling dangerous situations.

She owed them both an apology. *Damn.* She hated admitting she was wrong. Next to frogs, that was the thing she hated most. Maybe the drinks Tony carried to the table would help her wash down the crow she'd be having for lunch.

She rose to help Tony with his overloaded cargo. "What's this?" she asked as she took two of the cups from his hand. A lovely orangey-pink liquid practically over-flowed the rims.

"It's papaya refrescos."

Lacey took a sip of hers. "Mmm. That's delicious. What's in it?"

"Liquefied papaya and strawberry diluted with water and sweetened with cane juice."

Lacey took another sip. "I don't think I've ever eaten so well on an assignment. You're the best, Tony."

He grinned. "The rest of lunch will be out soon."

Before he could walk away, Lacey touched his arm. "Hey, I'm really sorry about my behavior back there. I didn't mean to put anyone in danger . . ."

Tony took pity on her and cut her off before she could choke on her apology. "Forget it."

Lacey took one of the two remaining cups and ambled across the landing strip to Luke, who had his head buried in the plane's engine compartment. She reached out her hand to touch his arm, and then withdrew it before she could make contact.

"Hancock."

Luke turned around, a frown of annoyance on his face. "Yeah."

Lacey handed the cup of refrescos to him as if it were a peace offering. She waited while he gulped down half the contents before speaking. "I'm sorry I put you and Tony in danger back there. It was not my intention . . ."

Unlike Tony, Luke took no pity on her. He just stood his ground and remained silent. She swallowed past the lump of crow that refused to go down. "I won't do it again." Before he could say anything, she headed toward the facilities.

Luke watched her walk away. He'd never thought he'd see the tough, hardheaded Lacey Sommers apologize. If he'd put money on it, he'd have lost.

He turned back to the plane. Tinkering, as his mother called it, was his outlet. Whenever something bothered him, he tinkered with things: his plane, his parents' old Jeep, the biodiesel generator on his house. The activity allowed him to think through his problems, just like puzzling through a mechanical issue.

Still unnerved from Lacey's self-inflicted predicament, tinkering helped put things back in perspective. When he saw her in the sights of that angry crocodile, his whole body had felt limp, like all the blood had been drained from it. He still had no idea how he'd managed to make his legs move.

Of course, he wouldn't want to see anyone in that kind of danger, but the visceral response to the situation was wholly unexpected. Then he'd been so angry he'd wanted to throttle her for almost getting herself killed, and while he saw the contradiction in that, he couldn't help it.

It had been so . . . personal . . . like seeing a loved one in danger. Why? Was it because she reminded him of Lisa? That must be it. After all, what else could it be?

He sighed. Lacey was a self-professed adrenalin junkie. Well, she could damn well get her adrenalin fix *after* her assignment here. He wouldn't tolerate anymore of her antics. If she put herself in harm's way again, he'd kill her.

Satisfied with his solution, he closed up the engine compartment and went to get lunch.

———

Following dinner, Luke's tension eased and agreed to a friendly game of Gin Rummy with Lacey and Tony.

After dealing the cards, Tony said, "Luke tells me you covered Afghanistan and Iraq. That must have been something. How long were you there?" He shifted his cards around.

"I was in Afghanistan off and on shortly after the war began in 2001 until 2003 when the Iraq war started, and then I transferred there."

While pretending to focus on his cards, Luke listened intently, hoping for some clue as to the events that had instigated the nightmare.

"Were you in Kabul and Baghdad?"

Lacey made her first play, taking a card from the deck, then discarding a two of hearts before answering. "I was all over the place. I was embedded with a Marine unit in Afghanistan, and later in Iraq. Men and women who served their country well."

"Do you still keep up with any of them?" Tony asked as he laid a meld of spades on the floor between the sleeping mats.

"Um, just a few. Some are still serving; others have gone home. Others . . . didn't make it home."

Luke glanced up from his hand in time to see a look of sadness cross Lacey's face. Lacey continued, her eyes distant, as if she'd stepped back into another place and time.

"I was in an armored personnel carrier convoy on the road to Kandahar when the vehicle behind us ran over an IED. Three men were killed, two others injured." Her vision appeared to refocus on them. "I often wonder how our vehicle missed it." Her lips lifted in a sad smile.

Lacey frowned then. Why had she brought that up? She didn't discuss the wars. Even now, years later, the experience was still too raw. Too . . . real.

She'd thought she was tough, but she didn't know tough until she got to Afghanistan. The soldiers she came to know and love were as tough as the armored vehicles they rode in. The first time her unit got caught in a firefight, she'd been scared shitless. Nothing in her life experience had ever prepared her for the hail of bullets. One of the soldiers saw her frozen panic and covered her body with his until the skirmish ended.

The men and women around her remained in control during the clash. They may have been just as frightened as she, but they kept the emotion locked away, never letting it show. They put their life on the line every day, and she'd be damned if she'd let her panic become a liability for them.

So she learned to swallow her fear. She had to in order to get the best photos possible. Robert Capa, world-famous combat photojournalist said, 'If your pictures aren't good enough, you aren't close enough.' That became her mantra.

Luke was silent as he digested the horrors she had to have witnessed and documented during her assignment there.

He tried to shake himself free of the images that Lacey had inadvertently implanted in his brain. What hell had she been through? He'd caught a brief glimpse of the vulnerability she frequently hid before the door closed and the bravado returned. With a sigh, he acknowledged he had lost his appetite for the game and folded his hand. "I'm beat. I'm hitting the shower and then the sack." He gathered his towel and a change of clothes before heading to the men's facilities.

Seeking to change the subject, Lacey asked Tony about growing up in Corcovado.

More than happy to oblige, Tony replied, "My mother's Boruca Indian. Her family has lived off this land for generations. When my father, a *mestizo* from the Guanacaste province, came to the area to pan for gold, he fell in love with my mother, and the land.

"My parents settled on land given to them just outside the forest preserve, in exchange for my mother's ancestral land. I was only five when we moved, but the forest was my home." His love for this deeply forested terrain was evident in both his voice and his expression. "I spent much of my childhood here."

"You seem . . . Americanized . . . I mean your English is excellent, and you have a familiarity with American pop culture." Clearly the game had been abandoned, so Lacey gathered the cards as she spoke.

"I spent a lot of time in the U.S., first with Luke and his family, and then later when I went to college."

"How did you and Luke meet?" Lacey settled back on her sleeping mat, rolling to her side and propping her head on her hand.

"Luke's family came here when I was ten," Tony explained. "Luke's father eked out a winter living here as a guide mainly for scientists and researchers who visited Costa Rica, long before the days of eco-tourism. In the summers the family returned to the Jersey Shore to run their inn. I sometimes went with them."

He shook his head, laughing at some memory. "I happened upon Luke and his sister one day, not too far from your crocodile encounter. They were covered in mud from head to toe, playing a game of *Lord of the Flies*. We became best friends."

"Wait. Luke has a sister?"

"Had. A twin. Lisa. She died when they were sixteen. Luke doesn't like to talk about." His closed expression barred any further discussion.

An awkward silence fell.

The desire to return to a more comfortable topic prompted her to ask, "Where'd you go to school?"

"U.T. on a full ride." He grinned with pride. Lacey whistled.

"Impressive. What major?"

"Business. Luke and I already knew we wanted to start our own company. In addition to guiding tourists and scientists, we wanted to educate the public about the importance of the world's rain forests. We believe that an educated public is an interested public, and the greater the interest, the greater the advocacy for the environment." Tony shrugged as if that philosophy was a no-brainer.

"Since I knew so much about Costa Rica's ecosystems, geography, and wildlife, I chose to learn more practical skills. I guess you could say I'm the brains of the outfit." His grin returned, lending a mischievous glint to his dark eyes.

Luke entered the enclosure in time to hear Tony's final remark. "He's right." Luke flexed a bicep. "I'm the brawn."

He was the brawn all right, she thought, frowning as her pulse stammered.

Luke swallowed hard. When he'd stepped into the enclosure and saw Lacey stretched out on her sleeping mat looking like a sleek cat, laughing at Tony's remarks, he'd almost tripped over his own two feet. *Damn, but she was hot.* He'd managed to recover his composure with a foolish show of muscle, but her frown had not been the hoped-for reaction to his joke.

She sat up, gathered her toiletries, and without looking at him, headed for the women's facilities.

When he first saw her at the airport, he knew he'd have to try for a piece of that action, but the more he learned about her, the more he realized he needed to back off. Clearly there was more to Lacey Sommers than a pretty face and a hot body. Their conversations had barely scraped the surface, but he could already see that she'd been through a hell he could only imagine.

She deserved more than a superficial sexual fling. She deserved a man who could uncover her ghosts and, perhaps, help her heal. But he wasn't that man. He had his own demons to exorcise. He didn't need someone else's.

CHAPTER FIVE

"Wake up, Sommers."

She groaned her disapproval.

"Wake up. It's time to get up." Luke shook her shoulder as he spoke.

She rolled over and gave him a baleful look. "What time is it? The howlers haven't even started yet." Just as she spoke, the deep bellow of a howler made a liar out of her.

"It's five-thirty. The howlers have been going at it for the last hour. I told you you'd get used to it."

Lacey groaned again. Her back ached from sleeping on the hard floor, sleeping mat notwithstanding. She must have been exhausted, since even the nightmares hadn't interrupted her sleep.

Her last remembered thoughts were of Luke's sister.

She knew how difficult it was to lose a twin. She'd seen it firsthand when her high school classmate, Samantha, lost her twin sister, Sandra, to cancer when they were only seventeen. The twin bond was incredibly strong and it took time for the surviving twin to learn to cope and to heal from the loss.

How did his sister die? What had it been like for Luke? How had he learned to cope? These and other questions had swirled in her head until she'd fallen asleep.

She felt rough, despite the decent night's sleep. Dressing in the dim light of the women's facilities, she splashed cool water on her face, running her wet fingers through her hair. Throwing on a Yankees baseball cap, she went back to the screened enclosure, considering selling her soul for a cup of coffee.

"Bless you," she said as Tony handed her a steaming cup as soon as she walked in. After her first sip, she wanted to grab him and plant a kiss on his mouth. The smell of breakfast reminded her that coffee was not the only sustenance she craved. *Huevos rancheros*. Lacey plopped down on her sleeping mat across from Luke and eagerly took the plate Tony handed her.

Luke noticed she wore the necklace and watch again. So far, he'd not seen her without them. Sentimental attachment? The guy must be 'The One,' if you believed in that sort of thing. Which he did not.

Her mouth full of buttery eggs and soft corn tortilla, she said, "You ever think of bagging this guy," she jerked her chin in Luke's direction, "call me. You're hired."

Tony laughed as he sat down with his plate.

Luke snorted in disgust. "You wouldn't last a week with her. Too stubborn by half." He washed his mouthful of eggs down with a gulp of coffee. "Besides, she wouldn't appreciate you the way I do."

That elicited another chuckle from Tony.

They ate in silence for a few minutes, serenaded by frogs and singing insects. The air was leaden today, and the frogs seemed louder, more animated than on the previous mornings.

As if reading her thoughts, Luke said, "We'll likely get rain today, so let's go right after breakfast."

As if they'd lollygagged every other morning, she thought.

"We'll hike the San Pedrillo trail today, so wear pants. It's pretty overgrown, but because of that, we'll be sure to see lots of wildlife," Luke said as he stood up, taking his plate with him.

"I thought San Pedrillo was closed to the public," Lacey said in confusion.

"It is. That's where Tony comes in handy." He wore a broad grin, an indication of pride in his friend. "He's a legend around here, so the park rangers give him free reign over Corcovado. Go change into pants and meet us out on the lawn."

It was well past six-thirty when Lacey stepped out onto the lawn, but dawn had barely made a dent in the darkness due to the heavy clouds. She'd likely need artificial light today if they came across any wildlife.

Lacey could see Luke with his backpack already strapped to his shoulders. As she approached, Tony stepped out from behind Luke, *a machete in his hand.*

She took an automatic step backward, then froze.

"Sommers, what the hell are you doing?" Luke asked, wondering why she'd chosen to stop mid-stride. "Let's go." The frustration left his voice when he saw her go rigid. "Sommers." He stepped closer and saw the unmitigated fear in her wide eyes. Following the direction of her gaze, his eyes stopped at the machete in Tony's hand.

Luke held his hands out as if trying to talk a jumper down from the ledge. "Sommers. Take it easy. It's just Tony."

He turned to Tony and calmly said, "Tony, put the machete down."

Lacey fought the wave of nausea. Her forehead beaded with sweat, and an uncomfortable trickle ran down her stomach. She could hear the blood pulsing in her ears, drowning out all other sound. Her rational mind told her there was nothing to fear. She knew Tony; she knew he wouldn't hurt her. But rationality had nothing to do with her reaction. A dark miasma engulfed her, making it impossible to reason her way out.

Tony dropped the machete.

Luke heard the quiet thud as it hit the ground.

"Okay, Sommers. I'm going to touch you now." Luke took a tentative step forward and, taking her wrist, pulled her toward him, forcing her to relax into him. He held her against him as her breathing eventually calmed, and he felt the tension in her muscles ease. "Sommers."

As soon as he said her name again, she pushed off and backed away. "I'm fine. Sorry," she said to Tony, "you just startled me, that's all."

Luke noticed she'd resumed her usual posture, a combination of athletic grace and stubborn independence with a hint of bravado.

"What's the machete for?" she asked in a casual tone.

It didn't fool Luke. "The last time Tony hiked the trail, it was pretty overgrown. We'll need the machete to cut away the brush."

"Well, don't feel you need to do that on my account. I'll be fine. Let's go. Time's a-wasting."

Luke sighed in exasperation, giving Tony a look that said 'give me strength.'

———

The morning proved productive, Lacey concluded. With the potential for rain, the frogs were especially active and easy to find because of their vocalizations. She'd gotten several more shots of the red-eyed tree frog, along with some shots of the rain frog, and the glass frog, careful not to get too close this time, thus avoiding a repeat of the other day.

They'd also encountered an agouti, two peccaries, and a two-toed sloth, not to mention several species of birds, including the keel-billed toucan with its multi-hued beak, and a pair of brilliant scarlet macaws. Unfortunately, there was no sign of the illusive quetzal.

She appreciated the fact that Tony tried to limit his use of the machete, but at times he needed to cut through thick vines to get through the forest along what remained of the trail.

No matter how she mentally prepared herself, she felt her shoulders flinch with each swing of the machete. Even when she looked away, using a photo op as an excuse, the sound of the machete making contact with the vegetation rattled her nerves. She'd been embarrassed yet again that Luke and Tony had witnessed her weakness and, even worse, that she'd momentarily given into it when she'd allowed Luke to pull her into his arms.

———

Luke silently watched her reactions to the machete, not fooled by her veiled attempts to appear unruffled. He tensed in response to each flinch, wanting to comfort and reassure her.

What the hell happened to her? he wondered. He thought of the vicious scar on her neck. Originally he'd thought it might be from shrapnel, the result of the roadside bomb. But now . . . that couldn't be from a machete, could it? What monster would take a machete to someone's neck? A woman's neck? His hands fisted in anger at the thought.

Whatever happened to her had left her with a strange amalgamation of bravado and vulnerability. He admired her strength in the face of her yet-to-be-identified adversity, but he also recognized the signs of the pain and fear buried deep beneath the surface. Pain and fear that would only continue to erode the shield she'd built around herself until it cracked, leaving her even more vulnerable.

He gave himself a mental shake. *Not my problem*, he reminded himself. *I'm an environmentalist and wilderness guide, not a psychotherapist.*

They took a break for lunch. The wind picked up, the trees swaying in first one direction, and then the other. Lacey ran a hand through her hair and smiled.

Her natural, unadorned beauty struck Luke anew as he watched her lift her face to the breeze.

Munching on soft tortillas, sliced avocado, cheese, and papayas, Luke attempted to occupy his mind with satiating one hunger instead of another. *Keep it in your pants, Hancock*, he admonished himself. He'd reached a decision last night that he couldn't give her what she deserved and he needed to stick to that decision. Yet, he couldn't take his eyes off her.

Lacey could feel Luke's gaze on her as she wrapped her avocado slices and cheese into a makeshift burrito. She wasn't particularly vain, but she thought she must look a fright. Covered in congealed sweat, hair plastered to her neck, and unless she was wrong, her deodorant had waved the white flag long ago. What could he possibly be looking at? She raised her eyes to his, lifting an eyebrow in question.

Luke lowered his gaze, a frown on his face.

"Luke, what's up, *amigo*? Why the frown?" Tony's question only prompted a deeper scowl.

"I'm just a little worried about the weather." He glanced up at the darkening sky. "We should get moving." He spoke as he gathered his pack and used his bandana to wipe his hands.

Lacey swallowed the last of her lunch, then washed it down with water before picking up her own pack.

After trudging through the thick growth another fifteen minutes, Tony suddenly stopped, causing Lacey to bump right into his backpack.

"Rain," was all Tony said, before he turned them around.

Confused, Lacey said, "Rain? I don't see any rain—"

"Tony can hear it. Trust me, we need to turn back. It's going to be a wet return trip, regardless."

They hadn't hiked more than five minutes before a subtle shower became a drenching rain. They stopped long enough to remove raingear from their packs. Luke took her camera bag and covered it in a plastic bag before stuffing it in his backpack.

The slog back to Sirena was quiet, with each person lost in their own wet misery. Even the birds were silent. The rain did little to cool things off, and the usually breathable Gortex jacket she wore became sweltering.

The fresh-cut trail became increasingly muddy . . . and slippery. Bringing up the rear, Lacey found it difficult to keep up and still keep her footing, and the last thing she wanted to do was fall on her ass in the mud.

Keeping her head down both to avoid the sheets of rain

and to dodge the rocks, roots, and vines in the path, she blindly used tree trunks along the trail to steady her. The mud sucked at her feet, threatening to pitch her forward as she worked to pull first one foot and then the other out.

When she grasped another trunk to right herself, a piercing sting like a white-hot needle shot through her hand. "Ow! Shit." She gasped in pain and squeezed her wrist as if cutting off the circulation would somehow make the pain go away.

Luke glanced back to see Lacey holding her right hand up in front of her face, her expression a grimace of agony.

"What happened?" He took her hand and saw the reddening welt on her palm next to a thin white scar.

"I don't know. I grabbed a tree trunk and . . . I think it bit me. Shit." She swallowed hard. *Suck it up, Sommers*, she reproached, *you've had worse. Much worse.*

Luke looked around, then found what he believed to be the culprit. "Bullhorn Acacia Ants."

Tony walked over to inspect Lacey's hand.

"Hey, Tony. You still have some papaya in your pack?" Luke asked.

Tony had already removed his pack. "On it. Give me a sec."

He took out half a papaya wrapped in wax paper and removed the seeds.

Luke held Lacey's hand out, while Tony squeezed papaya juice on the ever-growing welt. Luke longed to bring her hand to his lips and kiss away the pain. Instead, he attempted to distract her.

"The Acacia tree and Bullhorn Acacia Ants have developed a symbiotic relationship: the trees produce nectar to feed the ants; the ants protect the trees from unwanted insects and herbivores . . . and unwary hikers. The ant's sting is a bitch, but this should help," he said quietly.

Luke leaned over her hand, shielding it to keep the rain from washing away the papaya juice, their heads so close, he could hear her shallow breathing. "Sommers, take a deep breath."

Lacey inhaled the sodden air. The papaya started working. She peered up into Luke's face. So close. His eyes had become the gray-green of an ocean in a storm. They held each other's gaze, her hand still in his.

"You okay?" Tony asked in concern, breaking the spell.

She'd almost forgotten his presence. Luke released her hand as Tony reached for it, placing a slice of papaya in her palm. "Squeeze this into your palm. The juice will continue to penetrate the sting. You should feel better in a few minutes."

Lacey folded her fingers over the papaya. Her hand tingled, but not from the sting. Growing self-conscious over all the attention, she adjusted her pack with her left hand and said, "I'm fine. Let's keep going before we drown."

***

Back at Sirena Station, Lacey, weary and sodden, headed to the facilities to change into dry clothes, though in the current weather, the term 'dry' was relative. It seemed everything had absorbed the atmosphere's over-abundant moisture, making the dampness inescapable.

"How's your hand?"

The noise from the downpour obscured the sound of Luke's entrance to the enclosure.

Lacey stood hanging her wet clothes over a makeshift

clothesline someone had strung up in the enclosure. She glanced down at the red welt and shrugged. "It's fine. Looks worse than it feels."

"I'm sorry, I should have warned you about the Acacia trees."

"Don't worry about it." Her lips turned up into a wry grin. "I'm sure if you warned your clients about every potential hazard, you'd have to hold a weeklong orientation course before you took anyone out. I'll live." She returned to her task.

Luke watched as she squared her shoulders, as if in response to some internal command not to show weakness.

Tony joined them, running his hands through his hair, sluicing the water from it. "Luke, I just talked to the rangers. I've got good news and bad news."

Luke frowned. "Okay, what's the bad news?"

"The rain is part of a large weather system that's supposed to continue dumping rain on the peninsula."

It was Lacey's turn to frown. She was used to roughing it, but the thought of being stuck here for several more days was not pleasant. Maybe she was growing soft.

"Great. What's the good news?"

"The weather service said there'll be a short break in the rain in the next hour. You should take off, before the strip gets too wet and you get stuck here."

"What will you do?" Luke asked Tony.

"I'll be fine. I can bunk with the Rangers . . . sit out the rain. Once it lets up, I'll load the gear and food into my truck and take it back to the office in Puerto Jimenez."

"You sure?"

"Yeah, yeah." He leaned in to Luke and she heard Tony whisper, "Take Lacey back to the resort, where she'll at least have a comfortable bed to sleep in."

"Right." Luke turned to Lacey. "How quickly can you be ready to take off?"

CHAPTER SIX

The flight was treacherous. Luke gripped the yoke with white-knuckled force. The so-called break in the rain lasted long enough for them to take off, before it began pelting the plane with renewed force. This squall brought the added danger of strong winds.

Lacey braced for more stomach-dropping turbulence. She'd never hurled on a plane before, but this trip was shaping up to be a first for many things.

Luke spoke to air traffic control, but she couldn't hear the other end of the conversation. His face was grim. She didn't like that. "What?"

"The airport at Puerto Jimenez is closed, and they're closing Golfito as we speak."

"What are we going to do?" Lacey asked. From the look on Luke's face, she didn't want to hear the answer.

Luke pushed down on the yoke and pressed on the rudder pedals. The plane banked to the left, rising on a crosswind, before dropping precipitously. "We're landing on that dirt road."

Lacey peered out the window. In the distance, she could barely make out a short road running parallel to the coast. It seemed a road to nowhere. There appeared to be no buildings, no landmarks, nothing but forest and ocean.

Luke pushed down on the yoke a little more, bringing the plane in for a hard, short landing. Cutting the engine, he released the breath he'd been holding and shook out his aching hands. "Looks like we'll be spending the night here. Puerto Jimenez should reopen in the morning."

Lacey groaned inwardly. A night in a small plane was not what she had in mind. Aside from her desire to sleep in a real bed (she was definitely getting soft), the thought of sleeping in such close quarters . . . alone with Luke . . . elicited a response she'd rather not have. Covering the true nature of her thoughts, she shrugged. "I've survived worse."

Luke's brow knitted at her flippant remark, but he let it pass. "If you want to make a run for it, there's an outpost over there that serves pretty decent food."

"A what?" Lacey could barely see the building through the rain. "What on earth—out in the middle of nowhere—they can't get many customers."

"They cater mainly to the miners in the area who come down from the mountains every few months or so with their meager gold dust for a hot meal, a shower, and a bed."

"Okay. Sure, I could eat."

The two donned their raingear and sprinted across the sloppy meadow to a small, flat-roofed concrete-block building with a porch overhang. The glassless windows emitted a dim light. Smoke poured from a chimney and the enticing smell of refried beans and corn tortillas reached Lacey's nose, prompting a vociferous growl from her stomach.

Inside the dark, smoke-filled room, two women, one barely a teenager, toiled over a hot griddle, both standing barefoot on the dirt floor. The building had no electricity and clearly the chimney was not drafting well. Unable to stand the smoke any longer, Lacey returned to the relative fresh air of the covered porch while Luke ordered their dinner.

"*Señora Lopez, dos picadillos, por favor.*"

Luke brought out a couple of beers, handing one to Lacey as he sat down at a small wooden table across from her.

"Thanks," Lacey said, reaching for the beer bottle.

"I hope you're okay with warm beer. It's the safest thing to drink around here."

They sat in silence, sipping their beers watching the rain fall in sheets. Out of the monsoon emerged three figures stooped against the elements. The men were soaked through, their heavy beards and long scraggily hair dripping with the excess water.

"Miners," Luke said under his breath, "come to spend some of their hard-earned gold dust."

"*Hola,*" Luke said to the men as they stepped out of the rain and onto the porch.

The men returned the greeting before entering the makeshift outpost.

"Those men, and others like them, lead a hard life," Luke said, his voice gruff.

Surprised by the emotion in his voice, Lacey looked into his eyes and saw compassion in their stormy depths.

"Yes," she replied. "There are many in this world who lead equally hard lives, but the ones I pity most are the women and the children, many of whom have no way out, either for cultural or religious reasons, or because they have no education, no skills. Women whose lives have been torn apart by a war they didn't start and don't understand."

Luke's gaze held hers. He imagined she'd seen a lot of that in two war zones. He lifted his hand, intending to smooth away the lines that creased her brow.

"*Dos picadillos.*" The young girl's words as she placed their plates before them interrupted his movement, and he dropped his hand to his lap.

"*Gracias, Señorita* Amaya." Luke winked up at her smoke-smudged face as he took his plate.

"*De nada, Señor* Luke." Openly testing her feminine wiles on Luke, Amaya leaned over his shoulder, just brushing her long ink-black hair over his neck, before smiling and sauntering off.

Lacey smiled at the teenager's blatant flirtation. "Come here often?" she asked, eyebrow arched.

"Often enough. Oh, you mean that," he said, acknowledging Amaya's attentions. "I've known Amaya since she was a toddler. She's like . . . well, she's like a niece to me." He shrugged.

"I think she'd like to be more than that." Lacey laughed and shook her head at his horrified expression. Even teenage girls weren't immune to Luke's sex appeal.

"Oh please," he said around a mouthful of savory vegetables, "she's barely fifteen. I'm old enough to be her—"

"Father?"

He looked unpleasantly surprised by that realization. Hiding his chagrin, he took a gulp of his beer as Lacey sniggered. "Uncle. I was going to say uncle. And you're how old?" he retorted.

"Thirty-four."

"Old enough to be her mother—"

"As if," she replied with a snort. "Besides, I'm not the one she's infatuated with."

He let that pass for a few beats. "Do you have any children?"

She glanced up at him, her face aghast. "Definitely not."

"Got something against children?"

"No. I happen to love children, but with my job, do you really think I could be a mother?"

His mouth turned up in a wry grin. "Oh, you can be a mother all right."

"Ha! A wilderness guide *and* a comedian. Got any other hidden talents?" she asked as she speared a sweet plantain with her fork.

"Oh, a few. I'd be happy to show you some time." A wolfish grin replaced the wry one.

"You can just keep those, um, talents to yourself." After taking a pull on her beer, she asked, "How about you? You got any little beach bums running around?"

"Not that I know of." From the disgusted look on her face, his intended joke had fallen flat. "I'm kidding. No, I don't."

She nodded and they finished their meals in silence.

Luke took their plates and empty beer bottles and gave them back to the proprietress, thoughtfully saving her a trip, or rather, avoiding a repeat performance from Amaya.

While Luke chatted with *Señora* Lopez, one of the miners stepped out onto the porch to smoke. He pulled on the cigarette, turning his face upward. As that first draw reached his lungs, a look of sheer bliss spilled across his craggy features, transforming his face, like a woman biting into a rich dark chocolate treat. Lacey wished she had her camera. It made a great shot. She'd call it 'Better than Chocolate.'

Luke stepped out, stopping when he saw the slight smile on Lacey's face and the direction of her gaze. "That's probably his first smoke in months. I've seen a similar expression on your face."

Lacey spun toward him with a start, wondering when he could have possibly seen such an expression on her face.

Seeing her surprise, he replied, "When you get your first hit of coffee in the morning."

He gave her a broad grin, making her stomach do a little back-flip. "Oh." She felt the flush creep up her neck and over her cheeks.

How did he do that? Lacey wondered. Manage to make a jaded photojournalist blush with just a smile? Or maybe it wasn't just the smile, but also what his comment revealed. He'd noticed how much she enjoyed her coffee. And he'd remembered it.

"Let's go," he said as he picked up his jacket. "Rain's let up for the moment, and we should hit the sack."

Lacey reluctantly followed. Her previous thoughts of being alone with Luke returned with a vengeance after their little exchange.

Lacey watched as Luke crawled to the back of the plane and began moving boxes, backpacks, and supplies out of the way. He spread their sleeping bags out on the floor, side-by-side. They might as well have been sharing a bed for all the space between the two bags.

"We'll leave at first light," Luke said as he stretched out on his sleeping bag.

Darkness had barely fallen. The rain returned and blew against the plane, an occasional gust of wind off the water rocking it. Lacey hesitated.

"Don't worry," Luke said, eyes closed, "I'm not going to try anything." *Much as I'd like to.*

"As if I'd let you." *Okay, maybe.* She crept to the back in the dimming light, faltering when she encountered his large form blocking the path to her bag. Unsure what to do, she crawled over him, and for good measure, gave him a knee to the abdomen.

"Hey! Watch it!"

"Oh, I'm sorry, did I hurt you?" she asked, all innocence.

"Just go to sleep." He rolled away from her, giving her his back. But he didn't close his eyes to sleep. As if sleep was possible with Lacey lying less than a foot away from him. It was going to be a long, long night.

———

Ready to do battle, Lacey sat up swinging.

"Jesus!" Luke grunted as one of her fists found his rib cage. He grabbed her other wrist before she could take another swing. "Sommers! It's okay. No one's going to hurt you," he said, kneeling over her as he pushed her shoulders back down to her sleeping bag. Despite the darkness, he could see the terror in her eyes, her mind far beyond the cargo area of the small plane.

"Sommers." He reached up to brush the damp hair from her sweat-drenched forehead. Her chest heaved as she struggled to pull in a breath. "Calm down. You're okay." Her eyes focused on his face, and he knew she was finally alert and oriented.

"Get off me." She pushed at his chest as she tried to sit up again. "Christ, it's like an oven in this plane." She shoved her hair back.

Luke sat back onto his heels and handed her a bottle of water. "The rain's stopped. I could put a tarp down on the ground and we could sleep outside, although it'll be dawn soon . . ."

"No. Maybe if I could just step out and get some air." She averted her gaze, obviously too embarrassed to look him in the eye. He'd witnessed her nightmare a second time.

He opened the airplane door, climbing out first, before turning to help Lacey down. She must be feeling vulnerable if she let me help her down, he thought. He sat in the doorway and watched her pace, her arms outstretched to capture even the smallest breeze off the now-calm gulf.

Lacey inhaled the fresh salty air and tried to put the nightmare out of her head, as if it were possible. Darfur. Would she spend the rest of her life reliving that night in her dreams? The smell of death, the sound of sheer terror, the personification of evil, and the cut of the blade?

She'd lost her objectivity that night. And she'd almost lost her life.

The violence in Darfur had been at its height. The Janjaweed militia burned yet another village inhabited by non- Muslim black Africans. Women and children were fleeing the utter brutality. Covering two wars had done nothing to prepare her for the merciless massacre of an entire population.

She reached up to brush her fingers across the scar that would always remind her how short life could be.

Luke watched as Lacey stroked the scar, the significance of the action not lost on him, further confirming in his mind the link between the nightmares and the scar.

He came up behind her, placing his hand tenderly on her shoulder. She flinched at his touch. "I'm sorry. I didn't mean to startle you."

She straightened her shoulders faced him. The look of tenderness in his eyes almost unraveled her. She suppressed the overwhelming desire to melt into his arms and weep like a child.

His expression softened. "Come on. Let's get out of here," he said as he walked back to the plane.

Humiliation averted. So why the disappointment?

CHAPTER SEVEN

The brief flight to Puerto Jimenez had been smooth, and the refreshing shower welcome, notwithstanding the peeping squirrel monkey that had become a regular. After spending most of the morning reviewing her photos with her customary critical eye, organizing them, and uploading them to the magazine's intranet site, Lacey craved exercise to release her cramped muscles.

The sun had finally come out again. Maybe that last storm signaled the end of the rainy season. A run on the beach, followed by a swim sounded perfect. The endorphin release from the run would be icing on the cake.

Dressed in running shorts, bikini top, and running shoes, she jogged down the dirt road to the beach. The steep incline wound through the forest to the beach below. A dog barked as she ran past a beachfront bungalow nestled alongside the forest, but thankfully it didn't give chase.

Luke looked up from his canvas when Sandy started barking and saw Lacey run past the house. He watched as she sprinted across the sand, admiring her form. He dropped the brush he'd been dabbing in cerulean blue, cursing as it hit the deck. "Shit!"

Laughing at himself, he said, "Guess I need to pay attention to what I'm doing."

Lacey stretched out her stride when she hit the flat beach.

The rhythmic sound of the surf and the warmth of the sun relaxed her, allowing her mind to wander.

Although she lived on the beach in Florida (during her rare occasions home), it had been a while since she'd taken a run on the sand. She'd forgotten how it could be both exhilarating and relaxing.

The last two years had been grueling. The wars, Darfur, struggling to save her job, and with the nightmares plaguing her, it proved difficult to put it all behind her. She increased her pace as if she could outrun her demons.

When she'd reached the road back to the resort, she figured she'd run two miles roundtrip. Panting from the exercise and covered in sweat, she'd just toed off her running shoes when she heard her name.

"Sommers!"

No way. Thinking she was hearing things, she turned, and to her surprise, Luke approached, a rambunctious Yellow Lab with a Frisbee in its mouth running circles around him.

Astonished as she was to see him, she couldn't help but appreciate his bare torso with its light blond furring, muscular chest, and flat stomach. She narrowed her eyes. *What on earth could he be doing here?*

"I thought that was you," he said, stopping just short of her. "Been out for a run?" Of course he already knew that, but it was as good an opener as any other. He tried to avoid ogling her like a sex-crazed teenager, but without much success.

Still winded, the rapid rise and fall of her chest drew his eyes to her bikini top, where it revealed the swell of her breasts. Luke's fingers itched to follow a trickle of sweat that ran down her flat stomach only to disappear beneath the waistband of her shorts.

"What? Where did you come from?" She knelt down to give the lab an affectionate pat, which offered her an excuse to escape the desire she saw ignite in his eyes. Her stomach did a little somersault in response.

"I live here."

She looked up from the dog. "Here? On this beach?" *What the hell were the odds?*

Turning, he pointed to the tan concrete block house she'd passed earlier. "Right there." He glanced back at her, a boyish smile on his face. "The Frisbee addict who's currently in the throes of pleasure is Sandy." The Frisbee addict lay on her back, legs out, getting a thorough belly-rub from Lacey. "Aptly named, because if you're not careful, that's what she does—gets you sandy."

Lacey stood up and, taking the Frisbee from Sandy's mouth, launched it, laughing as the Lab jumped up and darted after it.

"Damn. You've got some arm."

She smiled at the surprise in his voice. "Thanks."

"Sandy and I were thinking about going for a swim. Want to come along? The water can be a little cool this time of year, but it's refreshing."

"I was headed to the water myself. No sharks here?"

"No. That's only a problem at the mouth of the Sirena River."

"Good." She shimmied out of her shorts.

Luke drew in a sharp breath. The rest of her body did not disappoint. Long muscular legs met a taut, shapely bottom. Instead of a string bikini, the choice of most sun-worshippers, she wore a simple sport bikini, the choice of women who'd rather play on the beach than lay on the beach.

The bright orange suit deepened the color of her skin. She reminded him of a bronze goddess. A tattooed Monarch butterfly sat on her back right hip as if perched on a flower. That she had a tattoo did not come as a surprise to him, but the choice of the decidedly feminine image did.

Lacey stood up and turned her head to look back at Luke. Following the direction of his gaze, she said, "College rebellion. My mother refused to allow me a tattoo, so I got it when I went away to college."

"Why the butterfly?"

She shrugged. "I just liked it."

Before Luke could warn of the impending danger, Sandy, Frisbee in her mouth, barreled into Lacey, knocking her right on her ass, and she landed with a *whoof*.

Laughing, Lacey attempted to fend off a cold, wet, sand-coated dog.

"Sandy, off!" Luke's terse tone succeeded where Lacey's giggles and playful shoves did not. Sandy showed no sign of remorse as she sat next to Lacey, her tongue lolling in triumph, the Frisbee at her feet.

"Sorry." He bent down and, grabbing Lacey's arm, hauled her to her feet before brushing the sand from her back and bottom.

"You can't say I didn't warn you."

Luke's hands on her bottom sent an electric shock up her spine. She stepped back, her laughter dying in the charged atmosphere. "It's okay. I've got it."

She continued to brush sand from her legs. Drawing a shaky breath, she said, "All the more reason to go for that swim." She spun around and ran for the surf. Diving in, the cold water took her breath away, but it cooled her heated body.

Luke watched her dive into a wave, then followed her lead, with Sandy bringing up the rear.

Lacey surfaced, brushing her hair out of her eyes.

Treading water, she studied the little block house and wondered if he owned it. It was a tidy structure. Simple, but sturdy. A row of solar panels covered the roof alongside a satellite dish and she spied what appeared to be a generator on the north side of the house.

Luke surfaced right next to her, spitting a mouthful of water at her before giving her a big grin.

"That's mature," she said dryly, as she swiped the water from her face. Without warning, using a powerful kick to give her momentum, she pounced on him, shoving his head and shoulders beneath the water.

Luke came up sputtering, her laughter and Sandy's yelping barks punctuating the air. "Oh, you'll pay for that!" he exclaimed.

"I don't think so," she sing-songed, before diving deep and swimming for shore.

"Damn," Luke swore under his breath, before diving after her. Through the bubbles, he could see her moving through the water like a sleek dolphin. She was fast, but he was faster. He reached out. Firm hand found trim ankle and latched on, pulling her backward. He could hear her gurgled curses as she twisted to fight him off.

Kicking with all her strength, she managed to nail him in the thigh, a little too close to the family jewels, before he let go. They both burst through the surface gasping for air.

Not about to give up the fight, he planted both feet and, reaching out, grabbed her hips thinking he'd pick her up and toss her farther out into the waves. Instead he lost his footing and she landed against him with a *thump*.

Grabbing his arms to right herself, she made full body contact, slippery, smooth, and hard. She heard his inhaled breath, saw his eyes widen, then felt his hands glide down her hips to her bottom.

Luke couldn't believe his luck. Lacey's breasts pressed against his chest, lungs heaving from the exertion. Their gazes remained locked for one heartbeat, two, before he lowered his mouth to hers, tasting the salt, feeling the warmth. Pulling her lower lip between his teeth, he nibbled the tender flesh. She fit so perfectly, her taut curves hitting all the right places.

Lacey gave in. Instead of kneeing him in the nuts like she should have, she lifted her arms, wrapping them around his neck, pulling his head down to hers to deepen the kiss. She grazed his tongue with hers, eliciting a moan deep in his throat. She shivered, partly from the cool breeze caressing her damp skin, partly from his kiss. But mostly from his kiss.

Her fingers tangled in his wet hair as his mouth moved over hers. His calloused hands roamed her back, down her spine, over her buttocks, finally lifting her hips against his.

Their bodies collided in the rolling surf, the rhythmic motion triggering a deep-seated need in him. He groaned. All previous thoughts of restraint fled.

The ocean's current had carried them several yards south, but he knew the perfect secluded spot. Just as he bent to scoop her up in his arms with the intent of carrying her to shore, Sandy barreled into them, knocking him off balance. He fell sideways, carrying Lacey with him as a rogue wave washed over their heads, sending all three of them tumbling in the wave's aftermath.

Sandy bobbed to the surface first, Frisbee still clenched between her teeth, followed by Luke, and then Lacey, all coughing and sputtering like old leaky radiators.

While Lacey laughed and Sandy snorted, Luke glowered.

———

"Do you kiss all your clients?"

He had the grace to look chagrinned at Lacey's question. "No. Not all," he prevaricated.

They trudged through the sand toward his house, studiously avoiding physical contact. Lacey had her running shoes in one hand and her shorts in the other, giving her an excuse. She tried to put their encounter out of her mind, but her lips still carried the imprint of his kisses.

Luke used her silence to change the subject. "Want to come up for a beer?"

Lacey's brain said no, but her mouth overruled. "Sure."

"Have a seat. I'll be right back."

Lacey spotted a large canvas and easel out on the deck, facing the rocky shore. Curious, she wandered over to find a lovely partially finished watercolor of the aforementioned shore and the deep blue waters beyond.

Frothy waves frolicked along the beach and caressed the great boulders in their path. White puffy clouds, tinged with gray, floated across the sky, all painted in short thick strokes capturing the essence of the subject, rather than its details.

Hmm. An artist. *And a rather good one. Who knew?*

She almost stumbled over a tackle box that had definitely seen better days. But instead of fishing lures and hooks, it contained watercolors, paintbrushes, and paint-stained cloths.

Lacey stretched out on one of the teak lounge chairs on the deck, overlooking the water. The sun glinted off the lapis- colored waves like yellow diamonds. A tuckered-out Sandy settled at the foot of the chair, head between her paws.

Here she was, playing with fire. Luke was just another playboy; a really hot, sexy playboy, but then again, weren't they all? She knew she wasn't the first female client he'd kissed, and of course she wouldn't be the last. She was also certain that he'd banged more than a few. She would not be the next notch in his surfboard.

Not that she was a prude by any stretch. Some might evencall her sexually adventurous, but she didn't need any entanglements, especially with a man who probably took his sexual partners about as seriously as he took his life.

Sandy's movement signaled Luke's return. Looking beach bum sexy, he carried two beers in one hand, and a towel in the other; around his neck hung yet another towel. Her resolve evaporated. What could a little fling hurt? She'd never see him again after she left. What happens in Costa Rica . . .

Luke settled in the chair next to her, crossing his tanned muscular legs at the ankle before handing her a beer.

"So, we have a Monet in our midst." At his look of confusion she gestured to the canvas with her beer.

Luke could feel his cheeks redden to his ears. In his haste to catch up with her he'd forgotten to put the canvas away. He preferred his work be finished before anyone saw it. "Uh, yeah, I dabble in watercolors, but a Monet I'm not." The corner of his mouth lifted in a slight smile.

"Well, I'm no art critic, but I think it's good."

He beamed, pleased that she approved of his work.

"Tony said your family has an inn on the Jersey Shore," she continued, changing the subject.

"Used to," was his terse reply.

Okay . . . "Where was the inn?"

"A small township on the north Jersey Shore called Ocean Park."

"Yeah, I know it," she said, brow furrowed.

How could she know it? Luke wondered. It was just a small, little-known resort town, until . . . He sat up. "Where'd you grow up?"

"New York City. My family sometimes took long weekends on the Jersey Shore."

He swung his legs back to the wood deck, comprehension dawning. "Sommers—Sommers Development Corporation. Your father is Gregory Sommers?"

Lacey observed the expression on his face: tight-lipped, jaw clenched, cheek twitching.

Now she remembered why the name was familiar to her. One of her father's companies had been involved in a court battle over the development plan for a parcel of land on the Jersey Shore. The plan had called for a high-rise luxury hotel and upscale restaurants and shops, but some of the landowners opposed the plan, especially those in the path of the multi-million dollar project.

She couldn't have been more than twenty when the court sided with her father's company. The property owners had run out of money, effectively ending the battle without an appeal. She recalled she and her father had disagreed vehemently over the case.

"Your avaricious father destroyed what *was* pristine oceanfront property," Luke said, voice vibrating with anger.

She might have disagreed with her father, but she wasn't going to sit back and let Luke cast aspersions. "My *father* created thousands of jobs in an otherwise economically depressed state, not to mention the tourism dollars that followed."

"Spoken like a true trust-fund baby. Daddy get your jobs for you too? That magazine part of his media conglomerate?"

"What would you know about hard work and dedication to a profession? You're just a devil-may-care beach bum and part-time wilderness guide. Maybe you should think about getting a *real* job! Thanks for the beer, asshole!" She stood up, throwing her towel in his face.

Luke lifted the soaking wet towel off his face, ready to light into her, but she was gone. "Son of a bitch." What was he going to do now?

He raked his hand through his hair. He still had several more weeks with the woman whose father had destroyed his father's livelihood.

Lacey fumed all the way back to her bungalow. So much for the endorphins. The cortisol now pulsing through her body was a real buzz-killer. She'd shoot an email to her editor and tell him she couldn't work with Luke —that he had to find another guide for the remainder of her assignment.

She was irate enough now to spit nails. How dare he? What did he know about her or her family? He assumed because her father had money that she didn't achieve her accomplishments by her own blood, sweat, and tears. Literally.

Lacey wasn't about to apologize for her upbringing. While it was true she had a trust fund, she'd never touched a dime of the money. She didn't even know how much money the trust fund held. If it weren't for the trust's restrictions, she would have donated it all to an international women's aid program to help the thousands of women ravaged by war rebuild their lives.

Born to Gregory Sommers and Clarissa Gentry, she and

her younger sister, Lilia, had grown up in New York in an apartment on Park Avenue overlooking Central Park, along with the likes of the Kennedys.

The family spent their summers in the Hamptons, their winter breaks in Aspen for skiing, or in Nevis for snorkeling and scuba diving. She and her sister had attended the best private schools. But her father had earned the family's wealth honestly, through hard work and intelligent decisions.

Clarissa, an avid socialite, came from old money. Lacey loved her mother, but if the adjective avaricious could be applied to one of her parents, it would be her mother.

Her sister, Lilia Sommers-Stanton, had followed in her mother's Jimmy Choo's. Married to a neurosurgeon, they now lived the self-indulgent lifestyle in Greenwich, Connecticut, near Clarissa.

Aside from DNA, Lacey had little in common with those pampered princesses.

As for her father getting her jobs for her, it couldn't be further from the truth. Her father wanted her to work for some glossy fashion magazine, even calling on friends and lining up interviews, but Lacey refused to give in. She couldn't think of anything more miserable than shooting a bunch of underfed, bitchy, fashion models.

Yes, she'd succeeded on her own merits, and she resented the fact that Luke thought otherwise.

She'd had to prove herself to her editor, to the troops, and to her father, who no doubt expected her to come home with her tail between her legs begging for that job with the fashion magazine.

Now that need to prove herself had become so deeply ingrained, had she lost sight of it for what it was: plain and simple insecurity? And here she was trying to prove herself all over again. To Luke. To her magazine. Maybe even to herself.

Running uphill had worked off most of her temper. Stripping off her still-damp swimsuit, Lacey headed for the shower hoping to scrub off the remaining funk of sweat, salt, and anger.

Adequately de-funked, she padded across the floor in her bare feet, wrapped in a towel. After giving it some thought, she wouldn't send the email after all. She had enough problems with the magazine without acting like one of those aforementioned spoiled whiney bitches.

She spotted a note under her door. Written on it in angry scrawl was the terse message:

We leave at 5:30 a.m. Sharp.
   s/ The Asshole

Lacey growled before ripping the paper to shreds.

———

Tony shut the door of his truck and strode up the drive to Luke's house. Before he got to the door, he heard a loud bang, followed by a string of curses peppering the air. Tony circled to the north side of the house and found Luke jumping on one bare foot, holding the other in his hands as he continued to spew obscenities.

"Uh-oh. What happened now?"

"Jesus!" Luke jumped, then swiveled to scowl at Tony. "You scared the shit out of me. How about giving me a little warning next time?"

"You wouldn't have heard me over the exploding f-bombs."

Luke gave Tony an eat-shit look. "And what did you mean by 'What happened now?' Who said this has anything to do with Lacey?"

"You just did." Tony grinned. "You're tinkering. You always tinker when something's bothering you."

"There's nothing bothering me." He turned back to the generator he'd been . . . okay, tinkering with. "The old generator is on its last leg. I'm hoping to get another six months out of it anyway," he muttered.

"Right." Tony waited patiently while Luke cleaned off his hands and put his tools away.

Luke released a heavy sigh. "She's Gregory Sommers' daughter."

Tony's jaw dropped open. "You're kidding me! How'd you find that out?"

"We were talking about our childhoods, and I put two and two together."

"Does she know? About your parents, I mean?"

"Oh, I let her know what her father did to my parents," Luke said with a self-righteous tone.

"Luke, man, it wasn't personal. Mr. Sommers didn't set out to destroy your family."

"What difference does it make? The end result's the same."

Tony didn't respond. He knew this was just one of Luke's many sore spots.

"She's just another rich girl like Caroline."

Tony winced at the vitriol in Luke's voice and as much as he wanted to defend Lacey, he held his tongue.

Luke picked up his toolbox and headed for the carport, Tony close on his heels. When he'd decided to move back to

Costa Rica and start his own business, Caroline had balked. She'd expected him to go to work for a big environmental consulting firm as a well-paid consultant, not to become, in her words, 'a glorified tour guide' in the jungles of Costa Rica.

He should have known that in the end, spoiled, pampered Caroline would choose money over him, and he wasn't about to beg her to come with him. Anyone who needed begging wasn't worth it to his mind.

He faced Tony. "Too bad you're going up to Guanacaste tomorrow with that family from Brazil. I'm not looking forward to spending two days alone with her. I'd even thought about terminating the contract with the magazine, but . . ."

"But, is right. This is a lucrative contract, one that could lead to more lucrative contracts with the same media corporation."

"I know. I know." Luke waved his hand in the air as if dismissing Tony's arguments. "I'm not bagging the deal. I'll just have to put up with the rich little—"

"Sins of the father, Luke?" Tony raised his brow in astonishment at his friend's narrow-mindedness. "She had nothing to do with the court case. For all you know she had no knowledge of any of it."

"She defended her father readily enough," Luke replied, his voice raised in anger.

"So, what? She loves her father. Is that a crime?"

"Why are you taking her side in this? You saw what that battle did to my parents . . . my father."

Tony came over and put his hand on Luke's shoulder. "I'm not taking sides. All I'm saying is you're condemning her for her father's actions, and that's not like you."

"Lacey Sommers seems to push my buttons," Luke muttered.

It's about time somebody did, Tony thought with a calculating grin.

CHAPTER NINE

The flight to the Monteverde Cloud Forest Reserve in northern Costa Rica, though mercifully short, was tense nonetheless. Lacey shot a glance at Luke. He'd had barely said a word to her. How would they spend the next two days together isolated in the Cloud Forest?

From her research, Lacey recalled the twenty-six thousand acre reserve straddled the Continental Divide and was home to an incredibly diverse ecosystem. Warm, moist air sweeping up the mountains off the Pacific Ocean cooled at altitude, forming an almost constant cloud-cover, bringing moisture to the forests, and providing an ideal habitat for frogs. *Super.*

To save time, they would travel on horseback to their campsite near the three hundred thirty foot San Luis Waterfall, the tallest waterfall in the Monteverde area.

Standing in the corral, Lacey's well-trained eye spotted a thoroughbred standing apart from the rest of the horses, like a princess standing apart from the peasants. She was a chestnut beauty. Standing at about sixteen hands, her well-chiseled head, long, slim neck, and trim, athletic body with its high withers, deep chest, and long legs made her excellent for jumping.

Lacey wondered what a horse of such fine quality was doing in a corral of workhorses like the Mustangs, Stock Horses, and packhorses, with a few mules sprinkled among them. She wanted her for the ride.

Luke spoke with a woman who apparently owned the horse outfitters. Lacey strode over to them, determined to ride the beautiful jumper.

"The two Mustangs will work, and Gustavo," Luke said, pointing to an indolent-looking brown mule.

"No." Lacey stopped just short of the two. "I want her," she said, pointing to the chestnut mare.

Luke turned to look in the direction of Lacey's outstretched arm, eyebrow lifted. "You must be joking. This is a trail ride, not a show ring."

"My money, I choose. And I choose her. Hi, I'm Lacey," she said as she stuck out her hand.

"I'm Mona," the woman replied as she shook Lacey's hand in a firm grip.

Lacey liked her on contact. Beautiful, even sultry, in a natural, earthy way, her long black hair was held back in a ponytail, and intelligent brown eyes sparkled from a friendly face devoid of makeup. Her jeans were worn, but clean, and her tank top revealed the well-defined arms of a horsewoman. She had no accent.

"You American?" Lacey asked.

"Yes. From Montana originally. Moved here when I followed husband *numero uno*." She shrugged, as if that explained everything. In a way it did.

"Well, Mona, nice to meet you. What's her name?" She jutted her head toward the mare.

"Sabina." Seeing the frown on Luke's face, she turned back to Lacey. "She's a handful. Spirited."

"Perfect."

Luke groaned. "Lacey, what did I say the other day?"

Lacey faced him, all innocence, and said, "Yes, my liege. I promised not to put you or Tony in danger again. And I won't." Effectively dismissing him, she turned back to Mona. "I take it Sabina's your personal horse?"

"Yes." Mona stared Lacey straight in the eye, apparently sizing her up. "But I do permit others to ride her. On occasion."

Luke groaned again, and marched off to saddle his own horse. "Your neck."

He watched as the two women talked, heads together, thick as thieves. Cinching the saddle on Nugget, a lovely mustang, he frowned. Lacey and Mona walked over to Sabina, Mona carrying the saddle, Lacey laughing at something Mona said.

This didn't bode well. It was clearly going to be two against one.

"How'd you find her?" Lacey asked as Mona lifted the saddle to Sabina's back. Lacey reached up to stroke the silky nose, earning a nicker of approval from the mare, the smell of horse, hay, and manure strong in the heavy atmosphere.

"A once-wealthy Spaniard lost everything in a pyramid scheme and was selling off his possessions for a song. Sabina came at multi-platinum record price, but a steal none-theless, and worth every *colón*." She smiled, affectionately patting the horse's withers.

"She's a beauty. I bet she soars over a jump like an eagle on an updraft." Lacey mounted the horse, leaning down to give her neck a pat.

"See for yourself." She smiled up at her.

"Seriously?"

"Why not? I trust you." Mona met her gaze and an undeniable bond formed.

From his perch atop Nugget across the paddock, Luke watched the exchange. He'd known Mona for years and they'd even had a short fling after her first husband left, but he'd never seen her take to someone so quickly. Usually Mona had to warm up to a stranger. She backed away from Lacey with a broad smile on her face, then gave a short, barely perceptible nod.

Lacey dug her heels into the mare, nudging her into a walk, circling the paddock a couple of times, before going into a trot, then a canter.

The expression on her face did not go unnoticed by Luke. She looked happy, relaxed. Guard down. She had a good seat. As he observed her form, the mare broke into a full gallop, circling the paddock once more, then charged at breakneck speed toward the paddock fence.

Luke watched, frozen in fear. Sabina sailed over the paddock fence with all the grace of a gazelle, before landing solidly on the other side, running up the trail as if a hungry puma dogged her heels.

"Sommers!" Luke kicked his horse into gallop and, closing his eyes in prayer to a god he didn't believe in, followed Sabina's path over the paddock rail, Nugget landing with a not-so-graceful thud on the other side.

There was no way in hell he was going to catch up to the leggy mare. She chewed up ground like she was running the Kentucky Derby. *Damn.* He kicked his little Mustang into a faster gallop.

Branches hung low on the trail that could unseat the unwary rider. The panic that filled him made it difficult to breathe.

Up ahead, Sabina slowed just enough for Luke to catch up to her. Reaching out, he grabbed the horse's reins, the sound of his shirt seam ripping as he yanked her to a stop, where she pranced with barely restrained energy.

"What the hell do you think you're doing?" Lacey turned on him, eyes ablaze with blue fire, chest heaving with her exertion.

"What the hell am *I* doing? What the hell are *you* doing?" In his anger, he tugged on the reins again, causing Sabina to sidestep in agitation.

"Get your hands off my horse," Lacey growled as she pulled the reins in the opposite direction, soothing Sabina as she did so.

"You mean to tell me that little show was intentional!" Luke's voice carried through the jungle, triggering birds to take flight. "Goddamn it, Sommers! You could have broken your neck and the horse's to boot. Clearly you've forgotten who your lord and master is."

His face was a portrait in rage, but she wasn't giving in. "Hancock! Shut it. I took state jump champion three years in a row. I've jumped horses all my life and besides, Mona gave me permission."

"I see promises mean nothing to you," he ground out. "Like father like daughter," he muttered.

"Fuck you, Hancock." She wheeled Sabina toward the paddock where they'd left their packs and camping supplies. "I promised I wouldn't put you or Tony in danger again, and I didn't. Nor did I put myself or Sabina in danger." Kicking Sabina into a trot, she continued, "You need to get over your hero complex. Not everyone needs rescuing," she shot, leaving Luke to seethe at her back.

———

Due to their late start, a consequence of her stunt, as Luke felt compelled to remind her throughout the ride, they arrived at their campsite just before nightfall. Lacey stubbornly set up her own tent and unpacked her meager supplies for the one-night bivouac, the distant sound of the waterfall providing background noise.

Luke set about making a fire on the damp ground, using the dry tinder Mona had supplied. Dinner would be cold, the campfire serving only to provide a little light, along with the camp lanterns, and to keep the animals at bay.

Lacey sauntered over to the edge of the campsite, seeking a little privacy.

"Don't stray too far, Sommers. As much as I'd like to feed you to a jaguar right now, it'd be bad for business if you got eaten by one."

"Be still my heart. Your concern is touching. Really." She threw him a look over her shoulder, dabbing at an imaginary tear. "Just need the little girl's room, if you don't mind," she said as she ducked behind some foliage for privacy.

Luke dug in the pack for the can of refried beans, tortillas, and avocado that would comprise their dinner, followed by a papaya for dessert. Not on par with Tony's fare, but better than an MRE.

Emerging from nature's privy, Lacey glanced over at Luke bent over their plates as he divvied up dinner. The firelight played off his features and turned his hair to spun gold. A little butterfly fluttered in her stomach.

The night in the airplane notwithstanding, this setting was by far the more intimate. And romantic, if you believed in that sort of thing. Isolated here in the cloud forest, only the two of them and the horses, as if they were the only two people in the world, like Adam and Eve.

Maybe she should tempt him with the fruit of the tree of knowledge, knowledge of her that is, in the biblical sense. Shaking her head at her nonsensical thoughts, she plopped down across from him.

She barely stifled a groan as her bum hit the ground. Her ass painfully reminded her of the long ride. It had been some time since she'd ridden more than an hour or two. Truth be told, the discomfort was more likely related to the gallop than the steady walk up the mountain. But she'd just keep that bit of information to herself.

Luke handed her a plate. Eyeing the skimpy meal, she raised an eyebrow.

"Hey, I never promised the Four Seasons," he said as he shoveled refried beans into his mouth.

"No kidding. I miss Tony."

"Don't eat then." Luke snarled.

Wrapping her refried beans and avocado in her tortilla, she made the best of it. It didn't make her top ten worst meals.

She frowned, recalling something Luke had said earlier. "Speaking of promises, why did you all but call my father deceitful and by association, me?"

"I have to explain that to you? Oh yeah, I forgot, Daddy Dearest can do no wrong."

"Fine. Never mind." The acid in his voice hurt more than she cared to admit. She picked up her plate, heading for her tent.

Luke released a gusty sigh. "Okay. Sit. I'll tell you, since you don't appear to know." His look conveyed disbelief over her lack of knowledge. "Your father financially ruined my family. He took away their livelihood. When they lost the inn, they lost their home in New Jersey. He could no longer afford to come to Costa Rica for the winter. A place he loved. Physically unable to work here as a guide anymore, he had no income."

"But my father gave all the affected business owners a fair deal."

Luke snorted in disgust. "Yeah, is that what you call it? Fair market value for the property? Big fucking deal. That did little to make up for the lost business. Another of your father's broken promises."

"What are you talking about? My father set aside millions of dollars for the affected businesses to cover lost income, moving expenses, start-up costs if they wanted to start their businesses elsewhere. He even covered employees who'd lost their jobs to tide them over until the new businesses opened and started hiring."

"Now what are *you* talking about? The court mandated fair market value for the real estate, nothing more."

"Right. The *court* didn't require any other settlement, but my father *voluntarily* financed a trust fund for those affected. They only had to come forward, complete some paperwork, sign a release, and they got the money."

Luke frowned. He vaguely remembered something about a fund, but . . . "Well, maybe that's what Dear Ol' Daddy told you, but my father is living on a small limited income." Supplemented by him.

His parents divorced a couple of years after they lost the inn, just too many losses for a marriage to handle, he guessed. His father had a breakdown less than a year later. His mother had remarried and was doing well financially with her husband's sporting goods store. But his father . . . his father still struggled.

"Hancock, I'm telling you the truth. Verifying it would be simple. A phone call. Even a web search."

"Quite frankly, I'm not going to rehash this with my father. Not much point. I'm sure the money is long gone. If it even existed to begin with."

"You're not going to rehash this with your father, but you are with me?" She narrowed her eyes.

"I didn't bring it up. You did. Now I'm ending it." His mouth drew into a tight line.

"Fine. Suit yourself."

CHAPTER TEN

L uke lay on his side, listening to the rain patter on the dome of the small tent. Ordinarily the rain's whisper would lull him into a deep, dreamless sleep, but tonight the thoughts warring in his head not only thwarted sleep, they triggered a headache.

He knew better than anyone just how stubborn and proud his father could be. He'd inherited some of those same characteristics. But surely even his father wouldn't cut off his nose to spite his face by turning down a settlement. It wouldn't be charity. It would have covered lost income and provided capital for a new business.

Luke rolled to his back, staring up at the tent without seeing it. He hadn't been there during the whole battle. He'd been finishing up his degree, and his father had convinced him to stay put, not interrupt his work, so every maneuver, every negotiation, and finally every legal argument had been filtered through his father, and occasionally his mother.

No. It's just another one of Mr. Sommers' stories to make

him look better in his daughter's eyes. His father was stubborn, not stupid.

A fat droplet of water landed in the middle of Luke's forehead with a startling *splat,* followed shortly by another. What the hell? Luke turned on his camp lantern and raised it to find an opening forming along one of the seams in the tent's roof.

Great. Just great. He had a spoiled, rich little daredevil for a client whose father was the root of all evil, he had a rip in one of his favorite shirts as a result of trying to save said daredevil, and now he had a hole in his tent.

Sliding his sleeping mat and bag out of the way, he tried to find something to catch the now constant drip. Grabbing his mug, he placed it beneath the leak, but with each *plink* of water into the mug, a splatter bounced out of the cup and onto his face. Not to mention the fact that if the rain kept up, the mug would soon be overflowing.

He would either have to wake up periodically to empty the mug or wake up in the morning to a wet sleeping bag. *Joy.*

———

Lacey tried reading a while, then tossed the book aside. She picked up her journal, scribbled a few lines, but couldn't concentrate. Finally, she picked up her camera and scrolled through the day's photos. They seemed pretty good, but she wouldn't know for sure until she could study them on the laptop.

She'd gotten more shots of the dreaded, but mandatory, frogs. She'd also gotten some great stills of orchids growing on the forest's tree trunks. Her breath left in a sigh when she came to a series of shots of Luke she hadn't been able to resist taking. First, sitting astride his horse, looking like a modern-day explorer. He had a good seat, she noted.

The next, a shot of him at one of the stops along the trail. Smiling, he had his forehead against Nugget's muzzle as he whispered some endearment to the horse. Finally, one of him kneeling by some huge beetle, studying it, his brow furrowed in concentration. All quiet moments when he hadn't realized she'd trained her lens on him.

He was so gentle, so respectful of the fauna they encountered. And despite their disagreements, he'd morphed into the consummate guide on the trail, so knowledgeable about the animals and their habitat, their behavior, and their importance to the environment.

What did it take to earn that same gentleness, that same respectfulness?

Setting aside the camera, she turned out the lantern and settled back to get some sleep. It seemed so lonely and isolated in the tent with the sound of the rain separating them.

Who was she kidding? More than rain separated them. The sins of the fathers—both perceived and real.

———

Lacey started at the sound of her tent zipper being slid open. Just as she laid her hand on her camp lantern, intending to brain the intruder with it, she saw Luke's wet form silhouetted against the outdoors.

"What the hell do you think you're doing?" she ground out.

"My tent has a hole in it," he said matter-of-factly as he tossed his rain-dampened sleeping bag next to hers.

"And you think you're staying here?" she said with a squeak.

"I'd stay in the Ritz-Carlton, but they're all booked up." Luke stretched out on the tent floor and crossed his arms over his chest.

"No way."

"Yes, way." He rolled over onto his side, his back to her. "Look, I'm tired and I'd like to get some sleep. Believe me, I have no plans of impugning your honor," he said, sarcasm heavy in his voice.

She didn't know whether to be angrier over his cavalier invasion of her space or his clear repugnance at the thought of having sex with her.

She rolled over in a huff. "Just stay on your side of the tent, Hancock, or risk losing a treasured part of your anatomy."

Luke's eyes flew open as he remembered that she'd yet to pay him back for revealing her frog encounter. Just to be safe, he tucked both hands between his thighs before drifting off to sleep.

———

Not again, Luke groaned. He forced himself to roll over. Lacey flailed in her sleep, her low, keening moans turning to whimpers of fear.

"Sommers." He shook her shoulder. "Sommers."

She sat up with a start, then searched the small tent as if trying to recall her surroundings.

"Jesus, Sommers. You need to do something about those nightmares. Get some help, for God sakes."

He rolled over again, ignoring her, as she attempted to pull herself back together.

Lacey huddled deeper into the sleeping bag. Tonight's nightmare had been a bizarre blend of Darfur and Tanzania, her attackers a sort of manticore: part man, part lion.

After she'd left the AP and started with the nature magazine as a wildlife photographer, her first assignment had been in the Ngorongoro Crater in Africa tracking a pride of lions.

One late afternoon, she and her African guides had come upon the pride as they brought down a gazelle. But instead of killing the frightened animal, they encircled it, taunting and snapping and batting at it with their enormous paws like a cat with a mouse. The bleating cries of the gazelle combined with the terror that she'd witnessed on the doomed animal's face proved too much.

She flashed back to Darfur and had a full-blown panic attack in the African Sahara, scaring the hell out of her African guides. These were the very photos she'd been paid to take, and she hadn't taken a single shot.

The Editor-in-Chief wanted her fired, but her editor stood up for her, giving her another chance with a nice, safe shoot in Costa Rica.

Lacey snorted. Crawling toward the tent opening, she unzipped it.

"Where the hell are you going?"

"Nature calls," she said bluntly.

"Yeah, well, just don't go too far, 'cuz if you're not back in five minutes don't expect me to come looking for you."

She rolled her eyes and stepped out into the cool, damp mountain air, breathing deeply to calm her frayed nerves. A fine mist still fell, and she held her face up to the refreshing shower.

Why did he have to crawl into her tent? Why did she have to wake him with yet another nightmare?

She was surprised to find that she'd even fallen asleep. At first she lay there considering her options for her yet-to-be- executed vengeance. The conditions were not favorable for the standard practical jokes: making him pee on himself by placing his hand in warm water, putting hot sauce on his lips, or a ripe tomato in his bed. Alas, she had no warm water, no hot sauce, and no ripe tomatoes handy.

Besides, those options weren't public enough. When he felt her retribution, and he would, she wanted witnesses. Only public humiliation would satisfy her thirst for revenge.

Then she'd laid there for a long time listening to the sound of his breathing, inhaling his scent, and feeling the heat roll off his body, thinking about how comforting it would be to slide over and spoon against his solid back.

She shook her head at her own asinine thoughts. *Get a grip, Sommers. Hancock might not mind shagging you, but he didn't seem the cuddling type.* And, come to think of it, neither was she.

Despite his nonchalant words, Luke waited until Lacey returned to the tent before settling back to sleep. Maybe he'd been unfair in his assessment of her.

He'd had his fair share of rich clients, most of them too pampered for their own good. They all wanted to play at 'roughing it' for a week, but many just wound up complaining about the heat and humidity, the bugs, and the lack of luxuries they were accustomed to. Lacey was different.

Given her father's money and power, he doubted she'd wanted for anything growing up. And yet, she'd spent several hellish years in two war zones, and now she managed the rigors of camping in a tropical environment, all without complaint. He'd discovered a newfound respect for her. Even if she *was* a pain in the ass.

———

L uke sighed with pleasure. The warm body molded to fit his in luscious, tempting ways. His hand rested on a firm cotton-clad breast, rising and falling with each breath. He mentally groaned as the womanly derriere nestled deeper into his hips. He smiled and drew in a long, slow breath. The scent of lavender and rosemary invaded his brain. His eyes shot open as he realized where he was, and with whom.

"Hancock! Get your hand off my breast!" Lacey ground out.

He pushed himself away from her, but his hand still bore the scalding imprint of her breast.

She sat up, holding the sleeping bag up to her chest as if protecting her modesty. "I should have known! I told you to stay on your side of the tent!"

"I didn't hear you complaining thirty seconds ago." He wore a rakish grin.

"Ooh!" She picked up her hiking boot to throw it at him. "Get out!"

He chuckled as he beat a hasty retreat.

Lacey sat in her tent, flustered, and not a little aroused, which only served to agitate her even more.

When she'd first floated to awareness and felt the hard body curled around her, she'd wanted to nestle deeper and sink back into oblivion, but the feel of the large masculine hand covering her entire breast led her thoughts down a different path.

Even after realization dawned, her pulse had quickened

at the intimate and all-too-delicious contact. It would have been so easy to roll over and take advantage of Luke's morning 'salute.' But she wouldn't give him the satisfaction.

"You coming, Sommers?" Luke called from outside the tent.

She bit back a juvenile giggle. *Unfortunately, no.*

———

L uke's gut clinched every time he visited a waterfall, but as a guide he had to get over it. It was the rare client that didn't want to see a waterfall, exclaim over the beauty and power, take hundreds of pictures and record megabytes of video. He tried to make the best of it.

The roar of the waterfall drowned out all other sound. Just coming off the rainy season, the falls cascaded over the cliff with impressive power. Breathtaking at three hundred thirty feet, relatively the same height as a thirty-story building, the cataract plunged into a deep pool at the bottom.

Luke watched as Lacey slid off her horse and out of her hiking boots. Though she hadn't complained, he'd seen the sweat rolling off her face, her clothes clinging to her in places he didn't want to dwell on too long.

"Water's cold," he shouted, in order to be heard over the roar.

Lacey turned and smiled at Luke's warning. She grew up swimming in the waters off New York. How cold could the waters in tropical Costa Rica be?

After their unintended cuddle, Luke had surprised her when she'd joined him for their makeshift breakfast by extending his hand in truce.

"Let's agree to disagree on our fathers', well . . . disagreement." His lips had turned up into a brief smile. "What's done is done, and neither you nor I can change it."

She'd peered at him through narrowed eyes, as if trying to figure out his angle. Taking his hand, she'd melted a little at the feel of his warm, calloused grip, remembering the feel of it on her this morning. "Truce, then."

"Oh, and I'm sorry about this morning."

"No you're not."

"Okay, you're right. I'm not." He wore a devilish grin that emphasized the dimple in his chin.

He'd been a little friendlier since and it made for a more relaxing, enjoyable ride. And true to his word, he hadn't mentioned his grudge against her father again. She tried to set aside the cynical view that he was just buttering her up because he wanted a roll in the sheets, *er*, sleeping bag.

Luke laughed as he watched Lacey jumped feet first into the icy pool, waiting for the inevitable scream as her body's nerves registered the fifty-degree water.

Lacey didn't disappoint. She shot to the surface with a high-pitched squeal, followed by a flood of curses. "Jesus Christ! Holy shit, that's cold!"

"Can't say I didn't warn you," he said, chuckling at her discomfort. After tying up the horses, he toed off his own boots and stripped off his shirt, intending to join her in the frigid pool.

He jumped in, cannonball style, soaking Lacey with a towering glacial splash. When he surfaced, he was met with another string of curses, eliciting another chuckle from him.

"Christ, Hancock! I just got my breath back."

Shoving the hair out of his eyes as he faced her, he found himself breathless, but not with cold.

Lacey stood in her usual ready-to-do-battle pose, her arms and legs slick with water, her thin tank top leaving nothing to the imagination, sodden shorts slung low on her hips. She looked like she belonged in one of those sexy cologne ads.

Thinking about this morning and the feel of her against him, a pool of heat gathered low in his abdomen. Her father had ruined his parents, but he wanted her just the same.

He'd never met anyone who made him so angry one minute and so horny the next. She kept him constantly off-balance. Any time he thought he'd gained the upper hand, she'd throw him another curve. Giving himself a mental shake, he turned his back on her and climbed out of the pool.

He'd resolved last night to put her father's actions aside.

She would have been in her twenties when this happened and surely had nothing to do with it. But she'd reaped the financial benefits in the end. *Enough*, he reminded himself. *It's done.*

Unaware of his inner struggles, Lacey paused to admire his bare back, the tan line where his shorts sagged below his trim waist, before she climbed out of the pool, shivering a little. Luke handed her a small camp towel that didn't offer much warmth, but it at least mopped up the excess water.

Lacey gazed up at the waterfall again. "Hey, Hancock, let's hike to the top. I bet the view is spectacular."

He froze. Only she would think of that. "No. I don't think so. It's an arduous hike, no trail, and we need to head back. You're on assignment, remember?"

"What, you think I can't do it?"

There it was again, that brash indignation. "Sommers, I have no doubt you can do it. You don't have to prove anything."

"Oh come on. We can take the time."

"No."

"Why not?"

Luke wouldn't turn around and look at her.

"Aw, come on, scaredy-cat," she teased, only intending to egg him on.

"I am not a scaredy-cat," he ground out as he whirled to face her.

She'd seen him angry just as recently as last night, but not like this. This was a desperate anger. A fearful anger. "Okay, then, I'll go."

He took a step toward her, his expression shifting from anger to pure fear. "No."

What was his deal? Putting a leash on her rising frustration, she cajoled, "Come on, Hancock, it'll be fun. It's a great way to warm up again, making another dip inviting."

Luke groaned. He knew she would go on her own, even if he threatened to take the horses and leave her behind. He could do this. Man up. Face his fear. Isn't that what his therapist in college had said?

But cold water notwithstanding, he didn't think he could take another dip with her without dragging her off to the jungle like some Neanderthal.

"Fine."

"Yay!"

He smiled in spite of himself. She looked like a little girl who'd just been given a pony.

———

Lacey had to admit, Luke was right. It had been an arduous hike, but the view was every bit as spectacular as she thought it would be. Taking out the ever-present camera, she stood on the river's edge and snapped on the wide-angle lens for some shots of the scenery.

Changing to the telephoto, she got some shots of two scarlet macaws on the wing, before spotting the elusive resplendent quetzal perched in a tree across the river. She inhaled sharply at its beauty.

The bird lived up to its name. His iridescent green body and vivid scarlet breast made him impossible to miss. The green tail feathers, over twice the length of his body, extended well past the branch on which he sat. He was quite simply magnificent.

The telephoto wasn't enough. Remembering her mantra, she searched for a way to get closer. The water raced over the edge of the cliff, but there appeared to be a protected area just north of where she stood. If she waded in there, she could get across.

She turned slowly to Luke, trying not to scare the bird off, and whispered, "Hancock, there's a quetzal. I have to get closer."

Luke followed the direction of her outstretched arm. "In all the years I've lived here, I've only seen the bird a handful of times. It's something, isn't it?"

Lacey left Luke watching the bird as she gingerly stepped onto the rocky bed, gritting her teeth against the cold water. Before she could take another step, the bird took flight. Seconds later, she understood why.

Luke grabbed her arm, jerking her backward, almost causing her to lose her footing. "What the hell are you doing?" he growled.

"I *was* crossing the river to get a close up, but you scared him away."

He grabbed her shoulders, his grip tightening. "Don't *ever* cross a waterfall, do you hear me?" He shook her for good measure.

She'd seen this look before, on the faces of soldiers as

they relived their combat experiences. Wide-eyed, tight-lipped, yet distant. In fact, she'd seen that same expression in the bathroom mirror after she woke from one of her nightmares.

"Okay, Hancock," she replied calmly. "It's okay." His grip didn't lessen. "Hancock, you're hurting me."

He refocused on her face. "Sorry. Just . . . don't do that again."

"I won't." She rubbed her arms as he turned away. Obviously she wasn't the only one with demons.

CHAPTER ELEVEN

Lacey stared at Luke's back as she followed him down the trail and replayed the scene at the river in her mind. In the short time since she'd met him, Luke had always seemed so sure of himself, so confident in his handling of all situations— including the crocodile encounter—that the look of abject fear in his eyes was like a knife to her heart.

What could trigger such a deep-seated reaction? A phobia of some kind? Clearly he wasn't afraid of the water, or heights, so what *was* he afraid of?

Luke guided the horse around an ancient strangler fig, trying to keep focused on the road, not reliving the horror at seeing Lacey so close to the edge. An all too familiar scene. Self-recriminations echoed in his head. If only he'd done that twenty years ago. If only he hadn't stood by and watched Lisa wade out into that violent river. If only they hadn't gone on that hike. If, if, if.

A year after Lisa's death, Luke had left Costa Rica, running away from the memories, the haunted look in his parents' eyes, and his inability to console them. And he kept running until he finally realized it didn't solve anything.

And neither did rehashing the event. It was a waste of time and energy. It wouldn't change the past. It wouldn't assuage the guilt, but most of all it wouldn't bring Lisa back.

Mona's warm greeting brought him back to the present. He couldn't even recall how he'd gotten down the mountain. Thankfully he knew the terrain like the back of his hand. Mona gave Sabina an affectionate hug, which the horse returned with an excited whinny.

As Lacey approached Mona, Luke watched the interchange between the two women, struck again by Mona's uncharacteristic openness toward Lacey. He shook his head. Women. They defied understanding.

He and Lacey were scheduled for a night hike in Monteverde and would stay in a local lodge before the flight back to Puerto Jimenez. As much as he needed some distance from Lacey and from the turbulent feelings she elicited in him, he'd welcome a hot shower and a comfortable bed, and he'd lay odds Lacey would, too.

———

Armed with flashlights and Lacey's ubiquitous camera equipment, she, Luke, and Enrique, a tracker and expert on Costa Rica's 'nightlife', slogged through mud in the hopes of spotting some of the forest's more elusive nocturnal inhabitants like the jaguar or ocelot.

A symphony of frogs and insects accompanied their night hike.

Everyone spoke in whispers, when they spoke at all, seeking to avoid frightening the introverted animals of the night.

Lacey turned in the direction of a rustling noise in the underbrush, her breath catching in her throat. She collided with Luke's muscular back, eliciting a grunt from her and a hissed, "Watch where you're going, Sommers" from him.

Lacey bit back the retort on the tip of her tongue. Luke was annoyed with her. Again. He must have a serious case of SRS (a.k.a. Semen Retention Syndrome). He definitely needed to get laid. But why did the thought of him with another woman make her blood boil?

"Oh, look," Enrique whispered as he turned his flashlight on a pair of beady eyes, "there's a kinkajou, there in that strangler fig."

Luke watched Enrique grab Lacey's hand, pulling her along next to him before stepping behind her, standing a little too close for Luke's comfort. Enrique had been putting the moves on Lacey since he'd introduced them a couple of hours before, and she'd been all smiles since.

The rapid click of Lacey's shutter punctuated the night before she moved on. Enrique pointed out toads and frogs for her benefit, leaning in to tell her little snippets of information.

Despite his best efforts, Luke found Enrique's interest aggravating. Yes, he and Enrique went way back, but did he have to openly carry on his Casanova routine? Helping her over fallen trees, holding back vines blocking their path, using any excuse to put his hands on her. And she let him. She, who spurned any offer of help he made.

Gritting his teeth, Luke glanced at his watch to see how much longer he had to put up with it. One more hour.

"Watch out," Enrique hissed. "There's a tarantula." He illuminated the arachnid with his flashlight as it scurried across the path not far from Luke's boot.

"Gah." Luke jumped back, landing on Lacey's foot.

"Ow! Shit!" She danced around on one foot, holding up her abused one. "Now *you* watch where you're going, Hancock. Jeez."

"Hey, *amigo*, you almost stepped on him, poor fellow," Enrique admonished.

A wave of apprehension crept under Luke's skin, making the tiny hairs on his arms and the back of his neck stand on end. Nausea bubbled in his stomach. He stood perfectly still, not moving even after the spider had crawled away beneath the undergrowth.

"Come on, Hancock, let's go." Lacey gave Luke a not-so-gentle shove before he started walking again, wondering what the hell the matter was now. Then, snickering to herself, it dawned on her. Mr. Tough Guy had a fear of spiders.

What kind of jungle guide was afraid of spiders? With a wickedness that would have made her Marines proud, she tucked that little tidbit of information away for possible future use.

———

After dinner, Luke used a headache as an excuse to turn in early. Lacey had seemed disappointed, having voiced the urge to play a game of Scrabble, but he needed solitude. Besides, if she wanted to play, why didn't she go find Enrique? As soon as that thought materialized, his hands fisted in anger.

Stretched out on his bed, he mulled over his contradictory physical and emotional responses to her. First, he wanted to bed her, then he wanted to keep her at arms' length. One minute he wanted to choke her, the next he wanted to protect her.

She'd gotten under his skin in a way few had. He should just tumble her; get her out of his system. Scratch the itch. That tactic seemed to work with other women. But their dinner conversation had thwarted that plan.

Sitting across the table from her had been almost more than he could bear. Freshly showered, smelling of earthy rosemary and rain-fresh lavender, slightly damp hair curling around her neck, she was more than irresistible, she was all-consuming. He winced when he noticed the bruises on her upper arms, no doubt from his grip on her at the waterfall.

He recalled their brief encounter on the beach, the almost dreamlike quality of this morning's embrace. Tonight he'd wanted more. Craved it like an addict craves his drug and was just as determined to get it. Especially after watching her interaction with Enrique.

Was she with him right now? He groaned and rolled over onto his side like someone had kicked him in the stomach. Why Enrique and not him?

She still wore the jewelry she never parted with. During the meal he'd reached out and touched the necklace at her throat, watching the pulse jump erratically in her neck. "I never see you without this . . . or the watch." His eyes lingered on her face.

"Oh, someone very special gave me the necklace," she murmured, touching the garnet, a soft smile on her face. "And my father gave me the watch when I won . . . well, when I won an award. And, I like to know what time it is." She smiled with a shrug.

Someone very special. That had settled it. He didn't sleep with women in a committed relationship, be it marriage or a live-in arrangement, no matter how evidently willing they were to be unfaithful. He had *some* scruples. Lacey would just have to remain an unsatisfied craving.

CHAPTER TWELVE

Unable to face another meal alone, Luke opted for Mariposa's restaurant. Even if he didn't have a dinner companion, at least he would be around people. The resort served excellent food, boasted an ample wine list, and the proprietors, Karl and Jill Snyder, often refused payment when he offered.

He had a good gig, and he knew it. Environmental Expeditions was the exclusive guiding company for the resort and, of course, when clients scheduled expeditions with him and needed a place to stay, he referred them to Karl and Jill. They were good people, committed to Costa Rica, the environment, and their community.

After visiting Costa Rica more than twenty years ago, they fell in love with the country and its people, so they quit their high-stress, big-city jobs, sold everything they owned, cashed in their 401(k)'s and built the resort. They hired the locals, shopped locally whenever possible, built a school, hired teachers, and provided books and computers for the students.

The resort boosted the economy of this remote area and

raised the standard of living for its inhabitants, while maintaining the pristine quality of the environment. It served as the poster child for Luke's philosophy that economic development and environmental sustainability were not mutually exclusive.

He called to Jorge, one of the bartenders, and took a seat at a small table overlooking the gulf. The restaurant was crowded with resort guests, some scanning the day's photos on their cameras, others looking over guidebooks to plan the next day's activities.

He spied Lacey and Tony out on the deck, heads bent over the game table, playing a game of checkers. Allie must be at her mother's, he thought, or Tony would be home this time of day.

Over the past week, he'd managed to avoid one-on-ones with Lacey, always keeping Tony close at hand. It was better that way. No temptations.

He watched as Tony said something to Lacey, making her laugh, a smoky, throaty sound that enveloped him in its warmth. She always seemed so relaxed around Tony. Open. A twinge of jealousy squeezed his chest.

His desire for dinner all but forgotten, he rose from the table and walked over to them.

"*Hola*, Luke." Tony's toothy grin could raise a smile from the dead.

Lacey raised her head in surprise. She knew Luke had been avoiding her. She wasn't obtuse. She just didn't know why. He'd lost his typical machismo around her too. "Hey, Hancock."

"Hey," was his pithy reply.

"She's beating the pants off me, and I'm man enough to admit it. I'm gonna need a raise to pay my gambling debts." Tony laughed lightheartedly.

"Tony, man, it's only checkers. Have some pride." Luke clapped Tony on the back.

"Yeah, but she's good. She makes Marion Tinsley look like an amateur."

Lacey laughed, blushing at the compliment.

"Yeah, but can she play chess, the Royal Game of Strategy?" He arched a brow as he caught Lacey's eye.

"It's been a while, but yes, I can play chess." She met his direct gaze with one of her own.

"Then I throw down the gauntlet. Care to pick it up?" She gave Tony a wicked glance. "Sure."

Tony got up to retrieve the chessboard and game pieces, scrubbing his hands in anticipation of what was sure to be the evening's entertainment.

"What were you and Tony playing for?"

"*Colones*, a *colón* a game."

"Well, let's sweeten the pot a little. Ten thousand *colones*." Roughly the equivalent of fifteen dollars U.S.

She raised an eyebrow. "Okay," she said, glad to see the machismo had returned.

"Ladies first," Luke said, after Tony set the board.

Lacey sat in front of the white game pieces, already determining her first move. She marched her king pawn forward two spaces.

"Game on," Tony said cheerfully.

Luke met her head-on with his own pawn and the battle was set.

Lacey called up her bishop pawn to join the ranks, moving it to stand abreast of his fellow pawn.

Luke promptly took out her bishop pawn with one of his own.

"Oh yeah," he said, "this is going to be a piece of cake."

Ignoring his comment, Lacey considered the board, her

poker face intact, took a sip of her beer, then advanced her king knight to face-off against Luke's victorious pawn.

Luke followed quickly by deploying his queen pawn.

Lacey chewed her lower lip as her queen knight rode forward, flanking her king knight in a show of solidarity, hoping to draw Luke into her territory. He took the bait.

After studying the board, visualizing the possible moves and the consequences of those moves, Luke swept his queen pawn in, knocking off Lacey's only other pawn currently engaged in the battle.

Aha! "Like taking candy from a baby," Luke said with a smirk.

Lacey ignored him again and contemplated her next move, casually munching on a tortilla chip. Her queen knight forged ahead and handily disposed of Luke's pawn.

Well shit. "Okay, giving me a run for my money," he said, a note of condescension in his voice. "Keeps it interesting." Luke met her challenge, summoning his queen bishop to join the skirmish.

"Got anymore clichés up your sleeve, or are you quite done?" she asked, her eyebrow lifted in challenge.

He flashed her with a devilish grin in response. "Bring it, baby."

With an eye roll, Lacey turned her attention to the lay of the land. She entered her queen into the fray, protecting her king from attack.

Luke couldn't help himself. He answered by attacking her king knight and encroaching deep into her territory. "Yes!" he hissed. "Sure you don't want to retire?"

"Yes, I'm quite sure. You win some, you lose some," she said, throwing out a cliché of her own with a confident smile. She charged her queen knight across the battlefield, effectively placing Luke's king under immediate attack, while ensuring her queen, queen bishop, and pawn protected her king.

If there was one thing she knew well, that was deploying defenses. "And *I* win this one. Checkmate."

"Holy shit, man! She beat you in only seven moves!" Tony chortled with glee. Examining the board, Tony continued, "That was brilliant! A check move from the queen and knight with no way to block the knight's attack, and no way to block the queen's attack because of the knight's attack."

Tony ran on excitedly, indicating the pieces on the board like a color commentator reviewing a replay. "And the king can't move anywhere because of the queen and the knight, and both the queen and the knight can't be taken because it's a double-check move. Awesome!"

Lacey bit back a smile at the look Luke shot Tony.

Luke, elbows on his knees, hands under his chin, stared at the board, recalling his moves, trying to figure out where he went wrong. Lacey had caught a lucky break that's all, despite Tony's Monday-morning quarterback review that painted her as the next Bobby Fischer.

Tony clapped him on the back. "Tough break, man. I told you she was good." Turning to Lacey, a grin on his face, he said, "Guess you got retribution for the frog incident?"

"Oh, no, this was just a friendly chess match. Retribution, when it comes, and it will, will be very, very public." She turned in time to see Luke blanch. "Pay up, Hancock," she demanded, hand out, a smug expression on her face.

"Best two out of three?"

"That wasn't the deal. If you want two out of three, that's ten thousand *colones* a game. Winner takes all."

"Fine," he growled as he set up the board again. "Your money to lose."

S everal chess games later, Lacey contemplated how to spend her winnings. With each successive win, Luke had called for another best-out-of . . . three out of five, five out of seven, before she, and Tony, insisted they call it a night.

After losing to Lacey, Luke harangued and cajoled, but Lacey refused any more matches. Even egging her on with absurd overconfident accusations that she feared she was losing her edge didn't budge her.

Her flippant, "Face it, Hancock, I'm just better than you," only served to inflame him more. He was determined to find something he could beat her at. Something physical. After all, he was stronger and faster than she was. Couldn't be too hard to get his revenge, right?

CHAPTER THIRTEEN

"Have you two," Tony waggled his brows and made an obscene gesture with his grease-covered fist, "you know?"

"What are you, reliving your adolescence? If you're asking if we've had sex, the answer is no." Luke turned back to the carburetor they were working on. The Jeep had been running rough the last few times out.

"Wow, man, I'm disappointed. Really. You being my idol and all."

Luke snorted in disgust. "You know I don't sleep with attached women."

"I didn't think sleep had anything to do with it, but what makes you think she's . . . attached?"

"You know the necklace she's never without? Someone very special gave that her." Luke made air quotes around the words 'very special.'

"Yeah. You're right, someone very special to most of us who were lucky enough to have known them."

Luke screwed up his face and gave Tony a questioning look.

His friend took pity on him. "The necklace is from her grandmother. Lacey's unattached, to use your word."

"How'd you find that out? She told you?"

"Yeah, man, it's called con-ver-sa-tion. You should try it sometime." He shook his head at Luke's obvious dimwittedness.

"Hmm." Luke considered this revelation. *Does it make a difference? Damn right it does.* Now maybe he could get the intriguing, infuriating, and altogether sexy Lacey Sommers out of his system. After all, she was only irresistible because he thought he couldn't have her.

As if reading Luke's thoughts, Tony clapped him on the back, leaving a greasy handprint behind. "Go for it, *muchacho.*"

Lacey scrolled through her emails. Seeing one from her father, she clicked it open. She'd sent a quick email to him yesterday to not only check-in, but also to ask him about the development fund set aside for the business owners on the Jersey Shore. She wanted to know if Luke's parents had ever collected the money, and if not, whether her father new why.

Hi Lace,

Things are fine here. Just putting the final touches on that deal to buy up three blocks of prime real estate in Queens. It's a great location for a multi-use building with apartments, shops, and maybe a restaurant or two.

Ran into your mother last week (picture me grimacing).

Lacey bit back a grin. Yes, her father would certainly grimace, or worse. Her parents divorced after Lilia went away to college, confirming Lacey's opinion not only of their marriage, but of marriage in general. She returned her attention to the e- mail.

I'm guessing you didn't tell her about your assignment in Costa Rica. She was pretty pissed when I told her. I know. What's new?

Poor Daddy, Lacey snickered. Is it any wonder she didn't tell her mother about her assignment?

Got to run. I have a meeting with the real estate attorneys. I'll get Margaret to look into Mr. Hancock's claim and get back to you.
    Miss you, baby. Come home for Christmas.

Christmas. She didn't know if she'd be finished with her assignment by then, but as much as she would love to see her father, she couldn't bear the thought of spending Christmas with her mother and sister and their whirlwind of society gatherings.

Speak of the devil. Lacey opened an email from her mother and groaned. *War and Peace* was shorter. Her mother had most likely dictated it to her personal secretary, a young woman who performed such illustrious duties as keeping her mother's social calendar, drafting regrets to the myriad invitations her mother received, and typing lengthy epistles to her rebellious daughter because Clarissa might chip a nail if she did it herself. As if she even knew how.

Scanning the email for anything she might even remotely be interested in, she caught her sister's name:

Lilia is following in her mother's philanthropic footsteps. She's featured in this months' New York Times Magazine *for her volunteerism.*

Her mother had served on numerous nonprofit boards over the years: hospitals, children's societies, homeless shelters, whatever happened to be in vogue at the time. But even if her mother's motives weren't entirely altruistic, the results were the same: the less fortunate were a little healthier, a little warmer, a little better off.

Yada, yada, yada, St. Lilia, blah, blah, blah. *Aha! A link to the article. That settles it.* Her mother's secretary definitely typed the email. The only links Clarissa knew anything about were those in jewelry from the likes of Tiffany, Cartier, and Harry Winston.

Lacey clicked on the link. The first page of the article featured a photo of a cool, elegant blonde standing in front of the fireplace in her Greenwich home.

Lilia was perfectly attired, coifed, manicured, and covered in her traditional war paint: Laura Mercier foundation, blush, lip gloss, shadow (plum, to play up the green of her eyes), liner, and mascara, the cost of which could feed a small family in Costa Rica for a year.

Scanning the article for any mention of her sister's philanthropy (so far it'd focused on her house, her decorator, and her husband's lucrative practice), Lacey finally found a brief mention:

Mrs. Sommers-Stanton has served tirelessly as the chair for this year's Hearts, Hands, and Hugs gala.

Translation: Lilia wrote a big, fat check to underwrite the cost of some overpriced bash where a bunch of wine-sipping snobs gathered to talk about how trying last year's vacation in the Hamptons was, while patting themselves on the back for their charitable giving.

Closing the link, Lacey returned to her mother's email.

Your father tells me you're in some remote jungle taking pictures of frogs. Darling, can you see me explaining that to the women at the club? Really, dear? Frogs? When will you ever settle down and find a nice man?

I understand Marvin Macy just got divorced. He'd be a good catch. I know he's twenty-five years older, but let's face it, at your age your options aren't what they used to be.

Gah! Marvin Macy. Not if he was one of only two men left on earth, and the other one was Mussolini. Lacey Macy. She groaned. Hell would freeze over first.

———

Luke strode into the bar, looking forward to an ice-cold beer, some male conversation, and maybe a verbal tussle or two with Lacey.

The she-devil of whom he spoke sat at the bar drinking a beer and chatting with Tony and Philippe, the bartender. The three laughed at some shared joke. Luke wondered again why she never laughed like that around him.

"How's it hanging?" Luke greeted Philippe in Spanish.

"Oh, it's hanging. Caught anything lately?"

"No, but I'm working on a tasty little *machita*," Luke continued in Spanish, pointedly referring to Lacey. He grabbed a bar stool next to Tony, using him as a buffer between himself and Lacey.

"I'm particular about who I let reel me in," Lacey quipped in Spanish, without missing a beat.

Luke's cheeks grew hot while Tony held back a snicker, almost choking on his beer.

"Four years of Spanish in college," she said with a shrug, taking another pull on her beer.

Luke turned to Tony. "Couldn't tell me she spoke Spanish?

What kind of friend are you anyway?"

"It never came up," Tony said with a half shrug and a mischievous grin.

Giving Tony a fulminating glance, Luke got Philippe's attention. "I'll take a Dos Equis."

"I'll take another myself," Lacey said, passing her empty bottle to Philippe. Since the generator for the bungalows was out, she'd decided to hang out in the bar where it was somewhat cooler. That, and her mother's emails always left her in need of alcohol.

"Careful there, Sommers, don't get yourself drunk and fall off the balcony," Luke said, barely giving her a glance as he propped his elbow on the bar and took a long pull from his beer.

"Please. Take a lot more than two beers to get me buzzed."

"What, three?"

She snorted. "At my worst, I could keep up with you. At my best, I could drink your beach bum ass under the table." So far, she hadn't bothered to look his way.

"You're on." It was the perfect challenge. He could win this hands down.

"What?" She finally faced him as Tony sat back, out of the line of fire.

"Put your money where your mouth is," he said with a cocky grin.

"What's with you and clichés? Fine. I could use a good buzz right about now, and I could use another ten thousand *colones* to add to the fifty thousand I won off you last week." She polished off her beer with an unladylike gulp. "Tequila shots. Tony can be the judge."

Luke's brows shot up at her preference for tequila shots.

Tony glanced from one to the other of them, giving each a questioning look.

Lacey continued with her recitation of the ad-lib rules. "After every five shots, Tony'll preside over a sobriety test. You know, walk a straight line, touch your nose with your index finger, count backward by seven. First one who fails the test coughs up the ten thousand *colones*."

"Okay, but none of that nancy stuff—no lime, no salt—just tequila shots straight up." Luke figured he had this thing nailed. She already had two beers in her. A little revenge for beating him at chess. Well, slaughtering him, actually.

"Deal." They shook on it. Lacey slid off her bar stool to go to the *baños*.

Luke followed her departure with a predatory smile.

"Philippe, a bottle of Cuervo and two shot glasses."

Philippe complied with the request, shaking his head all the while. "Luke, you know you and tequila don't mix," he whispered.

"Shh. Only cheap tequila. Besides, I might have to drink three, maybe four shots at most, before she's hammered." He boasted a confident grin as he winked at Philippe.

"Luke, man, what are you doing?" Tony's concerned

voice lowered as he saw Lacey return from the bathroom. "You're not planning to—"

"What? No. I don't sleep with intoxicated women either. This is strictly to prove a point."

"That you're a jackass?"

"What? No. Why would you say that?" Luke asked, giving Tony the stink eye.

Lacey returned to her barstool.

"Never mind," Luke quietly told Tony. He turned to Lacey. "Let the games begin." He poured two shots of tequila, handing one to her. *"Pura vida."* He lifted the shot in a toast before tossing it back. The liquid scorched its way down his throat, making his eyes water as he tried in vain not to cough.

Lacey followed suit, slamming the shot glass back onto the bar, seemingly unaffected.

Other resort guests seeking to escape the heat of their bungalows caught wind of the competition. Bill, a film and television producer from California, decided to get in on the action and started taking side bets on the outcome.

The wagers split evenly, with the women betting on Lacey's success and the men betting on Luke's.

Luke poured two more shots, and he and Lacey each tossed them back. After the five shot quota for Round One, each rose to perform the sobriety test.

Using one of the bamboo floor planks as a guide, Luke tread the line with the proprioception of someone accustomed to riding big waves.

His male supporters cheered him on, clapping him on the back and offering words of encouragement.

Then he stood on one foot and, holding his arms outstretched, successfully touched his nose with his forefinger, first with his right hand, and then with this left hand.

Finally, he counted backward from one hundred by seven. "100, 93, 86, 79, 72, 65—"

"Okay. My turn." Lacey danced along the bamboo plank in bare feet with the grace of a gymnast on a balance beam.

Her fans offered a chorus of "You go, girl" and "You show 'em, honey."

Luke watched her, admiring her form, those long legs, that hot, firm bottom encased in snug little shorts, and her bare feet. He'd never understood foot fetishes, but her tanned feet with their neatly trimmed nails made him think about how it would feel to have those feet glide up his leg.

Damn, he thought, *that tequila has already gone straight to my head.*

Performing a perfect pirouette, as if it were part of a choreographed routine, Lacey lifted one leg and blithely touched her nose with her index fingers, while simultaneously counting backward. "100, 93, 86—"

Show-off, Luke thought. "Wait, you memorized those—"

"Oh for Christ's sake, I'll start where you left off . . . 58, 51, 44, 37 . . ."

"All right. Back to the bar."

The impromptu gamblers gathered 'round, shouting words of encouragement.

By the eighth shot, Luke had a little trouble getting the tequila into the shot glass.

"Give me that." Lacey grabbed the bottle out of his hand. "Spilling perfectly good tequila is a sacrilege." She deftly poured two more shots and downed hers.

Luke hesitated a moment before picking up his glass and throwing the tequila down his throat. Beating Lacey was proving more difficult than he thought. She had to be at least as drunk as he was, if not more.

Lacey poured two more shots, her ninth and tenth, and the end of Round Two. After swallowing hers, she jumped off the barstool to perform her test while the women chanted, "La-cey! La-cey!" all the while.

He was still trying to figure out which one of the two shot glasses he saw was real and which one was a double. After a few swipes at one that seemed to slip through his fingers, he made a grab for the other one, knocking it over. "Shit," he muttered.

Philippe came over with a bar cloth to wipe it up. "You okay, man?"

"Yesh," Luke growled, "jush pour 'nother."

"Hey, man, I think you're done."

"Pour it." He gave Philippe a look that would turn steel into molten ore.

"It's your head," Philippe said, as he shrugged and poured another shot.

Luke managed to get his fingers around the glass this time and brought it to his lips. Closing his eyes, he emptied the glass.

The men shouted. "Come on, man, you can do it!" and "Show her who's boss!"

Luke gave his fans a thumbs up, then none-too-gracefully rose from his bar stool to weave his way over to the bamboo slat. If he'd been walking a ship's plank, he'd have hit the water after only two steps.

"I win!"

He heard Lacey's gleeful cry as if from a long distance away.

"No, you don'. I get 'nother chansh." He tried the plank again, falling off after the first step. "Never mind. I can tush my nose instead—"

"No way, Hancock. We agreed, the first one who fails the test, loses—"

"I haven't"—he hiccupped—"failed. I haf to take the whole tesh. Two out of free." He struggled to hold up three fingers, succeeding in holding up two fingers and his thumb as he wobbled on his axis like a slowing top.

"Fine."

After three unsuccessful attempts to stand on his left leg, he switched to his right leg without doing much better. Luckily, Tony stood next to him, or he'd have fallen on his face.

"Whoa there." Tony grabbed him by the shoulders to steady him. "Luke, *amigo*, I think you have to man-up and concede victory."

The women hooted and hollered, clapping their hands and jumping up and down.

"Yes!" Lacey pumped her arm in a show of triumph. "To the victor go the spoils. Pay-up, Hancock."

The women followed suit, telling Bill to fork over their winnings.

Why did she seem so defiantly sober? Luke managed to wonder through the murk of inebriation. *Something's not right about a woman who can follow two beers with that much tequila, and not be knee-walking drunk.* Luke reached into his pocket and after several missed attempts pulled out a wad of bills and handed them to Tony, mumbling something about paying the harpy.

Tony handed Lacey a ten thousand *colones* bill. She then kissed it and made a show of stuffing her winnings in her pocket.

"That's sixty thousand *colones* I've won off you Hancock. I'm beginning to like you more all the time." She wore a smug grin as she went back to the bar. Revenge was truly sweet, and she'd gotten it without even breaking a sweat. "That," she told Tony, "is what I call retribution."

Even through his tequila-soaked brain, Luke registered the appalling fact that she poured herself yet another shot, then raised it in a toast before tossing it back.

"*Pura vida!*"

That was the last thing he remembered.

CHAPTER FOURTEEN

L acey gazed down at Luke's sleeping form, sprawled across the bed, fully clothed, no doubt where Tony and Philippe had dumped him last night. He looked so angelic, his gold-tipped hair falling over his brow, a light stubble on his face, mouth soft in slumber, and thick lashes sweeping across his cheekbones. Looks were definitely deceiving.

When Luke didn't show up that morning for their planned trip into Puerto Jimenez, she and Tony figured he was still sleeping off his drunk. They were right.

"Luke. Hey, man, wake-up." Tony gave him another shove, but Luke didn't budge. Even Sandy's excited barking hadn't penetrated his drunken stupor.

The dog finally climbed up on the bed and began giving Luke wet doggie kisses.

Lacey held up her finger to Tony as an idea struck her.

With a mischievous grin, she crawled into bed and, leaning down, moaned provocatively into his ear, "Come on, baby. Is that all you got? Give me a little more."

Tony chuckled.

Luke sat up with a jolt, causing Sandy to scamper from the bed and Lacey to jump back, laughter bubbling to the surface.

"What the fuck!" Luke searched the room, wondering where he was before his eyes landed on Tony. "It's you." He dragged his hands through his hair. "God, I was having this crazy dream . . . Shit!" He started when he turned and saw Lacey kneeling on his bed. For a second he thought maybe he hadn't been dreaming.

"Good morning, Hancock," she chirped. "Sleep well?"

Ignoring her question, he smacked his lips and furrowed his brow. "Call a doctor. I think something furry crawled inside my mouth and died."

Tony and Lacey chuckled at his expense.

"Bastards," he growled. "Oh, sorry," he said, looking at Lacey as she rose from the bed. "Bitch."

Lacey just grinned in response, not at all offended by the remark.

"How the hell did you stay sober?" Luke sat up, holding his head as if it might roll of his shoulders and onto the floor. "And why are you so goddamned chipper this morning?"

"You forget who I've been hanging out with all these years: soldiers and journalists, most of whom were men, and most of whom spent their free time getting drunk on rot-gut alcohol. I had to learn to hold my own."

"What time is it?" Luke glared at his watch, but the numbers blurred, before disappearing altogether.

"Three hours past the time we planned to leave for Puerto Jimenez."

Luke leaned over and groaned.

"Hancock, if you're going to yack, I'm leaving," Lacey said.

"I'm not going to yack, but if you wouldn't mind, I'd like

a little privacy. You too, Tony." He grimaced as he stood up. The room listed to port, then to starboard, before righting itself. "I'll meet you at the resort after a shower, a gallon of coffee . . ." he smacked his lips again, "and an oral cavity de-furring."

"Sure, man."

As the two walked out, Luke watched Lacey punch Tony on the arm in response to some comment he'd made. He frowned. If Tony weren't a married, faithful-to-the-end type, he'd think the two were involved.

Suddenly he wanted Lacey to like him. Like she did Tony. And, oddly enough, not just because he wanted to get into her pants. He knew he could make Lacey like him. After all, most women did. He just needed to pour on the charm. She posed a challenge, but he liked challenges.

He'd start today, he thought as he stumbled to the toilet.

Right after he yacked.

Okay, so maybe starting today hadn't been the brightest idea Luke had ever had, especially since he'd been nursing the mother of all hangovers. But hey, he hadn't exactly been firing on all cylinders when he'd reached his decision.

The ride to Puerto Jimenez had been torture. Even through his sunglasses, the sun pierced his eyes like a knife in the hands of Norman Bates. Every pothole and dip in the road threatened to bring rancid bile boiling to the surface, while the marching band in his head performed a rousing rendition of "Stars and Stripes Forever."

Tony and Lacey sat in the front seats of the Jeep, chat-ting amiably, while Luke hung on for dear life in the backseat. He was afraid to open his mouth and join in the conversation for fear of tossing his cookies again. He may as well have stayed home for all the attention they paid him. So, he sat in the back and pouted like a child whose parents were pointedly ignoring him.

It didn't get much better once they reached town. He sweated profusely in the heat, soaking his shirt and plastering his hair to his throbbing head. Lunch at a local café proved his undoing, the smell of onions and garlic prompting a run for the *baños*.

That would leave a lasting impression on Lacey. A bad one.

When he'd reappeared minutes later, Lacey had taken pity on him, placing an ice-cold cloth on the back of his neck and forehead. Tony, asshole that he was, only grinned and shook his head. Luke wondered sullenly what he ever saw in Tony. The shit- eating grin was just too much to bear sometimes.

All he'd wanted was to go home, set his rarely-used air conditioner to frigid, draw the shades, and crawl into his bed. And stay. Forever.

———

The sun's rays just peeked over the horizon on the first day of December, but Lacey sat at the desk in her room reviewing photos she'd taken along the densely covered paths on the resort's property. She'd gotten some surprisingly good shots of a scarlet tanager.

She'd also gotten some decent pictures of a green and black poison-dart frog, as well as some frog that looked as if he wore an orange T-shirt and blue jeans. Luke would know the name of the frog.

"It's open," Lacey called at the knock on her door. "Good morning," Luke greeted cheerfully as he came in.

Lacey turned in surprise. He was the last person she expected to see, especially in her bungalow at this hour of the morning.

After they'd gotten back from Puerto Jimenez, Luke had beaten a hasty retreat, leaving her and Tony to shake their heads. She didn't see him the rest of that day. Still nursing a grudge and a hangover, she surmised.

In her ersatz pajamas consisting of a ratty tank top and gym shorts, she suddenly felt self-conscious about her disheveled hair and messy bed. "Back from the dead I see," Lacey said, a soft smile on her face as she furtively combed her fingers through her hair.

"Just call me Lazarus." He ambled over to take a look at the photos on her laptop. "Those are great. Where did you take them?"

"After we got back from town yesterday, I hiked along the resort's paths."

He leaned in over her shoulder to get a closer look. So close she could have turned and kissed his fresh-shaven cheek.

He smelled of the beach, clean and salty, and her heart pattered in her chest in response.

"That's a great one of the blue-jeans poison-dart frog.

They're hard to get." He straightened. "Good for you."

"*That's* what he's called? I thought he looked like someone dressed him an orange shirt and blue jeans." She laughed. She minimized the photos, revealing the one that served as the wallpaper on her computer. A picture of her with long hair standing in the middle of six soldiers, arms wrapped around shoulders, faces smiling into the camera.

"Was this the unit you were embedded with?" Luke leaned over her shoulder again.

"Part of them. That was taken in Iraq right before I left."

"You stay in touch with them?"

"Everyone but Matt," she said, pointing to a baby-faced young man. "He was killed a week after I left. Roadside bomb."

Luke stepped back, unsure what to say. "Sorry. That must have been tough."

"Not as tough as it was for his wife and kids."

Seeking to change the subject, he said the first thing that came to mind. "You had long hair."

She swiveled back to the photo with a frown. "Yeah. Cut it. It just . . . got in the way."

She faced him again, struck by his good looks, his hands shoved into the pockets of his cargo shorts, hair still damp. He wore a button-front shirt, rather than his usual T- shirt, revealing the light furring on his chest. Her fingers itched to reach out and touch—

"Come fly with me," he said, his voice warm and intimate.

His abrupt invitation interrupted her sexual musings, drawing her eyes to his in disbelief. Why was he being nice to her? She narrowed her eyes. "Channeling Frank Sinatra?" she asked to cover the unexpected reaction his request elicited.

Luke chuckled low. "No, but I could be if you'd like."

The sultry sound of his voice and the heated look in his eyes caught her off guard again.

"Thanks, but I have to get these photos to my editor." She turned back to her laptop. What the hell was he up to, anyway? A con to get his own revenge?

"Okay. How long will that take? I can wait." He sat on the corner of her bed.

"Who are you, and what have you done with Hancock?" She glanced around in time to see his lips pull up into a slight smile.

"I guess I deserve that. We didn't exactly get off to the best start."

She snorted. "It's been almost a month, and that's just dawning on you? Besides, it makes no difference to me whether you like me or not." She shrugged.

His smile vanished, making her sorry she spoke so abruptly. "Look, Hancock, you hate my father, and consequently, me. I get that. It's okay. You don't have to pretend to be nice to me. I promise I won't complain to the magazine about you. You'll still get your bonus."

"Dammit, Sommers. You can be so hardheaded. I came here to ask you to take a flight with me because I thought you might enjoy it." He jumped up from the bed, dragging his hands through his hair. "If you don't want to, that's fine, but I'm not trying to kiss up in hopes of a big bonus or something. Not everything is about money." He started to leave.

"Hancock. Wait." She almost apologized, but the words got stuck in her throat. "I'll go. Just give me time to get these photos out and take a shower. Maybe have some breakfast if that's okay . . ."

There was a heavy pause before he said, "Sure. I'll meet you out front in an hour. Can you be ready by then?"

"Yes." Maybe in that time she could also figure out his angle. "Hey, Hancock," she called as he left. "Where are we going?"

"It's a surprise," he said. "Oh, and bring your camera."

———

The best Lacey could tell, they flew northeast, across Costa Rica to the still-remote Caribbean Coast, with its large tracts of virgin lowland rain forests, where some areas of the coast were only accessible by boat or small plane.

According to Luke, the area was so remote from Costa Rica's populations in the Central Valley, that it had developed a culture all its own with a reggae beat, a Rastafarian ideology, and Creole cooking.

Luke still hadn't told her exactly where they were going or the purpose for the trip. The plane banked to the left, and as Luke pushed forward on the yoke, a grassy area came into view. A group of kids playing nearby spotted the plane and began running excitedly toward the landing strip.

Lacey then realized it wasn't a landing strip at all, but a large playing field. As the plane came in for a landing, she could see a few adults holding out their arms to keep the frenzied kids at bay.

The plane came to a stop and Luke turned off the engine, apparently the sign for the adults to release the mob, who came running at full speed toward the plane.

Boys and girls bobbed up and down in excitement, jumping from one foot to the other in their impatience for Luke to open the aircraft. When he finally opened the door and climbed down, he was swept up by the screaming throng, before the sea of bodies parted for a tall, dark-skinned man with long dreadlocks.

"Luke, my brother." He came forward, hugging Luke, clapping him on the back, the rhythmic lilt of his English-patois, pleasing to Lacey's ear.

"Akili." Luke returned the hug with the same gusto,

before turning to Lacey. "Akili, this is Som—, er, Lacey Sommers. Lacey, this is Akili Bongo."

"Welcome, sister," Akili greeted Lacey warmly.

The clamber began anew as Luke strode to the back of the plane and opened the cargo door, where he lifted a huge tarp revealing piles of net bags containing soccer balls and canvas bags of cleats, shirts, and shorts. Opening one of the net bags, he began tossing soccer balls into eager hands, laughing as the kids ran off kicking the balls in front of them.

Light-hearted laughter bubbled up from Lacey's chest. "Can I help?" she asked, arms out.

"Sure." Luke returned her smile. "Take these bags of shirts and shorts over there to those wooden benches and sort them into sizes. I'll grab the cleats."

Luke joined her, dumping the shoes out on the ground.

"Where did you get all this?" she asked. Surely he didn't buy all this equipment.

"A charitable organization in the U.S. collects and distributes soccer gear to kids in small communities in Central America. I volunteer from time-to-time to fly the equipment into remote areas of Costa Rica, Panama, and Nicaragua," he finished with a shrug, never taking his eyes off the shoes he sorted.

Lacey sat back in surprise. Volunteered? Huh. She thought he probably got paid good money for this. A stab of guilt shot through her. Luke hadn't done anything to make her distrust him and didn't deserve her unfounded conclusion.

"Did you bring your camera?" Luke interrupted his task to look at her.

"Yes. Why?"

"I thought you might like to take pictures of something

besides frogs." He tipped his head in the direction of the exuberant kids on the field.

Lacey stood to watch the boys and girls racing back and forth across the field, dribbling the balls as they went. A grin spread across her face. "Right." She jogged to the plane to retrieve her camera, leaving Luke laughing in her wake.

———

Hundreds of photos later, Lacey plopped down on the wooden bench, now empty of the shirts, shorts, and shoes the kids now proudly wore.

"Come, Lacey." Akili waved his hands at her. "Come, play."

Lacey left her camera on the bench and ran out onto the field, deftly stealing the ball from a young man, then laughing as he looked up in surprise over the now-absent ball. His broad grin told her he didn't mind a little competition.

Luke watched as she ran up and down the field, kids flocking to her to attempt to steal the ball from the tall, white woman. Was there anything the woman couldn't do, and do well? Spying her camera, he picked it up and began snapping pictures of her.

A little girl stumbled in front of her and Lacey picked her up, giving her a hug and brushing off her knees before putting her back down. She wore a smile unlike any he had seen from her. Open, honest, and pure. Beatific even.

She spun toward him and saw her camera in his hand, and they locked eyes. She smiled at him briefly, before an errant soccer ball landed a solid *thwack* on her thigh. He winced, but she just picked it up and head-butted it down field, laughing all the while.

Luke couldn't help but feel that he had caught a glimpse of a former version of Lacey Sommers, one that'd existed before she'd encountered the evil in the world that had made her so guarded, so tortured. And in that moment he knew he wanted to see more. He resolved to peel away the layers of Kevlar she wore and reveal the true heart of her.

He glanced up as she jogged over to him, breathless, sweaty, and disheveled, but beautiful. Her face glowed with the exertion, but it was the light in her eyes that compelled him to grab her and pull her into his arms for an affectionate hug. She stiffened briefly, before awkwardly returning his gesture.

She collapsed to the bench and he handed her a bottle of water, before sitting down beside her.

Giving him a playful shoulder-butt, she held the bottle to her lips. "Thanks. For today, I mean. It's been fun."

He watched the kids still running around the field with the same level of energy they'd had when he'd arrived, a satisfied smile on his face. He would make it his personal mission to bring out the best in Lacey Sommers, at least for the duration of her stay.

CHAPTER FIFTEEN

The next morning Lacey sat in the resort dining room, her laptop open, looking at the photos she'd taken, not only the soccer photos from the previous day, but all the non-work- related photos she'd taken since she'd gotten to Costa Rica.

There were photos of Tony, Luke, and Sandy, as well as some of Karl and Jill, and others of locals from Puerto Jimenez who were willing to have their photos taken.

Sundays at the resort were especially laid-back. Karl and Jill often had breakfast in the dining room, taking a rare opportunity to be waited on by their own excellent staff.

They'd been so great to her; generously allowing her to use the laundry facilities, inviting her to help herself to the kitchen if she got hungry or thirsty during their off-hours, even loaning her a coffee maker and supplies for her room, so she could partake of her favorite stimulant first thing in the morning.

Speaking of her gracious hosts, they approached and asked if they could join her. "Sure."

"You must have hundreds of pictures by now," Karl said as he took a seat next to his wife.

"More like thousands." Lacey grinned. She knew their story, and she couldn't picture either one of them in business suits, carrying brief cases, and attached to cell phones.

They'd apparently made the transition to the granola lifestyle with ease. Jill's short, brown curly hair showed streaks of gray, while Karl's balding pate only had a few strands of graying blond hair left. Instead of suits, they now wore wrinkled cotton, and instead of briefcases, they now carried coffee cups. They seemed to be attached to one another, rather than technology.

"Want to see the ones I took of you two?"

"Could we? That would be great," Jill said, sliding her chair over to get a better view of the screen.

"Oh, I love this one." Jill pointed to a photo of her and Karl in front of the resort's sign, where a Blue Morpho butterfly had spontaneously landed just as Lacey pressed the shutter. "Could we use that on the website? I mean, would your magazine mind?" Jill asked hopefully.

"I'd love for you to use it," Lacey responded enthusiastically. "It's my photo, so it's not a problem. If there are others you'd like, just let me know."

Luke strolled into the dining room and spotted the three bent over the laptop. Perfect. He'd gone to Lacey's bungalow to ask if she'd like to surf. Some nice swells were coming in as a result of a late subtropical storm off the coast.

"*Hola*," Luke called as he ambled over to the table. "You looking at Lacey's wildlife photography? It's pretty amazing."

Lacey blushed at the unexpected compliment. Luke appeared the prototypical beach bum this morning. Colorful board shorts, surfer T-shirt, and flips flops, his hair looked as if he'd already been for a swim, damp and a little crisp from the salt.

"No, actually we're looking at the photos she took of us," Karl said, grinning broadly. "Only in our younger days could those be considered photos of wildlife, right, baby?" He gave Jill a playful nudge, while she blushed and slapped his hand away.

Everyone chuckled over the former accountant's witty remark.

"Come on, baby, we've got to make some repairs in Number Twelve," Karl said to his still-blushing bride. "Apparently the guests tried to swing from the mosquito netting," he explained as they left the table.

"By the way, thanks for providing the evening's entertainment the other night," Karl threw over his shoulder as he left. "Took everyone's mind off the generator malfunction."

Luke made a face as Lacey laughed.

"Hey, how did yesterday's pictures come out?" Luke asked as he took a seat in Jill's vacated chair, the one closest to Lacey.

"See for yourself," she said as she turned the screen in his direction. He smelled of salt and virile male, making her heart give a little stutter.

"May I?" he asked. She nodded and passed the computer over to him.

While Luke sat quietly looking at the pictures, she grew uncomfortable with his silence, thinking he must be just going through the motions, or worse, that he didn't like them. Unable to stand the silence any longer, she spoke up. "Well, Hancock, the photos were your idea. You might tell me what you think about them."

"All right. I'll tell you. I'm thinking." He hesitated. "I'm thinking you have an uncanny ability to capture unguarded emotion on the faces of your subjects. It's almost as if you can see into their souls." He gazed intently into her eyes.

He looked like he wanted to lean in and kiss her, but instead, he turned back to the screen.

"Like this one." He pointed to a photo of a little girl, her black curly locks tumbling down her back in disarray, her tongue between her teeth as she concentrated on bouncing the ball on her knee.

"You can see her complete concentration on this one moment, this one joyous experience, when she can put aside all the deprivation that is her daily life, and focus on this one thing that makes her happy."

A beat or two passed while Lacey considered the photo and his comment.

"You should write about it," Luke said. "You got a journalism degree from Columbia. Why not put it to use?"

"Wait, how did you know that?" Her eyes narrowed in suspicion.

"I did a little research on you. Amazing what you can find with Google."

She shifted her whole body to face him, arm draped over the back of her chair. Their legs touched, sending a shimmer of electricity up her spine. "You *Googled* me?" She didn't know whether to be annoyed or flattered. "Why would you do that?"

"Curiosity." He shrugged.

"You could have asked you know. You didn't have to resort to the internet."

"I don't know . . . you're pretty tight-lipped about yourself."

"About my personal life, yeah, but I'd have told you where I went to school."

"What if I wanted to know more?"

"Well, if you wanted anything more personal than that, you wouldn't be able to get it off the internet." At least she hoped not. She didn't have a Facebook page or a Twitter account, or even a website, so what could he possibly have found? She returned her attention to the computer.

"Wanna bet?"

Her fingers froze over the touch pad and her stomach filled with dread. When she turned back to him, he wore a smug grin.

"You should Google yourself sometime."

Trying to sound casual, she continued clicking through the photos on her laptop. "So Mr. Woodward, what salacious details did you uncover?"

"Let's see, I'd already learned who your parents were." He laughed at the grimace that passed over her features. "Found a nice article about your sister in the *New York Times Magazine* recently. Pretty," he added as an aside, although she'd reminded him a little too much of Caroline. All polish, no substance, like a shiny sports car with no engine.

He tapped his temple as if trying to recall the results of his research. "You graduated from Bromley Academy with Highest Honors, attended NYU where you earned a BFA in photography. Followed up with a master's in journalism from Columbia. Impressive," he added. "In 2001 you joined the AP as a staff photographer."

Lacey thought he seemed quite proud of himself. "Well, congratulations. Let me know when the book comes out," she said, thinking he'd come to the end of his recitation.

"Wait. There's more," he said with enthusiasm.

She groaned inwardly.

"I found some charming photos of you and your family

at various charity events, gallery openings, and soirees. Poor Lacey," Luke said with feigned pity, "you were a rather tall, gawky teenager." Who'd grown into a hot, sexy woman. "Ow!" He'd earned a rather hard punch on the arm for that last comment.

"Are you finished?" she asked as she closed her laptop.

"No. Where was I? Oh yes. You were with the AP for eight years, finally leaving after a short assignment in Darfur covering the genocide there." He paused. "Funny, you didn't mention that you covered Darfur."

He felt Lacey tense before continuing. "In fact, you won a Pulitzer for your photo of a woman holding her newborn in a refugee camp just across the Sudanese border."

He'd seen many of her photographs: flag-draped coffins, a soldier grieving over a fallen comrade, innocent children caught in the insanity of war. All so powerful, so raw.

Luke had obviously been impressed by the Pulitzer, but when he saw the photo, he hadn't been surprised. Just like with the little girl playing soccer, she'd captured the poignancy of that moment so clearly, it was almost palpable.

Lacey sat very still, remembering the moments leading up to that photo. Watching the birth of that little girl, so determined to enter a world gone mad. Her mother's village had been destroyed only two nights before, and who knew what had happened to her father.

Luke tilted his head to look at her. "I wondered why you left." His eyes narrowed in suspicion. "But then you've covered some pretty rough stuff in your career, so you were probably due for a change."

She exhaled the breath she'd been holding. "Exactly." She shrugged. "You know, sometimes you're just ready to move on."

"Right."

She knew he didn't believe her.

Luke looked at her and saw tears in her eyes. His gut clenched. That had not been his intent, to make her sad. Before he could say anything else, she'd recovered, blinking away her tears.

What the hell was that? Lacey chided herself. She never cried. She was clearly going soft. In the head.

An awkward silence descended. Seeking to break it, she cleared her throat. "What's on tap for today?"

"Heard on the news a swell is coming in. You ever surfed?"

"Just body surfacing."

"Want to learn?"

"Um, sure. Why not."

"Great. Meet me on the beach in a half hour."

She swallowed hard against the knot in her throat and managed what she hoped was a convincing smile.

"Surf's up, dude. Gnarly, man," she said with a silly grin, her right hand forming the 'hang loose' sign, thankful for the change of subject.

"Okay, enough with the surfer lingo," he said with a grimace. "See you on the beach."

———

L acey plopped down on the sand next to Luke, spraying him with water as she did so. Reaching into the cooler, she grabbed a beer and unscrewed the top before taking a long, satisfying pull. "Ahh. Nothing better than an ice-cold beer after a salty swim."

She watched as Sandy swam out to fetch the Frisbee she'd just launched into the surf.

"You did great out there today. Makes me wonder if there's anything you can't do."

She waited a beat. "Cook. Can't even boil water." Then, grimacing, she remembered an incident involving copious amounts of alcohol and a karaoke machine. "Or sing." She took another gulp of beer, stealing a glance to gauge his reaction to her confession.

His mouth curved up in a half-smile.

"I'm guessing you're not surprised that I can't cook," she said with a little challenge in her voice.

He lifted a brow in question.

"Well, you probably figured—and correctly—that I grew up with a cook, so why would a spoiled little rich girl like me know her way to the kitchen, must less her way around it."

He chuckled. "Actually, that wasn't what I thought at all. Tony's wife, Allie, can't cook either, so the fact that you can't cook isn't an indictment of your childhood."

Satisfied with his response, she leaned back on her elbows, threw back her head, and closed her eyes, reveling in the warmth of the sun on her damp skin. A cluster of rocks surrounded them, forming a cozy alcove, concentrating the sun's heat.

Luke found himself irresistibly drawn to her. She appeared relaxed, a rare sight in his company. She *had* done well this morning; he wasn't just buttering her up. Surfing proved little challenge in light of her natural athleticism.

She'd taken to the longboard like, well, like a retriever took to water, he thought, watching Sandy swim to shore, Frisbee firmly between her teeth.

The surfing lesson had been a brilliant idea on his part. It allowed him to spend some quality time with Lacey while showing her what a nice guy he could be, and gave him the excuse to touch her while he instructed her on the proper positioning.

Lacey's strength, balance, and fearlessness made her an excellent student. If he weren't careful, it would be just one more skill she would eventually beat him at.

Her eyes were still closed, giving him ample opportunity to allow his to roam her body at will. Sleek and athletic, but all woman. Today she wore a bikini of deep blue, the color of her Bahama-blue eyes, same sport-style as the other, and just as sexy. He'd like to shimmy her out of those bottoms and—

"Like what you see, Hancock?" she asked, startling him and arresting his lurid fantasy.

Busted. He flashed a chagrinned smile and felt the heat creep up his cheeks at her observation of his frank appraisal. He considered his response. He could make a wise crack, deflect his embarrassment. Or he could take the direct approach. "Yes," he said, rolling sideways onto his elbow. "I do like what I see." His eyes lowered to her lips before leaning in, ever-so- carefully, to brush his lips against hers.

Lacey's pulse vibrated through her as he captured her lower lip between his. Sighing, she rose up like the tide to meet him.

He slid his fingers into her damp hair, cupping her head and pulling her closer, deepening the kiss.

Sandy chose that moment to divest her furry coat of water and sand with a fierce shake, showering them with the aforementioned detritus. They flew apart like an atom splitting, curses flying between the gasps of shocked outrage.

The offending canine stood there, tail wagging, Frisbee at her feet, her tongue lolling cheerfully.

Luke shot to his feet, hands on his hips, and gave the

oblivious retriever a fulminating look. "Sandy, down," he snapped. "Stay."

Sandy lay down on the sand with a whine, her head between her paws.

Brushing the gritty sand from her arms and legs, Lacey started laughing. She began to think the dog was jealously guarding her territory, although Luke appeared to have gotten the worst of the assault. Watching him as he tried to brush the sand off his back without much success only made her laugh harder.

"Think that's funny, Sommers?"

"Yes," she choked out between chortles. She didn't know whyit struck her so funny, other than it felt so liberating to laugh out loud.

"I'll show you funny." Luke leaned over and shook his head, spraying Lacey with a fresh coating of wet sand, as she squealed and tried to cover her head, laughing all the while. "Still funny?" He dropped down to his knees on the sand caging her between his arms as he grabbed her wrists and pressed her back against the sand, continuing his assault.

Lacey giggled uncontrollably, trying to fend him off and catch her breath at the same time, neither too successfully. She reared up her hips in an attempt to buck him off, but the sudden unexpected full-body contact was so shocking in its intensity that they both abruptly ceased their playful tussle.

Luke froze above her, before slowly lowering his body to hers and taking her mouth with his. He wrapped his arm around her and pulled her tight against him.

The voltage of the kiss sent shockwaves down her spine. His lips, searing and sweet, his body pressed against hers, hot and firm. Unrelenting breathlessness threatened to engulf her.

Sandy fingers gripped equally sandy hair, masculine legs intertwined with silky ones, breath mingled with breath.

Luke's hand slid down her waist to her thigh, lifting her leg up and over him. Her hips rose to meet his, and all coherent thought fled.

CHAPTER SIXTEEN

"Jeez, get a room."

Lacey froze. *Tony.*

Luke groaned as he rolled off her.

Tony stood a few steps away, hands on his hips.

"You two reenacting the love scene in *From Here to Eternity?*" Tony chuckled, clearly not phased by Luke's anger. "I love that movie."

Lacey scrambled to extricate herself from Luke's embrace, and standing, attempted to brush off the sand until she realized it was a hopeless endeavor.

Her face flamed. In the short time she'd known Tony, he'd become like a brother to her, and his respect was important. Her gut twisted with the thought of losing that respect by becoming just another of Luke's conquests.

She muttered something about washing off the sand and headed for the ocean.

Luke rose. "What the hell are you doing here?" he growled.

Tony's eyebrows shot up. "You asked me to drop by

sometime today to go over your notes for tomorrow's testimony, remember?"

Luke would spend the day in San José, testifying before the Committee for Environmental Sustainability on the potential effects of a proposed road between Puerto Jimenez and Corcovado. Many in the National Assembly, the legislative body of Costa Rica, believed it would boost tourism, and they were probably right, but at what cost?

Luke's knowledge of economics, environmental sustainability, and ecotourism made him one of the world's leading experts on the subject. And the letters 'Ph.D.' after his name didn't hurt either.

He turned to glance back at Lacey. "Yeah, well your timing could use a little work," he muttered.

"Well, I can always leave and let you get back to your . . . afternoon delight." Tony tilted his head and smiled. "I guess I'd be pretty frustrated too if I'd been caught *in flagrante.*"

"No. Sorry. Didn't mean to rip your face off. But seriously, man, you couldn't have occupied yourself for a while and come back later?" Luke added with his tongue in his cheek. He saw Lacey emerge from the water, then turned back to Tony. "Don't mention anything to Lacey about tomorrow."

Tony's brow creased in confusion. "Why not?"

"Because she thinks I'm just some beach bum and part-time guide, and I'd rather keep it that way."

"But—"

"I gotta get back," Lacey said as she bent to pick up her sand-encrusted shorts. "Got some work to do." She walked past the two men before realizing that, in her haste to retreat, she'd neglected her manners. She turned around and walked backward. "Hey, Tony."

"Hey, Lacey."

"Thanks for the surfing lesson, Hancock," she shot over her shoulder, as she turned back in the direction of the path. "Won't be long before I'm kicking your ass in that too."

Tony lifted an eyebrow at Luke, but he just shook his head, refusing to rise to the bait.

———

Lacey tossed her sandy shorts and bikini in the shower to rinse away some of the grit as she stepped beneath the spray. She had to admit the morning with Luke had been fun, but the almost-sex-on-the-beach had been electrifying.

She had no doubt that had Tony not interrupted their all- too-public display, they would have committed multiple violations of any number of laws prohibiting public indecency.

She had the hots for Luke, and he for her. That much was clear. The question was whether she should throw caution to the wind and enjoy a little fling, or put some distance between them and avoid the entanglement.

This was a relatively short assignment and she'd be moving on soon. She had high hopes of getting another more adrenalin- inducing assignment in the near future, so it seemed best at this point to avoid the entanglement.

Her mouth lifted into a wry grin as she rinsed the shampoo from her hair. Hell, with Luke factored into the equation, *this* amounted to an adrenalin-inducing assignment.

———

L acey grinned as she and Tony climbed out of the mud-covered Jeep laughing and good-naturedly jostling each other.

"Don't forget you owe me a beer," Lacey said as she reached in the back seat for her equipment bag. Thunder rumbled overhead.

"How could I forget, when you keep reminding me?"

After a heated discussion about baseball—Tony being a Rangers fan, she being a Yankees fan—Tony had bet Lacey that she couldn't name the pitcher who played for both the Yankees and the Rangers but was best known for swapping wives with his best friend, Yankee pitcher, Mike Kekich. He should have known better. He'd watched Luke lose more than one bet with her. Why did he think he could do any better?

She didn't even take time to think about it before she'd blurted out, "That's easy, Fritz Peterson."

That day, in Golfo Dulce, she'd gotten some great shots of macaws, many of the obligatory frogs, even a beautiful golden eyelash viper, so called for its patch of bristly scales above each eye.

She and Tony had conversed easily, and were equally as comfortable with companionable silences. But despite Tony's pleasant company, she found herself missing Luke's imperious directions and dictatorial mandates. She smiled. If she were completely honest with herself, she also missed pushing his buttons and trying his patience.

The day hadn't been all fun and games. She'd brought up Luke's sister again, but Tony had clammed up, refusing to talk about a subject he knew his friend wouldn't want discussed. He told her she'd have to ask Luke herself. Even her threat to do some research of her own hadn't budged him. She admired his loyalty to his friend.

A fat raindrop landed on Lacey's head, shaking her from her musings. She preceded Tony into the bar for the aforementioned beer just as the skies opened up. She stopped like she'd hit a wall, her rubber-soled hiking boots squeaking on the hardwood floor—thankfully concealing the gasp that escaped her mouth— causing Tony to bump into her with an audible *oomph*.

Luke stood speaking in hushed tones with Jill and Karl. It wasn't so much his presence in the bar that disarmed her, but rather his attire.

He wore dark gray suit pants, a white dress shirt, sleeves rolled up over his muscular forearms revealing a dress watch, and in place of his customary flip-flops, he wore black dress shoes. She spied his suit coat and a deep blue tie thrown carelessly over the back of a nearby chair. Aside from the surprise that he even owned a suit, her heart beat a staccato rhythm at the sight.

Growing up in the midst of Wall Street, suits were as plentiful as raindrops in Costa Rica, but there was some-thing about a man in a suit that still did it for her. He looked so different, so professional, and so . . . dashing. *Dashing? Where had that come from?* But really, he only needed a tumbler of Scotch and damned if he wouldn't look like a cover model for *GQ*.

Tony couldn't conceal his grin as he watched her obvious appreciation for Luke's transformation from beach bum to businessman. She scowled at him, but he merely flashed her a knowing look and stepped past her.

"*Hola*," Tony said to the room at large, causing Luke to turn in time to see Lacey's stunned expression.

Tony waited a beat, then said, "Hey, Lacey." He nudged her shoulder. "What's the deal? I'm thirsty."

Jill and Karl greeted her, and headed off in the direction of the kitchen as Karl said, "Luke, we'll talk more tomorrow. Got to get ready for the dinner crowd."

Giving herself a mental shake, before fully recovering her faculties, she strode over to the bar, suddenly all-too-aware of her sweat-encrusted skin, unkempt hair, and muddy feet. "Sorry, for a minute there I thought you were someone important."

"Yeah, I have that effect on people," Luke shot back. "How'd your, er, business meeting go today?" Tony asked as he grabbed a bar stool and ordered three beers.

"It went well. We can talk about it later," Luke hedged.

He pulled up a seat next to Lacey. "I'm surprised both of you made it back alive," he said to Tony. "I expected you to kill one another before day's end."

Lacey gave an unladylike snort. "Him, I like." She jerked her head in Tony's direction. "You, on the other hand, bring out my homicidal tendencies."

Luke took a gulp of his beer. "Yeah, I seem to have that effect on people too."

She eyed him again. The sudden, unbidden memory of their encounter on the beach the day before made her lips tingle and her body melt. The white of his dress shirt stood in stark contrast to his tanned neck and chest. She noted with surprise that he still wore the hemp bracelet. Oh well, you can take the man out of the beach bum, but you obviously can't take the beach bum out of the man.

Luke could feel her eyes on him. "You got something to say?"

"Just surprised that you'd wear a suit to discuss jungle-guide business. Wouldn't shorts and a T-shirt be more appropriate? I mean, you wouldn't want your prospective client to think you're more comfortable in the board room than in the rain forest."

He shrugged. "It was an important client." Something about his expression told her he was keeping something from her. Curious.

With a shrug, Lacey polished off her beer and gathered her equipment bag. "I need a shower—"

"I wasn't going to say anything, but . . ." Luke said with a smirk.

"Funny," she directed at Luke's back, afraid he wasn't joking. She suspected she smelled like a dead fish.

He watched her leave.

"Thanks again, Tony, I had a great day," she said a little too warmly. Let Luke see how much she'd enjoyed Tony's company, she thought.

"Any time, Lacey," Tony replied.

Luke frowned. "Hey, Sommers," Luke called out just before she left. "I'm having a little cook-out tomorrow after-noon at my house. Tony and Allie are coming. You're welcome too. Five o'clock."

Turning, she narrowed her eyes at the invitation. "Thanks." She dashed into the rain, arms and torso covering her equipment bag.

Luke watched her run past the windows, her hair already plastered against her head. By the time she got to her bungalow, she wouldn't need a shower.

"So, how'd your testimony go?" Tony prodded after Lacey's departure.

Luke turned back to Tony. "Fine. It's hard to tell really." Luke took a sip of his beer and reached for the bowl of tortilla chips Philippe had put on the bar and, crunching on a chip, continued. "The Committee appeared to understand the issues, but whether the rest of the assembly will understand remains to be seen. We can only hope."

He'd argued that tourists come to the region because of its pristine quality and relative isolation. A paved road, which would inevitably lead to more traffic, more development, and larger crowds, could eventually drive the more affluent tourists away.

Karl and Jill vehemently opposed the road, and most of the region's inhabitants did as well. Luke had been discussing the day's events with Karl and Jill when Lacey'd walked in with Tony.

"For everyone's sake," Tony echoed his sentiment.

Tony and Luke gave a passing nod to a couple honeymooning at the resort, before continuing the conversation.

"Tell me again why you don't want Lacey to know?" Tony asked, eyebrows furrowed in confusion.

Luke grimaced.

He shrugged and assumed an expression of disdain. "Because she's prejudiced, and I want her to see past the preconceived notions she has of people."

"By people, you mean you," Tony said, eyebrow lifted inchallenge. "Because I don't find her at all prejudiced."

Luke didn't respond. He didn't like the fact his friend could see right through him. Truth be told, he wanted Lacey to like him for who she thought he was—a ne'er-do-well beach bum—rather than a highly regarded expert on the environment.

"So, your plan is to teach her a lesson."

"Someone needs to. Might as well be me." His mouth lifted into a rakish grin. At Tony's dubious expression, Luke continued. "Hey, I'm doing her a favor."

Tony snorted. He was going to enjoy watching Lacey

turn the tables. She wasn't the only one with preconceived notions over who needed to learn a lesson. Or maybe two.

CHAPTER SEVENTEEN

Laughter floated up the dirt road as Lacey made her way to Luke's house. She carried a bottle of Shiraz she'd bought from the resort, her mother's admonition that one never arrived at someone's home empty-handed ringing in her ears.

She'd worried over what to wear, her limited wardrobe offering little outside of hiking clothes, running shorts, and swimsuits, finally deciding on the least battle-scarred pair of short shorts in khaki, a pale blue tank top, and flip flops. It wasn't exactly party attire, but it would have to do.

Eric Clapton drifted through the open windows, layered upon the rhythmic sound of the ocean. As she rounded the corner of the house to the beachside, the scent of burgers on the grill set her mouth to watering. She hadn't had a burger since she'd left the States.

Sandy's deep bark greeted her and she knelt down to give the dog a friendly pat on the head before approaching the deck.

Luke stood at the grill, spatula in one hand, beer in the other, laughing over something Tony had said. Seeing him dressed in his surfer's uniform of board shorts and T-shirt, his feet bare, revved her motor and shifted her pulse into fifth gear.

Tony spotted her first, greeting her warmly. Luke turned in her direction, and the look of appreciation on his face as his eyes swept up her bare legs made her feel warm and fuzzy inside. He grinned, waving the spatula in her direction. She glanced away as the heat crept into her face.

A petite raven-haired beauty lounged in one of the chairs. Allie, she presumed.

The woman stood and greeted Lacey. "You must be Lacey. I've heard so much about you from both my guys." Her Spanish accent and sultry voice lent her words a sensual quality. "I'm Allie."

Lacey still held the bottle of wine. "Here, let me take that." Allie jerked her head toward the men. "They don't always have the best manners, but I love them anyway." She smiled at Lacey, tilting her head charmingly.

Tony sauntered over and slipped his arm around his wife's waist and leaned over to buss Lacey's cheek. "Glad Luke invited you."

Luke was glad he'd invited her too. Maybe in a social situation she could relax and he could get to know her better. And vice versa.

After getting Lacey her drink of choice, Allie and Lacey settled in for some quiet conversation 'away from the *hombres*'.

Luke spoke to Tony. "Look at those two. Thick as thieves. What do you suppose they're talking about?"

"Us, I hope."

Luke's eyebrows shot up. "God, I hope not."

As Lacey and Allie chatted, Lacey learned in short

order that Allie served as business manager, accountant, and marketing director for Environmental Expeditions.

But Lacey thought Allie had missed her calling. She should have been an investigative reporter. Before Lacey could learn any more about Allie, she peppered Lacey with questions: Where'd she go to school? How long had she been a photojournalist? Even what size shoe did she wear? Her warmth and genuine interest made Lacey want to share her stories with her. A true test of a great reporter.

For Lacey's part, she finally managed to learn that Allie and Tony met at U.T. where she also earned her degree in business. They dated for a year, but she wanted to take some time to see the world after graduation and before she settled down, so she spent the next several years doing just that.

Instead of discovering the world, she discovered that she couldn't get Tony out of her head, or out of her heart, and returned to Costa Rica to sweep him off his feet.

Lacey enjoyed chatting with Allie. She'd never had a girl friend. Where the boys had been intimidated by her, the girls had been frightened of her. She hadn't been even remotely interested in the latest fashions, where to get the best manicure, or who committed the season's worst fashion faux pas, which had left little to talk about.

"What do you think of our Luke there?" Allie asked, as she looked in the direction of the men, a twinkle in her eye.

Lacey didn't know how to respond, so her response was less than candid. "He's been a great guide, very knowledge-able, very helpful in ensuring I get the photos I need for my assignment."

Allie tilted her head. "Hmm hmm. That's not what I'm talking about. He is sexy, no?" She lifted a delicate eyebrow.

Lacey caved. "*Sí*, he is sexy." She turned to look as Luke

tossed Sandy a hamburger patty from the grill, a boyish grin lighting his features, flashing the appealing dimple in his chin. "*Muy* sexy."

The two women glanced in Luke's direction and laughed, confirming Tony's suspicion and making Luke nervous. Luke had known Allie for several years. God only knew what stories she'd shared with Lacey.

"He's also a good man." She smiled at Lacey. "A great catch for anyone lucky enough, and determined enough, to reel him in."

"You ladies hungry?" Luke interrupted their conversation before Lacey could respond. "Burgers are done, and Tony's bringing out the rest of the food."

Allie rose, kissing Luke's cheek before patting it. "Aren't we two lucky to have our men cater to us while we put our feet up and sip our wine?"

Lacey colored at Allie's use of the term 'our' in reference to the men.

"All in a day's work," Luke replied with a devilish grin.

———

Lacey surveyed the remains of the meal on the table. They sipped the excellent Shiraz she'd brought. Chalk one up for Mother. She *did* know her wine.

Lacey relaxed in her chair, contented, as dusk turned slowly to night, the sky fading from violet to deep blue, and the first stars winked on. The moon, just shy of full, lit the night, eliminating the need for torches or candles.

The conversation was relaxed and cheerful, liberally salted with good-natured ribbing between Tony and Luke.

Witnessing the interactions between Tony and Allie made Lacey's cynical heart swell. Their playfulness, tenderness, and mutual respect for one another, something she'd never encountered in either her parents or other couples she'd known, touched her deeply.

Watching Luke's face when he observed their affection for one another made that same cynical heart ache. His unguarded expression and obvious envy for their relationship came as a surprise to Lacey. He didn't seem the type. Then again, neither did she, but after spending time in the couple's presence, they made you believe true love was not only real, but attainable.

Lacey gave herself a mental shake, looking with suspicion at her glass of wine. Maybe she'd had too much to drink.

Luke glanced at Lacey and then back at Tony and Allie. Tony'd found his perfect match in Allie. Despite his playboy persona, Luke sometimes thought about what it would be like to share his life with someone. Someone who understood him and loved him for himself.

If he were entirely honest with himself, he'd married Caroline for her beauty and her sex appeal. But not her heart. He hadn't loved her. He'd enjoyed her company and her body. But that was as far as it went.

And as much as Luke sometimes wanted his perfect match, he'd consistently take a step back from that daydream. After losing Lisa, he didn't think he could bear getting that close to someone again. He didn't think he could survive the loss.

The first notes of Van Morrison's "Brown-Eyed Girl" floated through the open windows. Tony rose, holding out a hand to his wife, then pulled her into his arms for a sexy salsa.

Luke smiled as he watched the couple mold their bodies into one and sway to the classic hit song.

Lacey rose from the table and started clearing the dishes, feeling a little uncomfortable watching such an intimate moment. Luke rose with her, grabbing the stack of plates from her hands before carrying them to the kitchen. She followed him with a couple of empty bowls.

On her way to the kitchen, she spotted the watercolor Luke had been working on the day they'd fought over her father. "You finished it."

"Yep."

"I like it." She stopped to admire it. Actually, she loved it. The finished product was even better than the earlier version she saw. The colors were richer, denser, adding depth and movement to the scene.

Luke paused behind her. It pleased him that she liked it. More than he cared to admit. "There's still something missing . . . I'm not sure what."

While Luke busied himself in the kitchen, Lacey took a few minutes to look around. The kitchen opened up to the small living room. Comfortable chairs and a sofa formed a seating area around a television. A colorful rug covered the painted concrete floor. Lacey slipped off her flip flop to test the floor. Cool underfoot as she'd expected.

Windows overlooked the deck where Tony and Allie laughed and swayed to the music. Beneath the windows stood a low bookshelf filled with framed photos, books, and a few odds and ends. But before she could nose around the photos, Luke walked back into the room.

He followed her out to the deck, but before she could pick up any other dishes, he caught her by the wrist and hauled her out onto the open deck.

"Hancock, what are you doing?"

"Dancing," he said as if it should be obvious to anyone

what he was doing. Fighting against her resistance, he gave her an awkward spin before gathering her into his arms.

"You really can't hold your liquor, can you?"

"I'm not drunk." Sliding his hand down her buttocks, he pressed her hips to his, executing a stirring rendition of dirty dancing, as he moved his hips in unison with hers. "At least not on alcohol," he continued with a rakish grin.

She laughed. "Wow. That's an impressively lame line. Does it usually work?"

"I don't know. You tell me," he murmured as his lips closed in for a kiss. A sweet, wine-scented kiss. Then he pushed her hip back, to give her another little spin.

Lacey giggled, thrown off balance by his seductiveness one minute, his playfulness the next, and his sweetness the next.

Van Morrison faded into Bob Seger's "We've Got Tonight." Tony and Allie's sexy salsa transformed into a sultry rumba that made even Lacey blush.

She tried to step away from Luke, but he held her tight around the waist. She looked up at him askance, eyebrow lifted in question. He lifted her arms up around his neck, then glided his hands down to her hips, moving them in a sweet, seductive circle.

As Seger crooned about loneliness, longing, and love, it seemed as if he were singing the words just for her. She might not be able to find love, but she could satisfy her long-ing, maybe even relieve her loneliness, if only for one night.

Lacey melted into Luke's hard, lean body, sliding a bare leg between his thighs, lacing her fingers into the silky hair at his nape, and burying her face into his neck, inhaling his fresh scent.

Luke's step faltered, surprised at the change in Lacey's body language, but he got her message loud and clear. She became pliant in his arms, as if her bones had melted into his. He cupped her head, bent to nibble her earlobe just above the scar that glowed white in the moonlight. A soft moan escaped her as his teeth captured the tender flesh, before soothing it with his tongue.

Lacey felt as if the rest of the world had receded. Only she and Luke existed in the tropical paradise. She didn't notice when Tony and Allie strolled out onto the beach, arm-in-arm. She didn't notice when the soulful song ended, changing to something slightly up-tempo. She only heard Luke's raspy breathing, inhaled his pheromone-laced scent, tasted his heat.

Luke grasped Lacey's hair, pulling her head back to expose the smooth column of her throat, kissing his way down, stopping at her grandmother's necklace, before retracing his path until he reached the scar, caressing the raised surface tenderly with his tongue.

Lacey gasped, pulling out of his arms and stepping away from him, resisting the urge to cover the scar with her hand.

Bemused, he asked, "Did I hurt you?"

"No." Her chest rose and fell with her shallow breaths. "Then I don't understand." His brow furrowed in confusion. "I should—I just need to go." She looked around, realizing for the first time that they were alone. Glancing back at the still-cluttered table, she said, "I'll help you clean up." She strode over to the table.

Before she could pick up anything, Luke's hand grasped her wrist. "No," he said, his voice quiet, but firm. "I'll clean up." His head still spun from the rapid deceleration of his pulse. And his desire. "I'll drive you back."

"No, I can walk—"

"Absolutely not. You are not to walk that road at night, do you understand?"

A sharp retort rose to the tip of her tongue, but she thought better of it. "Fine."

———

The short, uphill ride to the resort was quiet. Luke replayed the moment when he'd caressed the scar on Lacey's neck. Why did she react so violently to his tender gesture? Maybe she didn't see it as a tender gesture. Maybe she was ashamed of the scar, self-conscious over what she saw as a disfigurement. Maybe the gesture had brought back memories of what had happened to her. He wanted to ask her about it, but knew she wouldn't be receptive to the question, especially given her reaction.

Hands clasped tightly in her lap, Lacey contemplated her reaction. No one had ever mentioned her scar, much less kissed it. The two guys she'd been with since the incident had made a point of avoiding it; they didn't look at it, touch it, or kiss it. The moment with Luke had seemed almost too personal, too . . . intimate.

Luke's voice startled her. "Lacey, I'm sorry . . . if I did anything to hurt or offend you—"

"No—it's okay. I just . . ." Her voice trailed off. "You just surprised me, that's all." She fell silent.

"Did you still want to go to San José tomorrow?"

She'd almost forgotten that Luke had invited her to fly to San José with him so he could pick up Christmas gifts for his friends and family.

"Sure."

"Okay, I'll pick you up at eight."

They stopped outside the resort. The restaurant and bar were dark and quiet given the late hour.

"I'll walk you to your bungalow."

"I'm fine." She smiled. She was beginning to like his protectiveness. "You still have a mess to clean up at home."

He hesitated before leaning over to kiss her cheek. "Thanks for coming to dinner. Allie really enjoyed meeting you."

The corner of her mouth lifted in a smile. "Thanks for the invitation." She climbed out of the Jeep and walked through the moonlight along the path to her bungalow.

CHAPTER EIGHTEEN

To Lacey's surprise, the flight to San José was pleasant, notwithstanding the awkward and somewhat contentious start to the morning. But by the time they reached the city via a rental car, they'd fallen into comfortable conversation.

When she'd met Luke outside the resort office with her camera bag that morning, Luke had balked.

"You can't take that behemoth to San José. You might as well wear a target on your back for pickpockets and thugs."

"Then how am I supposed to take pictures?" She rarely went anywhere without her camera.

"I don't know, but you can't take that. And you need to leave the watch and necklace behind too."

Her watch-adorned wrist flew up to the necklace, before giving him a stubborn glare. "No. I'll leave the watch and the camera bag, and take my small digital camera, but I'm not leaving the necklace behind." She didn't tell him that it was a talisman of sorts. The only time she hadn't worn it since it was given to her had been when she was in Darfur.

"Then you'd better be willing to risk it." With that, he'd pivoted on his heel and strode to his Jeep.

The shops in San José were decorated for Christmas, but the decorations seemed out of place in the Central American heat, so different from the Christmases of her childhood in New York—or Tahoe, or Zermatt, or whatever posh location her family chose for the holidays. Of course, it had been many years since she'd spent a Christmas with her family.

The streets teemed with tourists, collecting souvenirs to mark their vacations, and purchasing gifts for friends and family members. The cafés and street vendors did a brisk business. The scent of roasting coffee permeated the air. First stop, a café for a hot, sweet, milky cup of *café con leche*.

Luke couldn't help himself. He watched as Lacey took a sip of her coffee. He loved the expression of bliss that never failed to grace her features after that first sip.

She opened her eyes to see him staring at her with a slight grin. "What?"

"Oh, nothing." He wondered if she wore that same expression after an exhilarating frolic between the sheets. Shaking his head to clear his thoughts, he continued as they left the café, "Pay attention to your surroundings, and guard your camera and wallet."

Lacey rolled her eyes. "I'm not a yokel. I grew up in New York City."

"The pickpockets in San José make New York look like Smalltown, U.S.A. Just be careful."

Lacey followed Luke into a couple of shops, looking with only limited interest at the goods they contained. She'd rather have a root canal than go shopping, but although she didn't go home for Christmas, she did usually send something along to her nieces from whatever exotic—or dangerous—locale she happened to be in at the time.

They ambled down Avenida Central when a window display caught Lacey's eye. In the window hung a lovely, simple cotton sundress of watery blues, soft greens, and pale turquoises all swirled together in a muted impressionistic pattern. Below the dress lay a pair of huarache sandals in pale green.

She glanced down at her khaki cargo shorts and the tank top in a color-formerly-known-as-green. She thought about last night's cookout and how she'd wished she'd had something nicer to wear. Looking back up at the dress, she decided she had to have it.

"Sommers?" Luke retraced his steps when he turned around to find her gone. "Did you want to go in?"

"Yeah. I need to get something for my nieces." He followed her in, but she stopped him, saying, "They're picky. It might take a while."

Despite his reluctance to leave her, he was impatient to finish up his shopping. "Okay. But meet me at that food cart," he said, pointing to a burrito stand a block away, "in an hour. That give you enough time?"

"Sure. Thanks." The bell over the shop's door tinkled as she stepped in. She sighed when the cool air touched her skin. A friendly clerk greeted her. "I'd like to see that dress," Lacey said in Spanish, pointing to the dress in the window.

"*Sí, Señorita.*" The woman hurried off toward the back of the store indicating that Lacey should follow.

Lacey found her size and asked to try the dress along with the sandals in the window.

Stepping out of the small curtained dressing room to stand in front of the mirror, Lacey barely recognized herself. She couldn't remember the last time she'd worn a dress.

Probably not since, well, since Lilia's wedding, and that had been under duress.

The dress fit perfectly. The neckline formed a deep V, with the thin straps crisscrossing over her bare back. The bodice fit snug at the waist and the skirt fell in soft folds to just above her knees. No ruffles, no frou-frous, no fuss. Just simple, flirty femininity. She felt womanly . . . and pretty for the first time in far too long.

She frowned, reaching up to touch the scar. She wasn't typically self-conscious about it, but it stood out in sharp contrast to the lovely dress. Sighing, she told herself it was there for good, a reminder that life was far too short.

Too short not to buy this dress, and these shoes . . . and maybe that bracelet, she thought, as she spotted a blue, green, and turquoise glass bead bracelet.

———

Luke had purchased his mother's favorite Costa Rican coffee and a bottle of *Café Rica*, Costa Rica's answer to Kahlua, for his father. He snagged a beautiful Biesanz Woodworks turned wood bowl for Tony and Allie, and for Jill and Karl he got a hardwood seedling to plant on the resort.

He had a few minutes to kill before his rendezvous with Lacey, so he stopped in a pottery shop. On a shelf, just to his right, he spotted a ceramic vase with a vivid hand-painted Monarch butterfly. Remembering Lacey's tattoo, and the sexy hip on which it sat, he thought it would be the perfect gift for her.

The fact that it was made by Peace Potters, an organization that trained low-income women to make pottery, sweetened the deal.

L acey juggled her shopping bags, quite pleased with herself. For someone who hated shopping, she'd done pretty well. She'd scored the dress, shoes, and bracelet. She'd also bought a pair of breezy white linen pants, a sheer cotton blouse, also in white, a pair of gold leather thongs, and a gold cuff bracelet.

Her nieces had each scored even better with some girlie hair accessories, a necklace, earrings, and matching bracelet, and little huarache sandals.

For Tony and Allie, she'd found a sumptuous hand-woven throw, and Jill and Karl, a hand-carved frame, which would display the photo of them and the serendipitous butterfly.

Luke had scored too. In another shop, she'd stumbled upon a beautiful watercolor set in a rich mahogany box—sustainably harvested, of course—to replace the beat-up tackle box she remembered stumbling over.

The box contained paintbrushes of the finest sable with handles of teak, also sustainably harvested, and watercolors made from organic pigments in luminous colors.

Excited about Christmas for the first time since child-hood, she could hardly wait to give everyone their gifts.

Completing her shopping in record time, her mood light and carefree, she headed in the direction of the burrito cart. She intended to treat Luke to lunch with some of the money she'd won off him.

At the corner of an alley stood a little girl with the largest brown eyes she'd ever seen. Her messy hair and dirt-smudged face couldn't conceal the child's angelic beauty.

Lacey fumbled in her pocket for her small camera, cursing the fact that she didn't have her telephoto lens. Just as she approached the little girl to ask if she could take her picture, the child ducked into the alley. Lacey quickly followed.

The child perched on a dirty stoop. She appeared to be about five years old, the age of Lacey's own younger niece. She put her shopping bags down, and speaking softly in Spanish, asked the girl if she could take her picture.

Before the girl could answer, her round eyes widened in fear as she cringed against the rickety stair rail.

Lacey was surprised that she had scared the girl so. Then she heard an ominous metallic *whisk*, like the sound of a switchblade springing from its bolster. She spun in time to see a young thug wielding a vicious-looking knife. He shouted to her in Spanish as he approached her, backing her up against the wall.

"Give me your camera and that necklace." He waved the knife in front of her face.

He could have made his demand in Portuguese for all she heard him. One look at the knife and she no longer cowered in that alley. She trembled in Darfur, where she could smell the smoke, the fear, the death, and the rank breath of her captors. A switchblade no longer threatened her, but a machete.

Her blood thrummed in her ears, drowning out all sound, as if they'd just filled with water. She held her breath, unable to fill her lungs, unable to scream. Her vision tunneled until she thought she might faint.

He shouted at her again. "Give it to me, or I'll cut you, bitch." He closed the distance between them and held the knife just under her chin, and then reached for the necklace.

Before he could rip the garnet from her neck, he

suddenly cried out in pain, dropping the knife and falling to the filthy pavement.

Luke kicked the knife out of reach, then bent down and picked up the mugger by his shirt before planting his fist in the guy's face, sending him sprawling to the pavement again.

Luke spun to look at Lacey, and the thief took the opportunity to make a run for it.

Lacey stood against the wall, paralyzed. Her breath came in harsh gasps, her eyes wide with fear, staring unseeing, her fists clenched at her side.

He cursed under his breath. Without a second's thought, he grabbed Lacey's stiff body and gathered her into his arms. Her body trembled as if she stood in an arctic snowstorm, instead of in a sweltering Costa Rican alley.

He whispered, "Lacey, sweetheart, *querida*. You're safe. He's gone." He rubbed his hands down her arms, chafing the chilled skin. The stiffness fled, and she suddenly went limp. Thinking she'd fainted, he wrapped his arms around her to keep her from falling. Her breath hitched, then came out in whimpers, before becoming racking sobs, her shoulders shaking with the effort.

"Shh. It's okay. You're safe, sweetheart." He began rocking her back and forth like a child, soothing her. "Lacey, *querida*, shh." He kissed her forehead, her eyes, her tear-streaked cheeks. She grabbed onto him like a lifeline. Her fingers clawing at his shirt, abrading the skin underneath, but he didn't care.

It killed him. Witnessing her anguish caused him physical pain. He'd seen many women cry, but not like this. This was torture. The flood of tears dampened his shirt. The sobs came from some deep, dark place, filled with terror and pain and grief. He recognized it because he'd experienced it.

No sign of audacity. No trace of bravado. This was Lacey completely vulnerable and exposed. She'd been stripped of all her armor and he hated it.

When he'd passed the alley on his way to the burrito stand, he'd spotted something out of the corner of his eye: a pile of shopping bags. He'd stepped into the alley to investigate and froze in fear at the sight of Lacey, her back against a wall, a lethal knife to her throat and the filthy mugger's hand reaching for her.

Something snapped in Luke. The only fights he'd ever been in were minor bar fights in college. He had no martial arts training, no boxing skills, but he had to do something, so he ran up behind the guy and kicked him in the back of the knee. By sheer luck the guy had dropped the knife where Luke could kick it out of reach.

After that, he had been so pissed that he'd picked the guy up and decked him. Only his concern for Lacey stopped him from continuing to pulverize the bastard's face.

He didn't know how long they stood in that alley, but Lacey's sobs finally gave way to short, hiccoughing breaths. He continued to rain gentle kisses on her face, whispering to her nonstop.

"You came for me," she said, her voice a harsh whisper, the words carrying a note of surprise. "You saved me."

He didn't know how to respond. "Of course I did, *querida*. What else would I do?"

Lacey didn't respond, not even to object to the endearment, she just pulled his mouth down to hers and kissed him. The kiss began gentle, tentative. He let her determine the tenor of it. When her hands rose to his neck and laced in the sweat-dampened hair at his nape, the tenor of the kiss intensified, and he welcomed it.

Cupping her head with one hand, he pressed her body

close with the other. He understood the need in her; the need to erase the last few moments; the need to release her pent-up emotions in a life-affirming embrace, and release the adrenalin coursing through her veins.

He allowed her free reign, giving her what she craved, letting her take all she needed, and then encouraging her take even more. The passion did not leave him unmoved. Far from it. Even as he gave, he took. And she offered.

The blare of a car horn brought them crashing back to earth. They both looked around the alley as if recognizing their surroundings for the first time.

Lacey took a step back, the Kevlar skin back in place. "I'm okay."

"No. You're safe, but you're not okay." His anger surfaced as Lacey's shield enclosed her, anger that she couldn't, or wouldn't, consciously admit her vulnerability.

"I'm fine." She brushed her hands brusquely across her cheeks, swiping away the tears, then ran her hands through her hair. "Anyone would have been unnerved by a knife-wielding thief."

Luke could see her hands trembling even still, as she walked unsteadily toward her shopping bags, then reached for the handles. He wanted to take them from her, but he knew it would only raise her ire, so he let her be. He'd give her some time to calm down, but then he intended to confront her, ask her what had happened to her, and God help him, see if he could help her.

CHAPTER NINETEEN

Lacey peeled off her clothes before collapsing naked onto her bed and closing her eyes, exhausted. She needed a shower, but she didn't have the energy to open her eyes, much less stand up. It seemed as if she wore a suit of chain mail.

It wasn't just the aftermath of the adrenalin overdose, but the constant weight of fear and the need to conceal it that wore her down, had been wearing her down for the past two years. If the incident in Africa hadn't been enough to expose her vulnerability, today's near-mugging was. Luke was right. She needed help.

When they'd returned to the resort after dark, he'd taken her hand before she could hop out of the Jeep. "Lacey." His voice had held a note of reproach.

"Go ahead," she said with resignation, as she clutched the heart-shaped garnet at her throat.

"Go ahead, what?"

"Go ahead and say 'I told you so.'" At his look of confusion, she'd continued. "For wearing the necklace after you warned me not to."

He ran his fingers through his hair, sighing. "I'm not going to."

She was shocked. He'd never hesitated to tell her, in no uncertain terms, when she'd done something he'd considered stupid. And she never deserved scolding more than she did now.

"You didn't ask for what happened to you today, no matter what I said this morning." His piercing gaze held hers for several beats. "Do you understand that?" he asked softly.

To her mortification, her eyes filled with tears.

He cupped her face, caressing her cheek with his thumb. "No one deserves to be the victim of brutality." A tear trickled down her cheek, and he caught it with this thumb. "Sommers. Lacey, what happened to you?" His eyes glanced at the scar. "Tell me."

Lacey shook her head, tears spilling over her cheeks. "I can't," she said in a choked whisper. She yanked her bags out of the Jeep and ran to her bungalow. His tenderness had almost been her undoing.

She could still feel the security of his arms around her in that alley. His tender kisses, his gentle caresses. He'd saved her. Again. He'd fought for her. Risked his life for her, not once, but twice.

Now, as she drifted off to sleep, she remembered him calling her by her first name. Something he'd never done before. It had only been her name, but it had touched her like an endearment.

———

Luke grew increasingly frustrated by Lacey's stubborn insistence that she was fine. Of course anyone would have been scared shitless if they'd had a knife stuck in their face. But her reaction went beyond the fear of the moment.

She hadn't been in that alley when he'd found her. Just like with the machete incident at Sirena Station, she'd been somewhere else in her mind. Somewhere black and sinister.

The fact was, as much as he wanted her to open up, admit she wasn't as strong as she pretended to be, it grieved him to see her so helpless.

He grabbed a bottle of soda out of the fridge, and swore. What had he gotten himself into? He didn't want or need entanglements. They never ended well. Besides, she would be leaving soon.

He stretched out on the sofa with a sigh. Sandy sat by him and put her head in his lap. As he absently stroked her silky ears, much to Sandy's delight, he pictured Lacey.

Yes, she was beautiful and sexy, and yes, there was definitely sexual attraction there. But it went beyond the physical. She was smart, funny, thoughtful, and thinking about her day with the kids, compassionate . . . as well as hardheaded, aggravating, and an altogether pain in the ass.

She'd gotten under his skin. And into his heart.

"Well, I'll be goddamned," he said, sitting up, spilling his soda, and startling Sandy. "Could I be falling for her?" He stared at Sandy for a minute before lying back down. "Nah."

———

Lacey awoke with a start, her hair matted to her head, the sweat-soaked sheets tangled around her legs.

She'd had another nightmare. No surprise given her ordeal earlier. The air lay heavy as a wet wool blanket around her, and she noticed the silence of the ceiling fans. *Great.* The generator must be out again.

She drew back the mosquito netting and squinted at her watch. Just shy of two a.m. In search of a breath of air, she stepped out onto the deck into the moonlight naked, but it wasn't much cooler. The rhythmic sound of the surf below invited her. The thought of the cool water beckoned.

After quickly donning running shorts and a tank top she hiked down to the beach, past Luke's house. The house was dark. She knew it was foolish to walk alone this time of night, as Luke had reminded her. She might encounter a big cat out for a nightly meal. But after today, she didn't much care.

Just as she passed the edge of Luke's property, Sandy started barking. Almost immediately, a light flicked on inside, followed by an outdoor floodlight.

"Shit," she muttered as she sprinted to the water, wading in up to her knees hoping Luke wouldn't spot her. She shivered in the comparatively cool water, but welcomed the relief from the intolerable heat.

———

Luke stepped out onto the deck wearing nothing but his shorts armed with an old cowbell. There'd been an inquisitive coatimundi hanging around getting into mischief the last couple of weeks. With no sign of the animal, Luke turned back to the door, then spotted a lone form in the moonlit water. A form he'd recognize anywhere.

"Sandy, stay," he said, then signaled the command with his hand. Sandy settled to the deck with a whine.

The sand felt cool beneath his feet as he approached the water's edge. Lacey looked so beautiful standing there in the moonlight, her clothes damp and clingy, her skin slick with the water that swirled around her thighs.

"Can't sleep?" he called as he waded out to her. "You know you shouldn't have come down here alone at night," he admonished. "You'd make a tasty snack for a puma or jaguar."

She had her back to him. "Yeah, I know. Generator's out. I just needed some air and maybe a swim."

"You're not wearing a swimsuit."

"Observant, aren't you, Hancock?" Lacey knew he didn't deserve her anger, especially after what he'd done for her in that alley, but she couldn't help herself. She wanted to lash out at something, and he made himself awfully convenient.

"Thanks, I pride myself on my skills of observation. Skinny-dipping, then?"

She swung around, a sarcastic remark ready to fly, but it froze on her lips at the look of desire on his face. *What the hell*, she thought, *maybe a little recreational sex was just what she needed.*

She waded back through the water with purpose, splashing him in her haste. Wrapping her arms around his neck, she drew his mouth down to hers, pressing her body to the length of his.

Stunned at first, Luke did nothing. When her tongue brushed his lower lip, he groaned, grabbing her hips and pulling her even closer, lifting her to her toes. The swell of the surf pushed her into him in a deeply primal rhythm. Her hands found the waistband of his shorts and she slid her fingers beneath to caress the warm skin beneath.

Luke drew back, gasping for breath, and held her at

arms' length. She reached for him again, her frustration clear. "No. I don't want just some roll in the sand from you."

"Then we'll go inside—"

"No. That's not what I mean. I won't be a physical outlet for your anger or your fear or whatever psychological pathology you have going on inside that Kevlar-wrapped mind of yours—not when you won't let me be an emotional outlet for you."

"Are you serious?" She couldn't believe he'd rejected her, all because she wouldn't pour her guts out to him. Since when did a guy care what her problems were?

"Dead."

"Fine." She spun to wade deeper into the surf.

He grabbed her arm. "You had another nightmare, didn't you?"

She glared with contempt at the hand gripping her arm, but didn't offer a response.

"Why won't you talk to me? Hell, I get more conversation out of Sandy. Something is eating you alive—something dangerous. The nightmares, the machete, your reaction to the incident in the alley . . . you're like a grenade with the pin pulled out—seconds from exploding. What the hell happened to you?"

"Look, I appreciate your concern, but I'm fine. And it's none of your business, so unless you're interested in a f— a roll in the sand, leave me the hell alone."

He watched her wade out into the shimmering waters before she dove in, coming up seconds later, her clean strokes slicing through the water as she swam out away from him.

He strode back to his deck and sat in the shadows watching as she exhausted herself with long angry strokes. Her splashes flashed phosphorescent in the light of a waxing moon. Despite her wishes to the contrary, he'd keep an eye on her to make sure she made it safely to shore and back to her bungalow.

"Christ," he said, patting Sandy's head, "sometimes I think she's got a death wish."

Sandy whined her agreement.

———

Lacey rolled out of bed, feeling groggy and disoriented, as if she'd downed a few sleeping pills the night before. She snorted in disgust. Maybe if she had she wouldn't have been swimming laps in the Pacific at two o'clock in the morning and making a fool of herself with Luke. What must he think of her? And since when did she care?

She stepped out onto the deck in the bright sunshine, shielding her eyes from the sun that glinted off the water below. She leaned against the railing with a groan. She'd thrown herself at him, and he'd soundly rejected her. What did that say about her that a playboy beach bum would turn her down. "Ouch," she muttered, a self-deprecating smile on her face.

But who could blame him? She was a certifiable headcase and he'd witnessed it first-hand yesterday. He wanted her to spill her guts, tell her story, even resorting to a Google search to find her secrets, but he'd be smart to run the other way. He didn't know how close he'd come with his analogy to the grenade.

Nevertheless, it was getting harder to resist his pleas.

Her defenses were crumbling, the pain and the fear that had been locked inside her for so long, threatening to erupt. What he didn't understand, what he clearly couldn't comprehend was that if she opened the floodgates, she might never get the torrent under control again.

No. She simply couldn't risk it. Without her strength, without her armor, she would collapse, like a building without its steel girders. Emotional intimacy just wasn't her thing.

Pushing off the railing, she stepped into her room and glanced around. It looked as if the aforementioned grenade had exploded in it.

Clothes were strewn on the bed and the floor, bed sheets hanging off the bed, like post-blast debris. The gifts she'd bought yesterday sat in disarray where she'd dumped them last night, and notes and papers littered the desk. The housekeeping staff would likely take one look, close the door, and move on.

Straightening her room would give her a good excuse to avoid Luke for the day, or at least a good bit of the day anyway. Maybe she'd look at the notes she'd made for the article she'd been thinking about ever since Luke had planted the seed.

She removed the gifts from their bags and set them on the bed. Christmas was the following week, so she'd better get them wrapped. She smoothed her hand over the gorgeous throw she'd picked up for Tony and Allie. Maybe Jill could give her some wrapping paper, since she'd forgotten to pick some up in San José. She also needed to ship her nieces' gifts.

She picked up the watercolor set she'd purchased for Luke, opening it to view the exquisite colors, the lavish brushes, imagining the scenes he would create with them. Her chest constricted. Scenes she would never see.

The day after Christmas they would leave for two days at Drake Bay, an isolated area on the northern end of the

Osa Peninsula. God, she hoped Tony came with them. She didn't want to spend two days—and two nights—alone with Luke. After her mortifying panic-attack in the alley and his humiliating rejection of her on the beach, her wounded pride couldn't take it.

Nor could her defenses. She couldn't chance Luke getting close again.

Her assignment was winding down. She'd likely be gone shortly after Drake Bay, certainly by New Year's, if not before. Why did that thought make her so sad?

CHAPTER TWENTY

"Man, you look like hell," Tony said as he sat down at Luke's kitchen table, amid the inner-workings of what appeared to be a now-disemboweled toaster. "Tie one on last night?"

"Hardly. Maybe if I'd had I'd be in a better mood," Luke grumbled, as he got up to pour another cup of coffee for himself, and one for Tony. It had been sometime after four a.m. before he crawled into his bed. Damn, but that woman could swim.

He thought she'd never wear herself out.

"Wow. That's saying a lot, since you're never in a good mood after a bender. So spill." Tony took the cup Luke offered, then helped himself to a mango muffin.

Luke picked up one of the parts, turned it over in his hand. "There was an incident in San José yesterday involving Lacey."

"What'd she do now? Antagonize a surly shop owner?" Tony asked with a grin.

"No. She was mugged. At knife point."

The smile evaporated from Tony's face. "Holy shit! She okay?"

"Well, let's just say she wasn't injured." Luke proceeded to tell Tony about the confrontation, including Lacey's reaction to it. He left out their late-night encounter on the beach.

"The nightmares," Tony said, remembering the first night at Corcovado.

"Yep. The nightmares."

"What do you think happened to her?" Tony's expression revealed his concern.

"I don't know. And she won't tell me."

"You don't think she was attacked with a machete, do you?"

"God, I hope not." Luke's voice came out in hoarse whisper.

"Maybe she'd talk to Allie," Tony offered.

"No. I don't want her to know I told you. She'd be pretty pissed." Luke picked up his screwdriver, started putting the toaster back together. "I'll figure out something."

Tony took another sip of his coffee, watching Luke's deft movements. He knew his friend well, and he was getting to know Lacey. Luke needed to rescue, and if Tony didn't know better, Lacey needed rescuing. Not that either one would ever admit it, especially to one another.

———

Lacey had barely scratched the surface on her clean-up efforts when someone knocked at the door. Her stomach knotted with dread, thinking it could be Luke, before realizing it was more likely housekeeping.

She opened the door to find Allie looking both as cool as a cucumber and as hot as a tamale. How did she manage that? Her generous hair was up in a casual twist with her jet-black curls spilling carelessly around her sultry face. She wore a sunny, sheer sundress and sandals.

"*Hola.* You feeling okay? Jill said she didn't see you for breakfast." She tilted her head, studying Lacey as if she knew about the alley mugging.

"Oh, yeah, I'm fine. Just, you know, trying to catch up on things." Lacey glanced back at the cluttered room, relieved to see that the throw was out of sight.

Allie surveyed the room, before stepping out onto the deck briefly, then back into the room again. "I'm going into Puerto Jimenez for some shopping, thought you might like to go . . . keep me company."

Lacey's first inclination was to say no, but thought better of it. It would be the perfect way to escape Luke's company. "Sure. I need to ship some things anyway. Can you give me a few minutes to change?"

"*Si.*" Allie sat on the edge of the bed.

Lacey frowned. Clearly Allie wasn't leaving. She quickly grabbed some clean clothes out of a drawer and went into the bathroom to freshen up and change.

"You coming to Luke's next week for Christmas Eve dinner?" Allie called into the bathroom.

Lacey paused from washing her face, surprised by the question. "Um, well, I haven't been invited." In fact, she didn't know anything about it.

"Oh, you're invited. Everyone will be there, Jill, Karl, me and Tony. It's sort of a tradition."

"I should probably wait for an invitation from Luke."

Lacey dried her face, slapped on some moisturizing

sunscreen, and ran damp fingers through her hair to eliminate the bed-head look.

She stepped out of the bathroom to see Allie peering inside the mahogany box at the watercolor set, feeling a little affronted by Allie's lack of respect for her privacy. Lacey bit back a sharp remark when she saw the expression on Allie's face.

Allie's hands passed reverently over the brushes and pigments. She had no doubt who would receive this gift. The thoughtfulness of it was not lost on her. It would mean more to Luke than, well, than a new plane.

He would never think to buy something like this for himself, and the fact that Lacey thought to buy it for him showed a level of sensitivity on her part that left Allie with a lump in her throat.

Allie looked up at Lacey, her emotions flickering over her lovely features. "He's going to love it."

———

A couple of hours and dozens of shops later, Lacey had purchased wrapping paper, and she and Allie stepped into the Environmental Expeditions office where Lacey could wrap and ship her nieces' gifts.

It was a small tidy office on the main street in Puerto Jimenez. She could see Allie's feminine touches, but it was also neat as a pin, very orderly, with its three desks, computers, a small copier and printer, and company brochures.

"Here," Allie indicated a desk, "this is Luke's, when I can tie him down long enough to use it. You can wrap the gifts. There's scissors and tape in the drawer. You'll find shipping labels on that shelf," she said, pointing to shelves on the back wall, "along with a Fedex box. I have to go to the little *chica's* room."

Lacey sank gratefully onto the desk chair that looked like it had seen better days. *Man, that woman can shop.* Lacey hadn't known what she was getting herself into when she agreed to go with her. Puerto Jimenez hadn't seemed that big when she was here with Luke and Tony. Obviously, Allie knew all the hidden nooks and crannies that held countless shops, and Lacey thought they'd hit them all.

She hoped Allie would help her wrap the gifts. Lacey could do it, but they always resembled the work of a five-year-old, all crooked edges and crumpled corners. Uncomfortable nosing around Luke's desk drawers, she hesitantly opened the central drawer to find a pair of scissors, but no tape.

Opening the top drawer next to her, she rummaged around beneath a pile of papers, finding a stapler, some miscellaneous paper clips, stray ink pens, but still no tape. When she picked up the papers to get a better look, an old Polaroid picture fell to the floor.

She leaned over to retrieve it, then lighting the desk lamp, she held the photo beneath it for a better look. Four people stood with goofy grins on their faces. One clearly Luke. He appeared to be a teenager, maybe sixteen, all arms and legs. Behind him stood a man and a woman. Luke favored his father. His father's hand rested on Luke's shoulder. His mother was tall and thin, her light brown hair pulled back from her face. In front of her stood a young girl, also about sixteen. Luke's twin, Lisa.

"We can head back after you get your package ready," Allie said as she came out of the back. "They'll pick it up tomorrow."

Lacey dropped the photo like she'd been burned. A flush crept into her face.

"Oh, that's a picture of Luke's family." Allie leaned over Lacey's shoulder. "That was taken shortly before Lisa's death." Allie released a pensive sigh. "The family was never the same after that. I guess no one ever is."

Hoping Allie wouldn't feel the same reticence to share the story that Tony had, Lacey asked, "Allie, how did she die?"

"About a month after that photo was taken, she fell over a waterfall while she and Luke were hiking."

Her hand to her stomach, Lacey closed her eyes in sudden horrifying understanding. She felt nauseous, like the after effects of a fist to the gut. It explained Luke's aberrant reaction to her attempt to cross the river at the waterfall, and it sickened her to think she'd unwittingly made him relive that gruesome experience. "He . . . he witnessed it?" she asked, knowing the answer already.

"*Sí.*" Allie grabbed some tape from her desk and, taking a seat next to Lacey, began wrapping Lacey's gifts. "I never met Lisa, but according to Tony, she had always been rash, reckless, acting without a thought for the consequences."

Bile rose in Lacey's throat as Allie continued her story.

God, no wonder he'd gotten so angry with her for the crocodile and horse-jumping incidents. He must have seen something of Lisa's behavior in her own.

"He left Costa Rica a year later, unable to deal with his parents' grief—and I guess his own. His parents divorced after they lost the inn, and his father has been living alone in California ever since."

Just when Lacey thought she couldn't get any more sick. Allie's story explained so much. Luke had every reason to be angry over the loss of his parents' inn. It had been more than just a business. It had been possibly the last tie between his parents. He undoubtedly blamed the divorce on her father, and no amount of money could have assuaged that level of resentment.

"Sorry to end the day with such a tragic story."

"I asked," Lacey choked out around the tears in her throat.

Allie studied her. "Lacey, are you sure you feel okay? You look a little pale."

"I'm okay. Just . . . tired." She tried to put on a cheerful face. "You shopped 'til *I* dropped."

Allie laughed, reaching for the tape and scissors. "All right, you fill out the shipping label while I wrap the gifts, and we'll head back to Mariposa."

As if Lacey didn't have reason enough to avoid Luke, after hearing about Lisa and his parents, and in light of her own past behavior, she wasn't sure she could ever face him again.

Claiming a headache, she asked Jill if she could have a dinner tray in her room. She knew she was being a coward. Of course she would have to see Luke again, but she needed time to get her thoughts together, decide how to best approach this situation.

She owed him an apology, but it wasn't something she could just blurt out. 'I'm sorry I made you relive your sister's death. I'm sorry I stirred up old resentments, old fears.'

Besides, he might get angry with Allie if he found out she'd told her.

Looking for an excuse to take her mind off her dilemma, if only for a short while, she opened her email and scanned the multitude of new messages in her inbox. One from Lilia, another from her mother. She'd read those later. They were guaranteed to raise her blood pressure.

Ah, one from her father. She clicked on it.

Hi Baby,

Sorry it took so long to get back to you. Mr. Wentworth,

the fund's trustee, has been in Europe on business.

Anyway, to answer your question, yes, there is still money in the fund. According to Wentworth, your Mr. Hancock is the only one who didn't apply for the payout. I don't know why. Apparently he never replied to any of the correspondence from Wentworth. The money is still there, should he decide he wants it.

Lacey frowned. So, Luke's dad never even inquired about the money. Clearly Luke hadn't been aware of it either. She sighed. If Luke's father had spiraled into a deep depression, which sounded possible, that might explain why he never responded to the correspondence regarding the development fund.

Another dilemma. Should she tell Luke, or would he resent her interference?

She shot off a quick thanks to her dad, then returned to her inbox. An email from her editor now sat at the top of the list.

Lacey,

We're good on photos. We've got everything we need, and then some. The shots you took of the sloths will be perfect for an article in the February edition on the continued deforestation of Central America's rain forests.

We'll cancel the Drake Bay trip next week, and we can make arrangements for you to be back in the States for the holidays.

Great job. I'd say you've redeemed yourself.

Spend some well-deserved time with your family. We'll talk about your next assignment after the New Year.

Best, Simon

Her next assignment. Maybe she'd proven herself to Simon and he'd consider a better one this time. There were several hotspots around the world. Elephant ivory was still a hot commodity despite the ban on its sale. Japanese whaling and the Chinese tiger bone market were also issues, as were black rhino in Africa.

Well, there went her excuse to avoid the holidays with her very own version of a TV reality show family. Thinking about Tony and Allie, Karl and Jill, and especially Luke, and missing Christmas with them, she grew melancholy. It would probably be a cheerful occasion, complete with good-natured ribbing, laughter, and . . . warmth. The exact opposite of the Sommers family holiday.

Of course, Luke hadn't asked her, and she wasn't going to crash the party, despite what Allie said.

It didn't matter anyway. She'd be gone by then. Shivering in cold, blustery New York.

———

Clearly Lacey was avoiding him, Luke thought, likely because of his rejection of her. She had no idea the mental—and physical—resolve it took to push away her warm, willing body. His restraint had been extraordinary, especially when he'd wanted her so bad he could taste it.

He'd gone to her room earlier in the day, only to have Maya, the housekeeper, tell him that she saw Lacey leave with Allie. He'd waited for her to come to dinner, but Jill said she'd sent a tray to her bungalow because Lacey wasn't feeling well. He thought about checking on her—seeing if there was anything she needed. Then he thought it could be female problems and abruptly changed course.

He wanted to invite her down for Christmas Eve. But he would have used any excuse to see her. It had only been a day, but damn if he didn't miss her.

Sighing, he raked his hands through his hair. He definitely had his challenges ahead. She wore more armor than a medieval knight. And every time he thought he'd found the chink in that armor, she'd solder it up again. But every fortification had its weakness. He had to find a way in, and time was running out.

The next morning, angry pounding on the door interrupted Lacey's work on her article. *Who the hell is that?*

She strode over to the door and yanked it open, ready to give the person a piece of her mind. Luke stood with his fist raised, ready to pound once more, his face looking like a thundercloud.

"Hancock, what the hell are you doing?"

He marched into the room without an invitation. "Why didn't you tell me you were leaving?"

She turned, open door still in her hand, shocked by his reaction. "I'm sorry you're losing the additional trip fees—"

He strode over to her, making her back up a step.

"Goddammit, Lacey, it's not about the fucking money!" After a few moments, he confronted her again. "I just thought . . . I just thought you'd at least tell me yourself, instead of leaving it to your magazine."

Before she could say anything, he continued. "And, well, I thought you might stay through Christmas at least. I mean, I know that Allie, Tony, Karl, and Jill were looking forward to it," he finished lamely.

Her heart fluttered in her chest, and an idea began to form. "Are you inviting me to your house for Christmas?"

He frowned. "Yes, I thought you knew you were welcome."

"And, how would I know that?" she asked, her brow arched in skepticism.

"Because you're always welcome at my house . . ." His voice trailed off. "But I guess it doesn't matter. You're leaving." He looked back at her, his eyes imploring her to stay, before he walked to the still-open door.

"Wait. You didn't tell me what time."

Stopping abruptly, he spun to face her. "What? Why?" he asked, his voice laced with confusion.

She couldn't help smiling at the impulsiveness of her decision. "Because I'm staying. At least until after Christmas. After all, I wouldn't want to disappoint Allie, Tony, Karl, and Jill."

Relief swept across his face. "Five-thirty?"

"Great. I'll bring the wine."

She'd gotten no closer to resolving her dilemma over Luke's sister and father, and all thought of his humiliating rejection on the beach and her desire to avoid his probing questions fled. All she could think about was spending

Christmas with her new friends. She was as giddy as a child awaiting a visit from Santa.

As soon as Luke left, Lacey sent an email to Simon to make sure he still didn't need her until after the holidays and to let him know she planned to stay in Costa Rica in case he did. He must have been sitting in front of his computer because he got back to her right away.

Sure. Whatever you want, but you're on your own dime.

CHAPTER TWENTY-ONE

Christmas Eve dawned sunny and warm. Lacey's gifts were cheerfully wrapped, thanks to Allie's deft hands. She'd even garnered a tasty bone for Sandy, and all the plans were in place.

According to Jill, everyone brought favorite dishes, and Luke grilled up the steaks. Lacey had purchased several bottles of wine from the bar and had them delivered to Luke's. Since she couldn't cook, it was her contribution to the feast.

The dress and sandals she'd purchased in San José lay on the bed, along with the bracelets. She felt like a teenage girl going to prom, or at least like she imagined a teenage girl would feel, since she never went. She'd even managed to dig up some lip gloss that her sister had insisted she take right before she'd left for Costa Rica.

Allie and Tony planned to swing by to pick up her, then Jill and Karl, since walking with food and gifts was impractical.

She looked at her watch. Now all she had to do was figure out how to fill the next eight hours.

———

Lacey and the gang, arms loaded with food and gifts, rounded the corner to Luke's deck, the sounds of Johnny Mathis crooning "White Christmas" out of place in the balmy tropical air.

"Wow, Luke really outdid himself," Allie said, looking around at the deck.

Festive paper lanterns hung from fishing line strung across the deck, crisscrossing the colorfully set table. While the music said Christmas, the decorations said *Cinco de Mayo*.

Playing hostess, Sandy gave a welcoming bark, her tail wagging enthusiastically, as if the party were all for her.

Luke stepped out of the door to greet them, wiping his hands on a towel, pausing when his eyes lit on Lacey. His knees wobbled. She looked so beautiful. The water soft colors of her dress bringing out the depth of her blue eyes, all that luscious bare skin, and were her lips shinier than usual?

Lacey felt his eyes on her and blushed, glad she'd bought the dress, glad she'd taken the time to fuss with her appearance. His expression made it all worth it, especially if he kept looking at her as if she was a tasty peach and he wanted to take a big bite.

Luke finally found his voice. "Hi, guys. Merry Christmas!" He sauntered over to Lacey and took the gifts from her arms, leaning in to whisper in her ear, "Wow, Sommers, you look amazing."

His breath tickled, sending a shiver down Lacey's spine. He smelled of salt, warm male, and . . . yeast? "Well, gee thanks, Hancock. Don't sound so surprised."

Luke drew back only to see the teasing light in her

eyes. He set the gifts under an outside Christmas tree decorated with seashells and wild poinsettia branches. Taking her hand, he gave her a little twirl. "That's some dress."

"Thanks." Lacey laughed. Although it was the hoped-for response, she felt a little embarrassed by his praise. "I'm glad you like it, especially since I bought it with the money I won off you."

He made a face, then answered her laugh. "If that's how you spend the money, I'll keep losing it. Happily."

"Luke, I put the salad in the fridge, the casserole's in the oven, and the dessert on the counter," Allie said, clearly comfortable in Luke's home.

He leaned over and bussed her on the cheek, making her blush. "Make yourselves comfortable. Steaks are marinating and the bread's in the oven." He walked back into the house.

Lacey tentatively followed him inside, unable to forget his warm greeting and whispered compliment. Unsure what to do with herself, she chose to stay out of the way. Obviously she'd be no help in the kitchen. Seeing the wine bottles and glasses on the bar, she offered to get everyone drinks.

"Sure. That'd be great." His eyes lingered on her again, a soft smile on his face, before he bent over the oven.

The house smelled of warm, yeasty bread. As she uncorked the wine, she watched Luke as he moved around the small kitchen, stirring something on the stove, a dish-towel thrown over his shoulder. He appeared to be at home in a space completely alien to her. A beach bum, a pilot, a wildlife guide, not a bad dancer, and now a cook. Luke Hancock was a jack of all trades.

What else did he do? What other hidden talents did he

have? She tingled, remembering the samples she'd tasted of another hidden talent.

He turned back to find her staring at him. "What?"

She jumped, clearly busted. "Hmm? Oh, what can I get you to drink?" she fudged as she reached for a wine glass.

"Red wine—that Merlot would be good."

She handed him the glass, their fingers brushing before she released it, sending a zing of electricity up her arm. Jesus, she thought, you'd think she was a teenager out on her first date.

Before she could walk away, he grabbed her hand. "I'm glad you came, glad you stayed."

She could feel the warmth in his eyes all the way down to her toes. "Me too."

Christmas Eve at Luke's was everything Lacey had imagined it would be. Surrounded by good friends, sharing great food, fine wine, and tall tales. And the more the wine flowed, the taller the tales became.

Tony told one about the time he and Luke had encountered a jaguar on the trail. To hear Tony tell it, the jaguar became a ten-foot tall man-eating cat. Allie rolled her eyes at his obvious exaggerations.

Lacey observed the jovial group. She'd never really been comfortable in her parents' world—society functions, gallery openings, and posh fundraisers. Although she'd held her own, she'd been equally uncomfortable with the raucous, somewhat lowbrow gatherings she'd been part of on her assignments. But here, she felt comfortable, welcome, part of this close-knit group.

"Can I get anyone anything else?" Luke asked at the end of Tony's liberally embellished account. Amid groans about full bellies, everyone responded in the negative.

Their *al fresco* dinner had been delicious. Tony and

Allie had brought traditional Costa Rican dishes, using their respective mothers' recipes, while Karl and Jill had provided time-honored American classics like sweet potato casserole, cornbread dressing, and pumpkin pie for dessert.

Luke had grilled the steaks to perfection and served them with a creamy bèarnaise sauce. She could also add another talent to his repertoire: baker. He'd made the yeast rolls from scratch. His own mother's recipe.

"Then let's get to the good stuff." Luke rose from the table, rubbing his hands together in great anticipation.

Kneeling in front of the Christmas tree, he picked up a gift and brought it back to the table. "Let's see, who could this be for?" He read the tag. "Lacey."

She looked up in surprise. She hadn't really expected to receive any gifts, especially since her decision to stay had been last minute. She felt uncomfortable being the center of attention, receiving the first gift. It was a small box, wrapped in shiny red paper.

"Open it . . . Yeah, come on, open it . . . Don't leave us in suspense." Everyone spoke at once.

The tag said it was from Tony and Allie. Inside the box lay a pair of small gold earrings. "Frogs?" Her brows shot up. Two tiny tree frogs dangled from posts.

Tony, Allie, and Luke burst out laughing, leaving Jill and Karl confused.

"We couldn't resist." Tony grinned from ear-to-ear, while Allie clapped her hands.

Jill and Karl looked around at everyone, curious about the obvious inside joke.

Luke leaned over to Karl and in a staged whisper said, "I'll tell you later."

Lacey gave him a warning look and everyone laughed.

"In pre-Colombian mythology the frog is the symbol of fertility," Allie explained.

Luke and Lacey's eyes suddenly met, before she glanced away. "Great. I'll keep that in mind." She put the earrings on and Luke leaned over to take a look, touching one of the frogs, setting it in motion. She raised her eyes to him in question, thinking he might kiss her, but he just grinned and moved back to his seat across from her at the table.

Lacey snapped pictures of the delighted faces of both givers and receivers alike, while everyone took turns opening gifts. Tony and Allie loved the throw. Allie hugged Lacey tight before exclaiming it would grace the sofa in their living room.

Jill and Karl admired the framed photo of them in front of their sign. "This will sit on the front desk for all our guests to see."

And Sandy lay under the table contentedly gnawing on the bone Lacey had given her.

Lacey saved Luke's present for last, handing him the wrapped box and biting her lip as he tore open the paper. Clearly the gift surprised him.

She watched anxiously as Luke's hand stilled when he lifted the box lid, then reached in to pick up one of the brushes, before putting it back and closing the lid. A ball formed in the pit of Lacey's stomach. He didn't like it.

———

L uke sat for a moment, aware of the multiple sets of eyes on him, but he didn't know what to say. Lacey's gift was beautiful, thoughtful . . . perfect. Just like her. He tried to swallow past the lump in his throat. Either she'd just gotten lucky or she understood like no one else did how important his painting was to him. He wanted to believe the latter.

When he finally looked at her, he met her gaze, hoping the appreciation shone through. "Thank you. Truly. It's beautiful."

Lacey smiled with relief and pleasure. Giving Luke that watercolor set meant more to her than all the gifts she'd ever given. Seeing his sincere enjoyment filled her heart with an unfamiliar warmth, making it feel whole.

"Finally, something to replace that pitiful tackle box," Tony said, breaking the spell.

"Hey, Luke," Allie said, a twinkle in her eye, "there's one more gift under the tree. I wonder whose that could be."

Luke cleared his throat and rising from his seat, said, "I don't know, let's see." Making a show of looking at the box, shaking it a bit, he walked over and handed it to Lacey. "Must be yours."

She gazed into his handsome face, her brow puckering in confusion.

"Go ahead, open it."

The box was heavy. Nestled inside it amid protective straw lay a tall glazed clay vase with a beautiful Monarch butterfly painted on it. She carefully lifted the vase to examine it more closely.

"It's made by Peace Potters," Luke explained. "All the proceeds are used to train low-income women in Central America to make pottery and sell it, helping them raise their standard of living."

"Oh, Luke, that's lovely . . . beautiful . . . what a nice gift," Allie and Jill remarked.

Lacey looked at Luke, then back at the gift. The vase itself was lovely, but the sentiment behind it touched her profoundly. Not only that he remembered her concern for women, but that he put that memory into action.

"Thank you. Really. I love it."

He gave her a big boyish grin, his eyes sparkling in the dimming light.

Brenda Lee started singing about rockin' around the Christmas tree and Tony lifted Allie to her feet and twirled her around to the cheers of the crowd. Luke rolled his eyes at Lacey and said, "It's not a party until Tony and Allie dance."

Dusk had fallen, and the colorful lanterns and citronella torches cast a warm glow on the festivities. Watching Tony and Allie swing to the beat reminded Lacey of another night on this very deck. After her previous reaction, would Luke ask her to dance again? She found herself wishing for the possibility.

Luke rose from the table, giving no indication of a repeat performance, and picked up a couple of near-empty casserole dishes before heading for the kitchen. Jill and Karl followed with empty plates and glasses, efficiently stacked from years of experience at their resort.

Disappointed, Lacey gathered up dishes as well. It appeared the evening was coming to an end. She wanted it to go on forever. Blinking to clear her suddenly blurry vision, she wondered how she'd gone so soft. What the hell was wrong with her?

Luke stood at the sink, his back to her, washing dishes. He looked so sexy there, up to his elbows in suds. She set her load on the counter next to him. "Hey, I can dry," she offered.

He gazed at her, his face flushed from the heat of the task. "Sure. Dry dishtowels are in the drawer," he said, indicating a small drawer in front of her.

Standing side-by-side, they worked in silence for a few minutes, listening to the sounds of laughter drifting in on the breeze. Every time Luke passed a dish to her, he felt as if he'd been shocked. The air between them sizzled and popped. It wouldn't surprise him if he saw a spark.

Luke had watched Lacey all evening. She seemed different.

She had a new softness about her, as if the hard lines and sharp edges had smoothed out. It wasn't just the clothes, but the body language. The change had been so gradual he'd barely noticed it until now.

Judy Garland began singing the poignant "Have Yourself a Merry Little Christmas." Luke turned to look at Lacey, and instead of handing her a dish, he took her hand in his wet, soapy one and drew her into his arms for a slow, rocking dance. He kissed the top of her head before resting his chin there.

The tenderness of the gesture caught Lacey off guard, especially after his previous rejection of her. The sexual tension between them remained as thick as the sultry tropical evening, but he seemed content just as they were. No groping, no suggestive remarks. Just this unbearable sweetness.

She wrapped her arms around his waist. It felt so good to be in his arms. Strong, protective steel bands that made her feel safe for the first time in far too long. She laid her head on his chest and could hear his breath, his heartbeat.

"Hey, Luke, we're going to head out," Karl said as he stepped into the house.

Lacey and Luke broke apart.

"Oh—sorry. Didn't mean to, um, interrupt . . ." His voice trailed off as he looked around the room at everything but them, a grin spreading across his bespectacled face. "Uh, Lacey, you ready?"

"Stay," Luke mouthed, his eyes beseeching her.

Lacey made a show of looking around the kitchen. "Um, you know what, I think I'll stay and help Luke finish the dishes."

"I'll give her a ride back," Luke interjected.

"Okay." Karl shifted from one foot to the other. "Well, thanks for everything. Had a great time."

Luke and Lacey followed him out to the deck where everyone gathered their belongings, the Christmas loot having already been loaded into the car.

Allie hugged Lacey tight and whispered, "Merry Christmas, *chica.*"

Amid hugs, kisses, and thanks, everyone left.

Without speaking, Luke took Lacey's hand and escorted her back into the house, closing the door behind them. "Grandma Got Run Over by a Reindeer" blared from the speakers, making them laugh and shake their heads at the ridiculous song.

"I always hated that song," Luke said, crossing over to the stereo to turn it down.

Lacey headed into the kitchen. "Well, guess we should finish up the—"

Luke grabbed her hand before she could finish her sentence and drew her into his arms. Lowering his lips to hers, he muttered, "They can wait. I can't." He'd waited patiently all night for this. No interruptions from dogs, best friends, or rogue waves. Just the two of them. Alone.

She rose up to meet him. He nipped her lower lip, then caressed it with his tongue, before taking it between his lips again. She groaned low in her throat, as she raised her arms to wrap them around his neck, twining her fingers in his hair. Luke dropped his head to press kisses along her jaw, inhaling the scent of her rosemary and lavender.

His head swam with it. With the feel of her body against his, the taste of her lips, the sound of her rasping breath. Why had he waited so long? *How* had he waited so long? Only her refusal could stop him now.

"Lacey . . . Lacey," he whispered. "So beautiful."

He returned to her lips again and again, unable to quench his thirst for them. Their sweetness only left him craving more.

The heat between them built to epic proportions. No matter how close they became, it wasn't close enough. One hand clasped the nape of her neck while his other hand slipped down her bare back, his fingertips skimming along her spine, raising goose bumps.

Lacey shivered in response. Her tongue grazed his, as their breath mingled in whispery sighs and soft moans. She slipped her leg between his thighs as his hands slid to her waist, before venturing further to her hips, pressing her snuggly against him.

His touch was like fire. It consumed her, and she willingly gave in to the greedy flames. Her hands slipped beneath his shirt, skimming her nails along his bare skin, his answering moan inflaming her until she thought she would spontaneously combust.

But something else lay beneath the passion. Something intangible, more intimate than the physical response alone. A nascent blossoming of some deep-seated emotion.

He lifted her dress, sliding his hands along her thighs, around to her bottom. Her breath caught, her legs trembled. She didn't know how much longer they would support her.

His hands glided back up her arms. "Say my name," he

muttered against her lips, as he slipped the straps of her dress from her shoulders.

"Luke," she whispered against his mouth.

"Again."

"Luke."

And it was the most beautiful thing he'd ever heard.

CHAPTER TWENTY-TWO

L acey's dress whispered to the floor as Luke's calloused hands skimmed up her sides to caress her bare breasts.

"My God, Lacey . . ." His breath snagged. "I have no words . . ." He lowered his head to taste the sensitive flesh beneath his hands, lathing and nipping her until her sighs rasped in her throat.

Lacey's head dropped back encouraging full access as she grasped his shoulders with the desperate strength of a woman trying to avoid a fall. Worshipping first one breast and then the other, Luke kissed his way back up the slender column of her neck to mate his lips and tongue with hers, while his hands and thumbs continued to work their magic at her breasts.

Torn between the desire to prolong the heady kiss, but desperate to feel his bare skin against hers, she stepped back and removed his shirt in one fluid movement. Unable to resist his bare chest, she paid homage to him in return, eliciting groans of desire as her tongue grazed his nipples, and his heart jackhammered against her palm.

Luke fisted his hand in her hair, drawing her lips back to his, clasping her tightly to his chest, her hardened nipples making contact with his overheated skin. The sweet-hot friction almost sent him over the edge.

Slipping his fingers beneath her panties, kneading the firm flesh of her bottom, he moved to draw her panties down the length of those gorgeous legs, his tongue following in their wake. He stopped to taste her, kneeling at her feet like a supplicant before a goddess.

She cried out at the sudden, unexpected rapture, completely undone by his touch. He caught her as her knees gave way and, boosting her up, said, "Wrap your legs around my waist."

A breathless moan escaped her as his lips met hers yet again, and she tasted herself there.

Luke carried her into the bedroom where he gently placed her on the bed. By God, she was beautiful. Hair tousled, lips swollen from his kisses, eyes glazed with desire. And her body, all soft skin and feminine curves, glowed in the aftermath of her fulfillment. His fingers blazed a trail from her breasts to her abdomen, her skin quivering in response. "I will never get enough of you."

"Please, Luke," Lacey whispered hoarsely. She'd never begged for anything, not even her life. But she swore she would burst into a million tiny pieces if she didn't have the feel of him against her, inside her.

He stripped off his shorts and climbed into bed. Opening the nightstand drawer, he removed a condom packet and tore it open. He rolled it on before covering the length of her.

Opening for him, she breathed his name as he entered her, filling her, with a slow, deliberate motion. She rose up to meet him thrust for ecstasy-inducing thrust, their fingers clasped, his name on her lips.

As Luke moved inside her, he gloried in the depth of their mutual passion, unlike any he'd ever experienced before. He'd expected a flash of white-hot heat, a flame that burned itself out in its intensity, excoriating everything in its path. What he experienced was a slow burn that seared as it slaked, the shimmering waves engulfing them in a molten river.

When it came, the climax devoured him in its radiant heat, leaving him shaken to his very core.

———

Tangled in the sheets, limbs entwined with his, Lacey rested her head on his chest, while his hand drew soothing circles on her back. He kissed the top of her head, wrapping his arms tight around her, the hum of the air conditioner providing background noise.

The honeyed sweetness of their union shocked her, leaving her bewildered and not a little afraid. The intensity of the experience went far beyond the physical, far beyond the passion. The emotion sparked by the encounter almost cataclysmic in its potency. His lavish attention made her feel beautiful inside and out. His sweet murmurings touched a part of her she thought she'd long since buried. And wasn't sure she wanted resurrected.

Covering the disquiet of her musings, Lacey did what she did best, sassed. "Santa must have thought I was a *very* good girl this year," she said, snuggling closer, forgetting she wasn't ordinarily the snuggling type.

Luke laughed. "Either that, or a very *bad* girl. My preference is for the bad girl." He rolled her over, kissing her until she couldn't breathe.

Sandy's bark, followed by a plaintive whine, intruded. Apparently fed up with being locked out of the house, she sounded her irritation.

Sighing and rolling off of Lacey, Luke said, "Sometimes I wonder why I got that dog."

Lacey watched Luke pad naked across the floor, wearing nothing but his friendship bracelet, the lights from the living room giving her an unimpeded view of his wide shoulders, slim waist, and sexy derrière.

Tonight, much to her extreme satisfaction, Luke had exhibited another of his many talents—twice.

She heard Luke say, "Bed," followed by Sandy's groan.

Lacey stretched and yawned, reveling in the feel of the cool air before looking at the clock. Almost midnight. She should go. Get Luke to drive her back to the resort.

Sex with Luke had opened a number of chinks in her armor.

Time to beat a hasty retreat. Now if she could just find her clothes . . .

"Where're you going?" Luke stood in the doorway, outlined by the light behind him.

"I should probably go. Back to my room." She stood, searching around the room for something resembling her dress, before remembering she'd left it in the living room, along with her shoes. And her panties.

"Don't go. Stay."

His voice caressed her. Staying the night, waking up together in the morning was tempting, but . . .

Luke watched the emotions flicker across her face. The desire to stay; the need to leave, to avoid the intimacy. He knew all about establishing emotional distance. The desire to keep people at arm's length so they never got a glimpse of the demons lurking inside.

"Stay," he repeated. "Wake up with me on Christmas morning." He hadn't moved away from the doorway. He knew if he touched her, kissed her, he could convince her. But he didn't want to influence her decision. Not that way. He wanted her to decide with her heart, not her body.

Lacey hesitated, her emotions at war with one another. God she wanted to stay, but the possibility of another nightmare giving him a reason to press her further made her reluctant.

Watching the indecision play over her lovely features, Luke thought, *Aw, the hell with his noble ideas.*

He wanted her to stay, no matter the reason for her decision. He pushed off the doorjamb and sauntered over to stand in front of her, and taking her hands, he kissed first one, and then the other.

"I'll make it worth your while," he said as he cupped her face in his hands.

Her breath lodged in her throat, the almost palpable heat in his voice kindling her desire. So, she did what any self- respecting lustful woman would do: she gave in to temptation, pulling his lips down to hers. "Damn right you will."

"Mmm, that is so good," Luke moaned. "Hmm mm," Lacey groaned in agreement.

"Don't talk with your mouth full," Luke instructed. "It isn't polite. Ooh," he said with a sigh, "you want more, don't you, baby?"

"Yes," she whispered.

Luke held the spoon to Lacey's mouth, watching as she took a heaping spoonful of Ben and Jerry's Chocolate Peanut Butter Swirl, before taking another bite for himself.

Sitting up against the headboard, Lacey peered into the almost empty half-gallon container between them.

"Oh God," she said around a mouthful of frozen decadence, "eating ice cream at two in the morning. I'm going to need to run five miles tomorrow."

"I can think of better ways to burn the calories." He gave her a wicked grin. "In fact, I'm sure we've already burned enough to offset the ice cream . . . and the steaks, the sweet potato casserole, the yeast rolls, the pumpkin pie—"

"Ow." She held her hands to her forehead. "Brain freeze."

"Poor baby." Luke leaned over, kissing her forehead. "It's the price you pay for sin."

"I think we committed more sins tonight than gluttony."

"And lust and greed are at the top of the list." But his expression lacked remorse.

"And tomorrow, sloth, because I won't be able to get out of bed after tonight."

"Last bite." He held the spoon out to her.

A glop of partially melted ice cream landed with an icy splat in the middle of her stomach, evoking a squeal.

"Oops. Waste not, want not," Luke said as he slid down the bed, a lusty gleam in his eye. Leaning over, he licked the icy blob off her stomach, eliciting more squeals. But these were squeals of delight.

———

The sun soared well above the horizon when Luke entered the room carrying a tray laden with a first-class breakfast of orange-papaya juice, poached eggs, bacon, toast, and jam. And of course, coffee, hot and sweet, just the way she liked it.

He almost dropped the tray when he saw Lacey. Lying on her stomach, the sheet draped over her hips, leaving her gorgeous back bare, Lacey looked like Aphrodite. He could see the butterfly perched on the smooth rise of her hip.

Unable to resist, he set the tray aside and knelt beside the bed, bending over to lay kisses along her spine from the swell of her luscious bottom to the base of her tantalizing neck.

Lacey sighed contentedly before rolling over and wrapping her arms around his neck. "Good morning." She smiled sleepily.

"Merry Christmas." Luke kissed her nose. And a wonderful Christmas it was. The best he'd had since before Lisa died.

Waking up in the wee hours of the morning, Lacey's delicious body snuggled against him, her deep, steady breathing lulling him back to sleep. It just didn't get any better than that.

She sat up. "Do I smell coffee?"

"I see where I rate," Luke said, rising with a chuckle to get the breakfast tray. "Coffee first, Luke second."

"Hey, I said good morning." She fluffed the pillows behind her back.

Luke carefully crawled into bed, balancing the weighty tray, and settled next to her.

"Jesus, Luke," she said, taking a steaming cup of coffee and eyeing all the food on the tray. "You feeding an army?"

"Well, I don't know about you, but I worked up quite an appetite."

She took a sip of her coffee and Luke watched as the now-familiar look of bliss crossed her features. "I do believe I saw that same expression last night. At least four times, but who's counting?"

Flushed with embarrassment, she grinned sheepishly.

He took a bite of toast, smiling broadly, pleased that he could fluster her.

Taking a bite of her beautifully poached egg, Lacey remembered the food Luke had served on their waterfall trip. He was an excellent cook. She wanted to ask him why they didn't get food like this when they camped at the waterfall, but she didn't want to bring up the waterfall. At least not until she'd figured out what to say.

He reached out and touched one of the frog earrings he noticed she still wore. "You want to tell me why you're afraid of frogs?"

"I'm not—"

"The lady doth protest too much, methinks."

"Fine." She released a long-suffering sigh. "When I was about twelve, my family and I were vacationing in Florida. The place crawled, or should I say hopped, with frogs, of the tree-frog variety. The second morning I woke up with a tree frog," she shuddered, "sitting in the middle of my forehead."

Luke started to chuckle, and she gave him a warning glance.

Closing her eyes in mortification, she continued. "I so 'girled-out.' I jumped out of bed, screaming, the frog's little suction-cup feet still stuck to me."

Luke's chest rumbled with suppressed laughter.

"Hancock," she warned.

"Sorry." He swallowed his chuckle behind a gulp of juice. "What happened next?"

"My father came racing into the room to see what was wrong, and instead of getting the little fu—, er, frog off me, he stood there and burst out laughing instead. Then my sister joined in, and then her best friend. And well, I've never heard the end of it since."

Luke's eyes were tearing up from the withheld laughter.

Finally, he could stand it no longer, and released a deep booming laugh that lasted far too long for Lacey's wounded pride.

"Great. See if I tell you anything else."

"I'm sorry," he choked out between chuckles. "You have to admit it's pretty funny though." He gave her a little shoulder- butt, and looked over at her. The corner of her mouth lifted ever-so-slightly, flashing the dimple he loved, before she recovered her forbidding expression.

"No. I don't." She sniffed.

Between snickers, he polished off his breakfast.

"Now it's your turn," Lacey said.

"My turn for what?"

"To tell me why you're afraid of spiders."

"I *am* not—"

"Oh yes you are. Admit it. When that tarantula ran across our path you almost jumped to the moon." She laughed at his dismayed expression.

"It startled me." His shoulder lifted in a gesture of nonchalance. He was met by Lacey's dubious expression. Hanging his head in defeat, he said, "Okay, I hate spiders."

Feeling no sympathy for his plight, especially after his reaction to hers, Lacey giggled in response to his confession. "How is it that you live in Costa Rica, you guide unwary tourists through jungles filled with insects, and you're afraid of spiders?"

"In case you didn't know, spiders bite. And some of them hurt, and some of them can make you very sick."

"Yeah, and so do snakes, and crocodiles, and Bullhorn Acacia ants."

A flush of embarrassment crept up his face. "I know. I know." He sighed. "But my arachnophobia is no different than your ranidaphobia."

"Fine. Let's agree we won't harass one another about our phobias." Lacey stuck out her hand.

Luke took it and they shook on it. "Deal." Relieved to have that topic behind him, he said, "Okay, next question."

She gave him an exasperated look.

"Why does that necklace mean so much to you?" He reached out, touching the garnet heart.

Lacey sighed with relief. At least this answer was not humiliating. "My paternal grandmother gave it to me before she died. It had been a wedding gift from my grandfather, so I know how much it meant to her."

"And you were close to her?"

"Very. She was the only one in my family who really understood me and encouraged me to follow my own path." She laughed. "You see, my Granma Madeline was a bit of a nonconformist. Some would say crazy, but since she had money, I guess the more appropriate label would be eccentric.

"Granma participated in the Civil Rights Movement as part of the group that marched to Montgomery, Alabama, in 1965. She also protested the Vietnam War, something she later regretted, because of the detrimental consequences to the men and women who served in Vietnam. And she supported the Women's Movement in the 1970s." God, it felt good to talk about her grandmother.

"Granma died while I was at NYU." She reached up to touch the necklace. "The last time I saw her before she died she gave this to me and said she would always be with me." Lacey grew thoughtful. "I think she knew then she didn't have long."

Luke leaned over, brushing his lips over hers. "Thank you for sharing that with me."

She didn't know how to respond to that. No one had ever thanked her for telling a story about herself.

He picked up the breakfast tray and rose from the bed.

"Don't go anywhere. I have another present for you."

She lifted a brow. "I've heard it called many things, but 'present' is a new one. Will it have a big red bow on it?"

Chuckling, he left the room, only to come back shortly with a large, wrapped rectangle.

"You really do have another present for me," she said in surprise. "You've already given me too much."

If she only knew how much more he wanted to give her.

"Don't be ridiculous. Open it."

She tore the paper, revealing the painting of the beach she'd seen on previous visits, only different. A woman stood in the foreground, her back to the viewer, the water swirling around her thighs, just below her bare torso. "Is that . . . me?" she asked almost reverently.

"Yes." He tilted his head, looking at the painting. "I've thought all along there was something missing." He glanced back at Lacey and his eyes held hers. "Then I finally figured it out. It was you."

Lacey's heart contracted in her chest. A combination of elation and panic. Luke's eyes flickered to her lips. He leaned in, a breath away from kissing her. "Thank you for staying with me," he whispered, before he kissed her with a sweetness that overwhelmed her.

Shoving down the panic that threatened to overtake her, she kissed him back, the desperation spilling over, intensifying the kiss until it left her dizzy and weak.

Luke drew back, his breath heavy and raspy. "Come on," he said, taking her hand. He had a little fantasy he wanted to fulfill.

"Where're we going?" she asked, her brow furrowed in confusion.

"Shower."

Baffled, Lacey shook her head at the rapid change in his demeanor, again throwing her off balance. But then again, a hot, soapy shower with Luke sounded *very* appealing.

———

Luke watched Lacey pad around his house wearing nothing but one of his T-shirts and thought it was the sexiest thing he'd ever seen. Well, with the exception of Lacey's naked body, slick with water and soap, as he'd scrubbed her back this morning. Or was it this afternoon? Didn't matter. It was a sight he wouldn't soon forget.

She plopped down on the sofa next to him, camera in hand scrolling through the pictures she'd taken last evening, the sounds of NFL Football emanating from the television.

"Let me see." He leaned over to get a better view of the camera's screen and caught the scent of his soap on her skin, which sent a little jolt of desire straight to his abdomen.

She stopped on a photo of Tony and Allie looking into one another's eyes and laughing. She'd captured their feelings for each other on camera.

"I'll say it again. You're not a wildlife photographer.

People are your best subject." He tossed some popcorn into his mouth, chewing thoughtfully. "You're wasting your talent."

"You're starting to sound like a broken record." She gave him a playful nudge with her shoulder.

"Maybe. But I'm right about this." A thought occurred to him. "Hey, why don't you look into Peace Potters? Take some photos of the women learning their craft, others who've made a success out of selling their pottery, and write an article about it?"

His enthusiasm grew as he spoke. "Search out the happy stories. You can write about the good people in the world who don't get the recognition they deserve. People quietly doing good in the world, unnoticed and unsung, giving back with no expectation of recognition beyond the thanks of the grateful people they help."

"I don't know." Lacey smiled at his rhapsodic description. She hadn't said anything about the article she'd started because she was still skeptical. "Magazines and newspapers aren't going to pay me to photograph and write about . . . happy people."

The crowd erupted as Dallas scored a touchdown.

"Then freelance."

"I repeat. People are not going to pay me to write touchy-feely stories."

"Okay, then how about a blog? I don't know, Good Vibrations or something."

"What are you, channeling the Beach Boys?"

Luke shrugged and turned his attention to the game. He'd learned not to press her—to let her come to the decision in her own time. "Just something to think about."

She settled back onto the sofa, and taking a handful of popcorn, nestled into the crook of his arm, both of them content to watch the snow fall on Green Bay on this warm Costa Rican Christmas Day.

———

The next morning Luke entered the bedroom, a spring in his step. Again, Lacey presented a stirring picture lying on her stomach, the sheets down around her shapely calves. He'd have to paint her like that some time. Soon, he amended, and grimaced at the thought of her leaving.

Smacking her on her gorgeous bare ass, he dropped down on the bed beside her, laughing as she yelped in dismay.

"What the hell was that for?" she said as she rolled over, rubbing her abused bottom with one hand and her eyes with the other.

"Well, if you're going to flaunt that beautiful derrière of yours like that, you got to expect an appreciative smack now and then."

The grin he gave her made Lacey's pulse do a little dance.

"How long would it take you to pack a bag?" he asked, light sparkling in his eyes.

"Why? Where're we going?" she asked with the petulance of a child.

"Drake Bay."

"But that trip was cancelled," she said, the confusion plain on her face.

"Just because your assignment is over doesn't mean we can't go to Drake Bay."

CHAPTER TWENTY-THREE

Tony walked into the office in Puerto Jimenez. Allie paced the floor, the ever-present headset hooked to her ear, arguing in Spanish with someone.

God, Tony loved it when she was in a temper. She became a little spitfire. Her eyes flashed, her face flushed, her hands gesticulated, and her already rapid Spanish hit warp speed. It never failed to turn Tony on, even when that anger was aimed at him.

He perched on the corner of the desk patiently waiting for her tirade to end. He didn't know what the guy did to piss her off, but whatever it was he'd lay odds he regretted it now. Tony winced at her last well-delivered threat against a cherished anatomical body part, before she hung up.

Tony chuckled as he slid from the desk and sauntered over to his sexy hellion of a wife. "I'm sure he didn't mean it."

"Ooh! That . . . man. He delivers a case of pink copy paper and then tells me I ordered it! What would I do with pink copy paper? The man has rocks in his head." Her hands still gesticulated wildly.

Tony gently removed the headset and tossed it on the desk before wrapping his arms around her waist and nuzzling her neck.

"Want to sneak into the backroom for a quickie?" He lifted his head and waggled his brows comically.

"Oh you!" She swatted at him. "I think you've got rocks in your head too. Can't you see I'm working off a temper?"

"What better way to work it off?" He shrugged. "I'm only trying to help."

She lifted a delicately arched brow, clearly not buying his argument.

He gave her a devilish grin, then kissed her nose before releasing her.

"What are you doing here anyway? Weren't you and Luke flying to San José to pick up supplies for Jill and Karl? Something wrong with the plane?"

"No." He sank into the chair behind the desk that served as his on the rare occasions he came to the office, propping his feet up. "Luke has other plans." At Allie's questioning look, he continued. "He's taking Lacey to Drake Bay."

"But I thought that trip was cancelled."

"It was."

"Then why?"

"Guess."

It only took her a moment. "So he could be alone with her?

Since when does he worry about discretion with one of his fly-by-night relationships? Didn't he screw that one woman from L.A. in the plane's cargo area while you fished on the beach not fifty yards away?"

Allie was no fool—she knew Luke was an operator—and loved him despite his skirt-chasing tendencies. As long as he was single, who was she to judge? But Lacey deserved more than a casual fling.

Tony sat quietly, toying with a paperclip. "This one's different." He related his previous suspicions and the encounter with Luke last week that had confirmed them.

"Well, I'm not surprised." Allie'd had a feeling Christmas Eve when she saw them together. The looks, the gestures, the signs of affection when they thought no one was looking.

Allie sat on the edge of the desk and studied her husband. He was Luke's best friend. He knew everything about Luke, the good, the bad, and the ugly.

And there was plenty of ugly: the death of Luke's sister, the subsequent break-up of his parent's marriage, his father's breakdown, and his own divorce. But there was a lot of good there too, if someone took the time to look past the devil-may-care exterior to see the man underneath.

Tony's lips lifted in a wry grin, but his eyes were full of concern. "They'll either screw each other's brains out or kill each other, or both."

"I just hope Luke doesn't break Lacey's heart."

"I hope *she* doesn't break Luke's," Tony countered quietly.

———

On the flight north to the opposite end of the Osa Peninsula from Corcovado, Luke had explained that Drake Bay was just as undeveloped as the southern tip. Its very remoteness lured the adventurer, with little to do but swim, snorkel, dive, canoe, and sport fish. Getting into, and out of, Drake Bay was difficult at best, with often muddy roads, and a small airstrip, serviced only by charter flights, that was subject to tide conditions.

When they'd checked in, her insistence that she pay for the room since he'd paid for the fuel, caused a minor tiff, in front of the desk clerk no-less.

"Oh come on. Surely your manhood can survive me paying for the room."

"Dammit, Lacey." He turned to glare at her. "Let's get one thing straight. I don't need your money." Then returning his attention to the desk clerk, who clearly wished to be anywhere else but there witnessing the argument, Luke had smiled and rolled his eyes as if to say, 'women.'

A minor bump in the road, and one she'd quickly gotten over when, in the seclusion of their room, he'd pulled her to him and kissed her until all cognitive function fled and instinct took over.

The bungalow at the resort, with its mosquito-netting-draped king-size bed and sweeping vista of the Pacific and Caño Island beyond, had all the trappings of a romantic getaway. A bucket of chilled champagne and a basket of fruit had awaited their arrival.

Lacey checked her reflection in the mirror and smiled at her uncharacteristic interest in her own appearance. The frog earrings dangled from her ears, she'd fluffed her hair with her fingers, giving her soft wispy waves a slightly disheveled look, and swiped on a little lip gloss.

On a whim, she'd packed the linen pants and cotton blouse she'd bought in San José. The resort where they stayed was a slightly more upscale version of Mariposa Lodge, and she didn't want to show up in the dining room wearing the hiking clothes she'd grown so tired of.

But if she were completely honest with herself, she'd

brought the clothes to please Luke, and in an act of daring, she wore absolutely nothing underneath the outfit.

She noticed in passing the watercolor set she'd given Luke for Christmas sitting on the desk. He leaned on the railing looking out at the cobalt waters, a few pelicans bobbing on the surface.

Luke turned when she stepped out onto the deck. He drank her in, as his breath snagged at the sight of her, so sensual, so natural, so sexy.

"Wow."

Although Lacey craved his attention and approval, she nevertheless felt self-conscious under the heat of his gaze. No one had ever looked at her that way—with a combination of lust, admiration, and respect.

"You too," was all she could think to say in response. Dressed in a pair of easy-fitting slacks, tropical silk shirt and sandals, so different from the usual board shorts and T-shirts he wore, he looked like he belonged in a Tommy Bahama ad.

She gestured to her outfit. "I also bought this with the money I won from you."

He shook his head and laughed, but his eyes never left her. She grew increasingly uncomfortable with the intensity of his stare. "Um, you hungry?"

He approached her at last, kissing her. "Oh, I'm hungry all right," he muttered against her lips, before reluctantly stepping back, "but we have dinner reservations."

The dining room bustled with wait staff carrying trays loaded with food that smelled delicious, and diners huddled in quiet conversation.

The hostess led them to a table by a window overlooking the water, Luke's hand at the small of Lacey's back.

After placing their orders, they sat sipping their wine,

both seemingly at a loss for conversation. They'd just spent two days and nights together, most of it in bed, but in this setting, it felt more like a first date.

Lacey wanted to ask questions, about his family, about his sister, but she didn't want to bring up anything that could lead to a quarrel or distress. Maybe she could talk to him about his love for, and appreciation of, the environment, but before she could get the first word out, a ruckus at the table next to them interrupted her.

Everyone in the restaurant had turned to see a guy still on his knees with what appeared to be his new fiancée waving her arms in glee, laughing and crying at the same time. "I'm getting married!"

The diners applauded, toasted, and offered their congratulations to the happy couple. Luke and Lacey raised their glasses in a silent toast of their own.

God, Lacey thought, *how embarrassing . . . and risky, on the part of the guy at least*. What if she threw her drink in his face and said no? She shook her head.

"You disapprove?" Luke asked.

"What?" *Busted*.

"Of marriage I mean?"

"Um, no. I mean, I guess it works for some people. I just think guys who propose in public are either really brave or really stupid." She shrugged, embarrassed that he'd clearly read her mind.

"I guess love makes people both brave and stupid." He smiled. He reached across the table and took her hand, giving it a little squeeze that corresponded with the squeeze of her heart.

"Yeah. I guess." She surveyed the couples in the room, most making goo-goo eyes at each other, holding hands across the table like they were afraid to let go even long enough to eat their dinner. She frowned, wondering if that's what she and Luke looked like.

At least he released her hand when the waiter brought their food.

"Tell me about your job with the AP. What made you take on such a dangerous assignment?" he asked, taking a bite of his fish.

His question only provided limited relief. At least they weren't talking about love anymore, but questions about her job would eventually lead to questions she didn't want to answer.

"My father wanted me to stay in New York, work for some overpriced fashion magazine filled with underfed models. No thanks."

Luke smiled, imagining Lacey on location with a bunch of pampered, whiney models. They wouldn't last the day.

"I wanted to cover the important stories, the ones that made history. So when the AP announced opportunities for photojournalists and reporters to cover the war, I put my hand up, got selected, and next thing I knew I was on a plane to Kabul."

Lacey explained that it hadn't been easy when she'd first gotten to Afghanistan. For the first time in her life, she'd had to prove herself. There weren't many female journalists in Afghanistan at the time, and she had to work twice as hard as a man, just to earn half the respect. She had to prove she was tough enough to handle the rigors of covering the war.

"The soldiers, male and female alike, didn't trust me at first. When I was around, they became more formal, careful about their behavior. 'Yes, ma'am, this' and 'no, ma'am, that.' I couldn't get the real images I wanted."

She shrugged. "No surprise, I guess. How was a girl

raised in the Upper East Side supposed to relate to soldiers from places like Briarcliff, Arkansas, or Wallins Creek, Kentucky? Men and women who might not make it home, and even if they did, not in one piece." She paused as she remembered those who didn't make it home.

"But after a few weeks in their company, they began to loosen up, and after a few months, I became one of them. Drinking with them, joking with them, even bunking with them at times."

Luke listened with interest as she talked about the boots-on-the-ground training she got, how she came to know the men and women in the unit she covered, and how hard it was to leave when she was re-assigned to Iraq, and had to leave them.

Luke noted how she waved her fork in the air when she got excited, taking a break every now and then to take a sip of wine and a bite of food.

He liked it when her eyes lit up while talking about e-mails she'd gotten from some of the soldiers after they'd gone home; or winced when she laughed at some of the outrageous practical jokes the troops played on one another, grateful that he'd only had to endure an ass-whooping at chess and tequila shots.

Lacey talked through dessert and after dinner drinks, finally pausing when she saw the corner of his mouth lift in a small smile. "I'm sorry," she said, her brow furrowed. "I've talked *way* too much."

Luke laughed. "No. I enjoyed it. It was way more than I could learn on Google." The chagrin was plain on her face, but he didn't want to stop the free flow of stories. He'd learned so much about her, and he didn't want it to stop when he'd just managed to get her to talk about herself.

"Let's continue this story on the beach." He rose, and

before she could stand he came around and pulled out her chair, taking her hand and ushering her out of the restaurant and onto the deck.

She stepped out into the fading sunlight, which shone through the sheer fabric of her pants and blouse, lighting her from behind and casting her sumptuous curves in silhouette. A bolt of desire from the blue struck him, and he inhaled sharply.

Before she stepped onto the cool sand, she bent over and slipped off her sandals, giving him an even better view of her sweet little bum. Jesus. He wondered if there were any secluded caves around here.

When she glanced back to see what was keeping him, he could see through her blouse and pants, making it clear that she wore absolutely nothing underneath. "Good God." His breath left in a whoosh. "You're killing me woman."

Pleased with his reaction, Lacey laughed, deep and sultry.

"You mean to tell me that you blithely sat across the table from me during dinner and beneath those clothes you've been *au naturel* . . . all evening?"

She just lifted her brow in response.

"Come on." He grabbed her hand.

"Where're we going?"

"To the room," he growled. "I'll never make it to the beach."

She just giggled as he hauled her along behind him as if his life depended on it.

CHAPTER TWENTY-FOUR

Luke's hand drew a path, soft as a sigh, along Lacey's arm. Cocooned behind the mosquito netting, listening to the rise and fall of the surf, it felt as if they were the only two people in the world.

Lacey's head rested on his chest where she could hear his heartbeat and breathing slowing to normal rhythms.

They'd barely made it through the door of their room before he'd stripped her of the only two pieces of clothing separating her from him. His hands and lips had worshipped her body until she could no longer stand.

Just as she thought her legs would crumple beneath her, he'd picked her up and carried her to the bed, before continuing his exultation of her. Intoning praise, whispering endearments, until she'd implored him huskily, "Now."

His hand stilled and his breathing deepened, making her think he'd fallen asleep.

"What made you go from photojournalist to wildlife photographer?" His hand resumed the soothing pattern on her arm.

Physically and emotionally drained from their intense

lovemaking, she didn't even have the strength to readjust her armor.

She thought about it a moment, and then with a heavy sigh, explained. "After so many years of taking photos of death and destruction, trying to maintain my objectivity in the face of the atrocities I'd witnessed and documented, I began to feel that with every snap of the shutter I lost a piece of my soul. Until I had nothing left."

She spoke so quietly Luke had to strain to hear the words, but the pain in them rang clear as a bell. He reached down to cup her face and lift it to his. Their eyes held for a heartbeat, then two.

He skimmed his fingers along her side, stopping at the Monarch perched on her hip. "Did you know many cultures believe the butterfly symbolizes the transformation of the soul?" His hand returned to cup her face. "It's there, Lacey," he breathed. "You just have to reawaken it."

Lacey reached up and wrapped her hand around his wrist, making contact with the hemp bracelet he always wore. She felt certain she already knew what it meant, why he wore it like a talisman, just like she wore her necklace. Taking a deep breath, she asked, "Did Lisa give this to you?"

He stiffened and dropped his hand from her face.

Lacey propped herself up on her elbow and gazed down at his face, his lips drawn together in a tight line. "Talk to me, Luke." He raised his hand to cover his face and, taking a deep breath, nodded.

Then the words came, the story of that day twenty years ago when he'd watched his sister tumble over the waterfall to her death.

Although Lacey'd heard the story from Allie, it hadn't prepared her for Luke's account, for the horror and the grief; the emotions so raw it was like it'd happened only yesterday. There were no tears, just his voice, hoarse and grating.

"As with most twins, we were inseparable. We did everything together, and Lisa kept up with all of my strenuous physical activities, but where I carefully considered my more daring stunts, she had been brash, reckless." He inhaled deeply. "Her recklessness proved fatal.

"Our family had gone backpacking and camping in the central highlands south of San José. We'd had such a great day. We'd actually seen a quetzal." He smiled briefly. "Even at sixteen, we played silly explorer games, you know, the quest for the Seven Cities of Gold or El Dorado. That day we'd been on a quest for Atzlán, the mythical ancestral home of the Aztec, when we came to a river.

"It had been a particularly wet rainy season and the river rushed past like a freight train, before dropping off precipitously into a turbulent waterfall.

"Lisa was determined to cross it even though it was flooded." He stopped, drew in a gulp of air and then released it. "I never thought she'd go over the falls." He closed his eyes. "To make matters worse, I made some flippant remark about not crying to me when she sprained her ankle on a rock. I never should have let her go." He scrubbed at his eyes, as if he could erase the vision from his memory.

"It's so surreal. Your brain doesn't register what your eyes are seeing. One moment she was there, the next, I heard a wild cry, watched her try and get her balance, then she was gone. My beautiful, brave sister. The other half of my soul." Silence fell, louder than any cries of anguish. "I tried," he choked, "I tried to save her, but I couldn't get to her in time.

"My parents never blamed me, but that didn't alleviate

the guilt that almost swallowed me whole. Even now, I haven't been able to forgive myself."

"It wasn't your fault, you know," Lacey whispered in the dark.

He nodded again, but it failed to convince her that he actually believed it.

"Tell me about her," Lacey said softly.

He hesitated, as if trying to decide whether he could talk about her or not. "She was funny and sassy and sweet, smart and determined, and brave, all rolled up into this never-ending bundle of energy. She embraced life, soaked up all it had to offer."

Luke realized how good it felt to talk about her. He hadn't talked about her in the almost two decades since she died. He didn't need to with Tony. Everything went without saying. And he'd never wanted to talk about her with Caroline. But sharing her with Lacey just felt so . . . right.

He laughed. "She could just about outdo me in anything." He looked at Lacey, his eyes sparkling with unshed tears. "In other words, she was a lot like you."

Lacey's chest felt tight, and she had to swallow hard past the lump in her throat as he drew her into a hug kissing the top of her head.

"God, how I miss her. It's like I lost a vital piece of myself that I'll never get back, and yet at times, I can feel her . . . as if she is right next to me." Luke lifted Lacey's chin to look into her eyes. "Crazy, huh?"

She kissed him, a gentle kiss both warm and sweet. "No. It's not. I'm glad she's with you."

And I'm glad you're with me too, he thought, as he tucked her head beneath this chin and drifted off to sleep.

———

Lacey lashed out, fighting to save the woman from the brutality, but she was too late. The woman lay in a heap at her feet. She screamed her fear and frustration into the night.

"Lacey." Luke grabbed her wrists as she continued her battle. "Lacey, wake up."

She awoke with a start, sitting up, her chest heaving, her heart thumping, her face covered in sweat. After looking around the room to get her bearings, she collapsed back onto the bed in exhaustion.

Luke reached out and cupped her neck, his thumb touching the scar, feeling her pulse jackhammer beneath it. "*Querida*. Tell me. Please."

She nodded almost imperceptibly and released a shuddering breath.

He brushed the hair from her forehead and waited patiently until her pulse slowed to a steady gallop.

Lacey spoke to the room, as if she were alone, verbalizing for the first time the brutality she'd witnessed in Darfur. Brutality that in the end was turned on her.

Of course Luke had followed the stories on the news and in the papers, but hearing Lacey's bone-chilling descriptions of events far too graphic for television or print gave him a whole new gruesome perspective.

"We hid in the brush along the roadside, overlooked by the Janjaweed in their thirst to wipe out the village, the chaos covering the click of my shutter." She shook her head. "I'd never encountered such a scene."

"A woman, a mother desperate to protect her baby, faced off against her attackers, the infant screaming in her arms. One of the men snatched the infant from its mother's arms before silencing it forever." Shuddering, she paused, wiping the sweat from her brow.

"I waited. The UN Peacekeepers usually ran a patrol through the area around nine p.m. But they hadn't come. I couldn't stand back any longer and do nothing. Unarmed, I knew I'd be no match for the militia, but I didn't care."

As the story unraveled, Lacey relived the senseless violence, plunging deep into the terrifying abyss, no longer in the room with Luke's protective arms around her.

"I ignored David's admonition to remain hidden and ran to help the woman, even as the men began to beat her. By the time I reached them, the woman lay on the ground, either unconscious or dead."

She sobbed. "The men turned on me. I tried to run, but one of them grabbed my ponytail and pushed me to my knees. The other men surrounded me. After taking my camera, one of them yanked my head back and sliced my throat with his machete. I thought I was going to die. I remember hoping they wouldn't rape me. In that moment, I thought of my family and wondered if they would even get my body back."

As she described her capture, Luke held his breath. Every fiber of his being wanted to rescue her, even though it happened over two years ago. It didn't matter how irrational the emotion, the anger he felt now over his helplessness to save her then overwhelmed him.

"In that instant, you think, 'this can't be happening to me.' But it is . . ." Lacey couldn't finish. Great racking sobs erupted, choking off any further words. She cried for herself, but she cried for the woman she couldn't save. And for her infant.

Tears seared Luke's chest as he held her to him and began rocking her like a child. "Shh. *Querida*. My love.

Shh." He kissed her head, murmuring soothing endearments. The pain he'd felt in the alley washed over him again and, as anxious as he'd been to learn how she'd escaped, he didn't want to push her.

Sometime later, the sobs subsided, leaving her exhausted, but she continued her story.

"Suddenly, headlights pierced the darkness even before I heard the low thrum of engines over the violent din. My would-be executioner released me, shoving me to the ground, before he and the other men ran to their vehicles. I lay there, afraid to move, afraid to attract attention to myself, until a gentle hand touched my shoulder, and a calm voice with a French accent asked me if I was hurt. UN Peacekeepers saved my life.

"After they treated my wound, the UN peacekeepers delivered me back to the group of journalists I traveled with. David had been shocked to see that I'd survived." She released a laugh bereft of humor. "His relief at seeing me rang false.

"He hadn't even tried to save me. I knew the truth. He'd wanted the scoop on the photojournalist who'd lost her life to the Janjaweed. With him, the story meant everything. The only thing. But I asked anyway how he could've left me like that."

Luke tensed in anticipation of the answer.

"He said what I did was stupid. That I should have known better than to lose my objectivity. That he wasn't about to risk his life for my stupidity."

"You and David were . . . lovers?" He could barely get the last word out before jealousy sank its claws into his chest.

Lacey just nodded.

Now he understood Lacey's statements in the alley, her

surprise at being rescued. Luke swore that if he ever met up with the son-of-a-bitch he'd make damn sure he paid the price for abandoning Lacey to those animals. *Fucking bastard.*

Luke felt her anger seething just beneath the surface. He preferred that to the gut-wrenching pain and fear.

"What did you do?"

"I punched him." Lacey remembered with pleasure the jaw-breaking punch, the sound of cracking teeth, notwithstanding the fractured knuckle she'd received out of the deal. She'd left Darfur without looking back.

"That's my Lacey," he said as he gave her a hug. He had no doubt she'd left her mark. "So brave."

Her heart squeezed at being called 'his Lacey.' Spent from her emotional purge, her eyelids grew heavy and her breathing deepened. It felt like the weight she'd been carrying for the past two years had lifted. Like she could finally fill her lungs with air again.

"I've lost my objectivity before," Lacey continued, "and I carry other scars as a result. But I've always considered those scars badges of honor."

She held up her right hand. "Like the one on the palm of my hand I earned while helping a medic stem the flow of blood from a soldier's wounded leg, the result of the IED. A piece of shrapnel cut right through my glove, requiring stitches." The corner of her mouth lifted up in a smile. "The soldier not only survived, he kept his leg."

"But this scar," she touched the scar on her neck, "represents a badge of shame. I failed to save that woman. And probably got what I deserved for losing my objectivity and foolishly charging in like the Light Brigade."

"No. Don't." Luke tenderly kissed the machete scar. "You're courageous and beautiful, with the heart of a warrior. You should wear that scar proudly, like any warrior would.”

A peace descended. Something she hadn't known since before she'd left to cover the wars.

Luke ran his fingers through her sleep-tousled locks. "So, the hair."

"Yeah. The hair. I swore it would never be a detriment to me again." Embarrassed by the absurdity of her impulsive act, she said, "Silly, I know."

"It won't happen again." His arms tightened around her. "You're safe."

Silence reigned for a few heartbeats.

"My assignment here was a test of sorts," she continued, "to see if I could still do my job."

"What do you mean 'still do your job?'"

"I had a little . . . flashback in Tanzania."

"What triggered that?"

Lacey told him the story of the lions and the gazelle.

Luke frowned into the darkness, imagining her association with the gazelle's plight.

Although he was glad she left the AP and its often dangerous assignments, he wished she'd consider the good-news freelance idea. *Because, let's face it, the life of a wildlife photographer isn't exactly low-risk.* Lacey had and would continue to get herself into trouble.

Hoping to nurture the seed he'd planted, he said, "On New Year's Day I'm making another flight for charity. Shoes this time. Come with me. Take some photos, talk to some folks, write something and see what comes of it." He lifted her chin, kissing her lips. "Who knows, you might just find your soul again."

Lacey sighed. New Year's Day. She really needed to have her departure plans in place by then. The weight that had lifted was suddenly replaced by a new weight, one that not only threatened her capacity for breathing once again, but also created a fissure down the center of her heart.

She kissed him again. "Sure." She'd go with him on New Year's Day and then she had to leave. No more excuses.

————

Physically and emotionally drained, Luke suggested they fritter away the morning lying in bed, dozing in each other's arms. They spent the afternoon diving off the coast of Caño Island, followed by an afternoon nap, that didn't include much in the way of sleep.

Luke pointedly avoided the issue of Lacey's departure. He knew it was inevitable, but postponing the topic was vital to the enjoyment of their last few days together. Neither discussed the future, clearly choosing instead to live in the moment. And the moment was pure bliss.

They ordered room service for dinner, neither over-joyed with the idea of dressing for dinner and eating among the other guests. Not when they could lie in bed, wearing nothing but their smiles.

"Do you have any strong feelings about fishing tomorrow?"

He poured her another glass of wine, handing the glass to her.

"No. Why?"

"What would you think about spending the morning in bed?" He leaned over, nuzzling her neck, then planting kisses along her shoulder, before retracing the path back to her neck.

"Have I complained about it the last three mornings?" She shivered in response to his butterfly kisses.

"Well, I had something a little . . . different in mind."

"How different?" She pulled back, arching her brow at him and smiling seductively.

"I want to paint you. Nude."

She drew back even further. "Me? Nude?"

"Who else would I want to paint nude?"

"Why?"

"Does that even require an answer?" At her continued silence, he said, "Apparently it does. Fine. You're gorgeous. You have the body of a goddess, sleek, yet voluptuous." He skimmed his hands down her side. "All luscious hills and valleys, graceful sweeps and curves. You're the perfect subject."

Feeling a flush creep up her cheeks at his effusive description of her body, Lacey couldn't help but ask, "Have you ever painted a woman nude before?"

"You're the first."

That pleased her far more than she realized it would. With Luke, she found herself giving in to things she never would have considered doing before. "Okay. I'll do it. But I'm going to feel *very* self-conscious."

"No, you won't. I won't let you, I promise. I'll only make you feel what you truly are," he kissed her nose, "beautiful."

Draped across the bed like one of Titian's women, Lacey did indeed feel beautiful. Luke's eyes, lit with passion and longing, told her constantly how beautiful he thought she was.

Stepping closer to adjust her arm to better see her face,

he leaned over and said, "You're doing great. You're a natural." He stepped back to the canvas, a frown on his face. "But don't get any ideas about doing this full-time."

"No worries about that," she snorted. "I can't imagine doing this for anyone else."

He looked back at the canvas, face beaming in response to her remark.

"When can I see it?" she asked.

"When it's done."

"When will that be?"

"When I say it is."

She rolled her eyes at his parental tone.

Lacey lay on her stomach in that pose for what seemed like hours. Who would have thought lying still could get so uncomfortable? "Luke, I'm getting stiff." She winced at the whine in her voice.

"So am I," he said, with a waggle of his eyebrows.

She rolled over, propping herself up on her elbow. "Poor baby. Why don't we see if we can do something about that?"

He wasted no time spearing his paintbrush into the cup of water before diving onto the bed to join her.

CHAPTER TWENTY-FIVE

Lacey couldn't wait for their fishing expedition the next day. The resort packed a lunch, Luke chartered a boat, and they headed off in the direction of Caño Island.

She could now add boat captain to the ever-growing list of Luke's talents. She loved water sports, but she'd never been sport fishing before, and she looked forward to the challenge. A clear sunny morning promised good weather but very warm temperatures later.

Their destination, a forty-minute boat ride from their resort, was once a refuge for pirates. The hulking stone mass of Caño Island was studded with trees and now held a biological reserve. The waters off the island boasted sailfish, blue, black, and striped marlin, and yellow fin tuna.

Luke had finally shown Lacey the portrait last night. She couldn't believe it. He was a much better painter than he gave himself credit for, and he'd made her look like something out of Greek mythology. If that was his vision of her, she was beyond flattered. She was blown away.

The sheets draped across her calves in soft swirls, leaving the rest of her body visible. Her skin appeared luminous, as if glowing from the inside out. Her eyes were soft and dreamy, and the subtle smile on her lips promised secret delights. Luke depicted the butterfly on her hip in such stunning detail, it seemed as if it would flutter its wings and fly away at any moment.

"Is that how you see me?" she'd asked, awestruck.

"That's how you look," he'd said matter-of-factly.

Luke cut the engines, interrupting Lacey's reverie. He dropped anchor as the thirty-one foot sport fisher bobbed and rocked on the waves. A few other boats dotted the ocean's surface, glittering now with the sun's rays.

Luke watched as Lacey slathered on sunscreen. Seeing her run her hands up those gorgeous legs, he wondered what he'd been thinking when he'd suggested fishing. Even after five days (and nights) of almost constant togetherness, he couldn't get enough of her. He remembered all too clearly what lay beneath that bikini, and his hands itched to strip if off and fill his hands and mouth with her.

This morning they'd given a whole new meaning to the phrase 'long hot shower.' Even after the hot water ran out, the heat had lingered. As an environmentalist, he'd clearly set a bad example.

It wasn't just the sex, which was the best he'd ever had, he enjoyed Lacey's company, even at her prickliest. She was low-maintenance. None of that 'I might break a nail' or 'mess up my hair' crap.

She had a wicked sense of humor, and beneath that tough exterior beat the heart of a humanitarian. Who else would think to fight off the Janjaweed barehanded to try to save a complete stranger?

"Hey, Luke. We going to fish or what?" Lacey stood, hands on her hips, staring at him with a perplexed expression.

"Hmm? Oh yeah. Sure." But fishing was the furthest thing from his mind.

———

An hour and a couple of nibbles later—from the fish, not Luke—Lacey finally caught something, the line *zizzing,* the pole bending in an arc as the fish took the bait and ran with it. "Whoa." Lacey's grip tightened on the pole as she fought to reel in the fish.

"Need help?" Of course he knew the answer.

"No."

Luke never thought of fishing as a spectator sport, but he couldn't resist. He locked his pole into its stand and watched as Lacey and the fish played an all-out game of tug-a-war. Bare feet planted, she wrenched back on the pole, revealing her considerable biceps. Inspiring to behold.

"Give it some slack. Let it run a little, get tired," Luke instructed.

The sailfish leaped from the water, fighting the pull of the line.

"Holy shit!" she gasped. "Who knew a fish could be this strong. It's got to weigh a hundred pounds!"

Luke didn't have the heart to tell her it was likely closer to sixty pounds, on the smaller end of the sailfish spectrum. She learned fast, listening to his instructions and following through on them. Luke watched as she continued to work the line, letting the fish run in between reeling it in.

But he could tell she was getting tired. Sweat coated her body, the muscles in her arms and back bunching with every pull.

"Lace, come on, take a break."

No one except her father called her Lace, but she liked

hearing it from Luke. "No," she responded stubbornly, even though her arms felt as if they would break.

Luke rolled his eyes behind his sunglasses, reached inside the cooler for a beer and opened it. He held the icy bottle to her lips so she could drink before taking a pull himself.

"Thanks," she panted.

He'd just wait her out. At some point she wouldn't be able to continue.

"Jeez, he doesn't seem any closer to the boat. How long does this usually take?"

Taking another sip of the beer, he replied casually, "It can take up to an hour, maybe more, depending on the amount of fight in the fish."

"What! Jesus. How long has it been?"

Luke glanced down at his watch. "About fifteen minutes."

Lacey groaned. No way she could keep this up for another fifteen minutes, much less another forty-five.

Luke offered her another sip of beer, finally trying once again. "Lacey, let me work it a while, then when he gets close, you can pull him in." At her lack of response, he added, "Even grown men need help pulling in a fish." No response. He sighed. "You're going to have to stop soon. Wouldn't you rather take a break now and have the joy of pulling him into the boat at the end?"

"Oh, all right," she gave in, exasperated. "How do we do this?"

"I'll help you get the rod into the stand and lock it down, then I'll pick it up."

Together they maneuvered the rod into the stand, with Luke standing behind her, her body pressed close to his. The feel of her sweat-slick body against his bare chest was just as alluring as it had been in the shower this morning. *Down, boy*. They had a fish to reel in.

"God. I need another beer," Lacey huffed, leaning over the cooler. She could barely lift the bottle to her mouth her arm shook so badly.

After claiming possession of the rod, Luke worked the reel before giving the fish some slack, enjoying the heat of battle.

Lacey collapsed onto the cooler, watching with avid interest as the muscles beneath his skin rippled and flexed.

Luke worked on the fish for half an hour, before giving the rod back to Lacey for her to reel in her catch. She hefted the sailfish from the water while Luke held out a giant net. The two struggled to get the tired but determined fish onto the boat.

"Oh. My. God." Lacey bent over, bracing her hands on her knees, winded from the exertion. "My arms are going to kill me tomorrow."

"Great job, Lace." He clapped her on the back like one of the guys, practically knocking her over in her fatigue.

"Thanks. What do we do with it?"

"First, we get a photo of you with your catch."

"Then what?"

"We release it."

"We what?" she yelped. "I fought to bring that sucker in and the only reward I get is a photo op and sore muscles?"

"That and the satisfaction of knowing this beauty will get another chance at life. That's why it's called 'catch and release.'"

"Fine," she grumbled. "But the picture better be damn good."

———

L acey was reluctant to leave their corner of paradise. Not that the southern tip of the peninsula didn't offer its own version of paradise, but leaving meant facing reality. And dealing with it.

She had to return to the States. Even if she could stay until Simon came up with her next assignment, she'd have to leave eventually, and it might be better sooner rather than later.

Truth be told, she'd never been able to handle that much togetherness with anyone, much less a guy. And while these past few days with Luke had been heaven, he'd given no indication that he wanted anything more.

And when it came down to it, did she? Or had this just been a pleasant interlude? A memory to be stashed away, only to be recalled on lonely nights? Then why did the thought of losing that, of leaving him behind, make her physically ill?

She should just bring it up for discussion, but in this one area she was a coward of the first order. With past relationships, she'd just ridden the high, let them take their natural course, until they'd fizzled out, or in the case of David, crashed and burned. What end would this one meet?

The short fifteen-minute flight back to Puerto Jimenez had been somber, with each of them lost in their own thoughts. There was a scary moment when oil spattered the windshield. Lacey knew next to nothing about planes, but she knew that couldn't be good.

Luke had handled it with the composure of a well-seasoned pilot, explaining it was likely an oil leak. They'd made back to the airport just fine, but it meant Luke would spend the next morning working on the plane.

Luke lifted Lacey's duffle out of the Jeep, noting that

she let him, and placed it on a bench outside the lodge's reception area.

He took her by the shoulders, ran his warm, calloused hands down her arms before clasping her hands in his. He pulled her in for a long, potent kiss.

"I had a great time," Lacey said with a sigh, her mind now in the gutter thanks to that kiss.

"Instead of spending money for your bungalow, why don't you stay"—Luke swallowed hard—"with me?"

"I don't know, Luke. Do you really think that's a good idea?" Trying to lighten the mood, Lacey said, "Besides, are you really ready for that type of commitment? You know, my panties in your drawer, my tampons in your medicine cabinet?"

He visibly winced, making her snicker. "Yeah. I thought not." She stepped back. "Maybe it's just best if I go back to my bungalow and I'll see you in the morning."

"It'll be more like afternoon. I've got to go back to Puerto Jimenez in the morning, check on the plane."

"Oh, right. Well," she said, rising up on tiptoes, clasping his chin, and kissing him again. "Good night then." She could feel the separation begin as she picked up her duffel and headed in the direction of her bungalow.

CHAPTER TWENTY-SIX

Luke cursed up a blue streak as he drove the rough road to Puerto Jimenez to meet the mechanic. He'd rather spend the morning with Lacey, but oil leaks could be serious if they weren't found and corrected. That's why he left that kind of work up to the experts.

After a week of nightly companionship, he'd had a sleepless night. The bed had seemed cold and empty without Lacey next to him, and Sandy served as a poor substitute. "Get used to it," he admonished himself.

He usually welcomed the reprieve. Clingy females rubbed him the wrong way. But he found himself missing Lacey's company. He knew of course that she couldn't stay. She had a career, and she had to move on to her next assignment. He needed to move on as well.

But he'd finally managed to break through her protective shield, and he liked what he saw underneath: warmth, courage, and integrity. And the vulnerabilities she'd laid bare only made her more appealing.

He'd accomplished what he set out to do. Now what?

———

Rubbing her sleep-deprived eyes, Lacey tried to focus her attention on the article. She'd finally given up on sleep about four that morning. She missed the security of Luke's strong chest as she nestled into his body, the feel of his protective arms around her, even his light snores. And missing the scorching hot sex went without saying.

"Focus." The article had grown from a short human-interest piece to a full-blown article on the underserved needs of kids in Central America. Clicking through various websites she'd found a plethora of small foundations filling a myriad of needs from Mexico to Panama, but there always seemed to be more needs left unfilled.

Taking a break to pour herself more coffee, she stepped out onto the deck. Dawn broke over paradise and she was loath to miss it. Her days here were numbered. A keel-billed toucan perched in a jacaranda tree and watched her curiously. God, she would miss this place. How often could she say that about a place? And how much of that had to do with Luke?

She watched a few more minutes as the sky faded from deep violet, to fuchsia, to gold, and finally to pale blue. She leaned out over the rail to see if Luke's house was visible, but the dense vegetation blocked it from view.

She wondered if he was up, if he'd already left for the airport. Hopefully he could get the plane repaired so they could still make the 'shoe run' tomorrow. What a generous thing he did. Aviation fuel wasn't cheap, especially now. He at least deserved recognition for it.

With an idea forming in her head, she returned to the desk and started jotting down notes. *How had he gotten into these charity flights?' 'How many did he do a year?' 'How did charities find out about him, or vice versa?' 'Was there a network of pilots who volunteered?'*

Pulling up Google, she searched for 'pilot charity flights' and got over a million hits. *Wow.* After reviewing a few of the websites and making some notes, she typed in 'Luke Hancock Costa Rica.'

A fairly common name, so she got a few hits. Scrolling through the list she came across an article on economics and environmental sustainability by William Lucas Hancock, Ph.D. The same name also appeared on various environmental websites, the U.N.'s website, and the Costa Rican National Assembly's website. Her skin prickled.

Clicking on the U.N.'s Environment Programme web page she saw a decidedly more formal picture of Luke, but it was her Luke nonetheless. The caption read, 'Dr. Luke Hancock, international expert on economics and sustainability, speaks before representatives of the U.N.'s Environment Programme,' and was dated November of the previous year.

What the hell? She clicked on a link to his bio.

After earning a bachelor's degree in Environmental Sciences and a master's degree in Environmental Risk Analysis from the University of Southern California, Dr. Lucas Hancock went on to obtain his Ph.D. in Economics and Environmental Sciences from U.C. Santa Barbara.

Dr. Hancock has published numerous articles on economics and sustainability, focusing primarily on enhancing eco-tourism in Central America. He has consulted for international environmental groups such as World Wildlife Fund and The Nature Conservancy.

The more she read, the angrier she got. Why wouldn't

he have told her? She cringed at the memory of their fight when she'd called him a devil-may-care beach bum who needed to get a real job. Come to think of it, with his education and expertise, why did he choose to bury himself in the jungles of Costa Rica as some glorified bush pilot?

She stood to pace her bungalow. What else hadn't he bothered to tell her? Maybe he had a wife somewhere. Maybe he'd lied to her about not having kids. Maybe these charity flights weren't for charity after all. What, did he create a different persona for each woman he slept with?

How dare he? "Tell me, *querida*. Tell me all your deep dark secrets," she mimicked. While he kept choice bits of information, important information, about himself a secret.

"Damn." She'd let him in, let her emotions get the better of her. She'd been such an idiot. Well, that would end now. At least this would make it easier to leave.

Her bungalow suddenly closed in on her. She needed a good long run. She tugged on her running shoes knowing she could ask herself questions all day and not discover the answer.

What had moments earlier seemed like paradise now seemed more akin to hell. Apparently even paradise was a state of mind. She was reminded of Milton's line from *Paradise Lost*: *'The mind is its own place, and in itself, can make a heav'n of hell, a hell of heav'n.'*

She began running even before she left the resort gates. She heard Jill calling her name, but she just picked up the pace.

She ignored the voice in her head that accused her of overreacting, that said if she hadn't been so blinded by her own prejudices she might have asked him about his profession, his life. Instead, she'd just assumed he was a smart but uneducated beach bum and guide. Not that his education mattered to her, because it didn't. But the fact that he'd never bothered to tell her did. He let her preserve her prejudices against him.

And that's his fault? a voice asked. She ignored the voice again.

Lacey let her breathing and the sound of her feet hitting the dirt road that led to the beach take her mind off her anger, and her hurt. Then the sound of the surf and the wind filled her ears. She forced herself to look straight ahead as she passed Luke's house, heard Sandy's deep bark.

Clouds built in the moist atmosphere, billowing into towering thunderheads. She'd welcome an all-out tempest right now. It suited her mood. When would she learn she was better off on her own, pursuing her career, avoiding complicated entanglements? As for the article, she'd just bag it. She was a photographer, not a writer.

Thunder rumbled overhead. A fat raindrop landed on her nose. The wind rose. She kept running.

She wasn't the type to sit behind a desk anyway. She needed to be outside, she needed the thrill of danger. Always had. Maybe that was the problem. She'd been lollygagging here. She'd grown far too soft. That's why she'd given in to Luke's charm. Well no more. Lacey Sommers, tough girl, was back.

Pleased with her resolve, she turned back to the resort just as lightening pierced the sky and the heavens opened up.

By the time she got back to the bungalow, she was soaked, panting, and determined. She would tell Luke she was leaving tomorrow.

After a hot shower, she sat down to send an email to Simon, only to see she'd received one from him instead, with the subject line: 'New Assignment ASAP' and an exclamation point marking the message 'urgent'.

> *Lacey,*
>
> *You need to get to Nassau, Bahamas, ASAP. Steve was there shooting photos for a story on the shark- diving business when he got drunk at a bar and fell*
>
> *and broke his leg. Bonehead. Anyway, if you can get to San José by tomorrow or the next day, I can get you to Nassau via private jet.*
>
> *Time is of the essence.*
>
> *Simon*

Shark diving. Lacey grinned. Perfect. A chance to use her diving skills *and* her underwater photography skills. She'd been hoping for this type of assignment.

She sent an email to Simon telling him she was on it and would get back to him with the details of her itinerary. Then she grabbed her duffle bag, which she'd yet to unpack from her trip to Drake Bay, and began stuffing her things into it.

She supposed she'd have to ask Luke to fly her to San José, although she didn't look forward to that. She wanted to say goodbye to Allie and Tony too, but maybe it was best to just leave. She hated goodbyes anyway.

CHAPTER TWENTY-SEVEN

L acey called "Come in" to the knock on her door, expecting housekeeping, or even Jill, since she hadn't stopped to see what she'd wanted earlier. Instead, Luke stepped through the door, wet and disheveled. And looking about as sexy as she'd seen him look.

"Hey, Lace." His warm greeting skidded to a halt as he surveyed the room in confusion. "Going somewhere?" he asked quietly. He had a sick feeling in his gut.

She returned to her packing, trying to keep her pulse under control. "Well, if it isn't *Dr.* Hancock, international expert on economics and the environment."

He cringed. "Lacey, I can explain." Cringing again, he thought he sounded like a guy who'd just been caught with another woman.

"Here you've been beseeching me to tell you my deepest secrets, when all along you haven't been honest with me. I feel like I don't even know you." Lacey's eyes stung with tears, but she refused to let him see her cry over him. "You know what, Hancock, it doesn't matter." She waved her hand in dismissal.

Luke took a step forward, reaching his hand out to touch her shoulder, but dropped it. So he was 'Hancock' again.

"It's not like we had a relationship or anything, right?" she continued, cramming more clothes into her bag. "It was just great sex."

She might as well have kicked him in the stomach. His breath left in a rush, leaving him deflated. The last five days hadn't meant anything to her. Just sex.

He couldn't overlook the irony of the situation. He supposed he deserved it. How many times had he been on the giving end of this same conversation? Now he knew how it felt to be on the receiving end.

"Where're you going?" he asked softly.

"Bahamas. To cover a shark-diving story."

"Are you fucking crazy?" He spun her to face him, grabbing her by her shoulders. "You're going down where you'll be surrounded by blood-thirsty sharks after what you've been through? You're just asking for flashbacks and more nightmares."

"It's my job. Now let go of me."

He dropped his hands from her shoulders, but he didn't back up. He could smell her scent, feel the heat of her anger rolling off her. "Jesus, woman!" He raked his hands through his damp hair, before turning to stride away from her. He had to get some distance before he threw her onto the bed.

"Even diving in a cage won't keep the flashbacks at bay."

At her silence, he glanced back at her. Eyes wide, she avoided looking him in the face. Her expression told him everything. "You won't be in a cage." He could barely get the words out, his breathlessness making it difficult to speak.

"Jesus, Lacey, when will you realize you don't have anything to prove?"

But she did. Lacey returned to her packing. "It's safe. They have divers armed with spear guns to protect you." Her voice sounded small.

"Bullshit! Did you know a client died a couple of months ago? Had his leg bitten off by a tiger shark, bled to death before they could get him medical attention?" His legs felt weak. The thought of Lacey, with no cage to protect her, diving among chum-frenzied sharks made his blood go cold.

Luke stepped up behind her. "That's why your magazine's covering the story."

"The 'why' doesn't matter. I just take the photos."

"I won't let you go," Luke said so quietly he didn't know whether Lacey heard him. Her reaction confirmed she had.

"*You* don't have any say in this." Her eyes spit blue fire as she turned on him, pointing her finger at his chest. "It's none of your goddamned business. Just because we slept together doesn't mean you can control my life, *Dr.* Hancock. Now, if you don't mind, I have things to do. I leave tomorrow."

"And just how do you plan to get to San José?"

"You," she replied, brow lifted, as if it was obvious.

He shook his head. "I have a charity flight tomorrow. I'm not bagging that." Before she could speak, he continued. "And even if I wasn't already booked, I wouldn't take you. Not if you're going to be so goddamned reckless."

"Fuck you, then," she said, turning back to throw more clothes into her duffle.

"You already did," Luke shot back.

Recoiling as if she'd been slapped, she could feel tears stinging her eyes. "Get out."

He slammed the door behind him. Her gaze landed on Luke's paintings before she sank to the bed and wept.

———

"What's eating you?" Tony asked.

"Nothing," Luke answered as he scowled into his coffee cup. Even after he'd gone to bed sometime around three a.m., he'd failed to fall asleep, greeting the dawn with a massive headache and no closer to figuring out how to get Lacey to stay. One hell of a way to spend New Year's Eve. He'd gone from the best Christmas to the worst New Year's in the space of a week.

After he'd left Lacey, he'd considered going to the bar and drowning his sorrows, but he didn't want to fly with a hangover. And he didn't want to run into Lacey. Instead, he'd resorted to a run on the beach with Sandy, a long swim, and making some repairs on the Jeep.

Every time he thought of Lacey surrounded by sharks, he felt physically ill. It wasn't just the physical danger she would be in, but the emotional danger as well. What if she had a flashback? What if she had another panic attack like the one she'd had in Tanzania? She could lose more than just her job this time.

He and Tony sat at Luke's breakfast table, neat little color-coded spreadsheets filled with numbers courtesy of Allie spread around them. He didn't have the patience for numbers today. Hell, he didn't have the patience for much of anything.

"Is it Lacey again? Man, I've never seen you give so much thought to a woman before." Tony took a sip of his coffee, then gestured to Luke with it. "I think you've lost your edge."

Luke frowned, anger starting to bubble up inside him, mixing with the impatience for a volatile cocktail. "What do you mean?"

"Well, you were just looking to get in her pants, right? So what do you care about the emotional or psychological baggage she's carrying? It's her body you wanted, it's her body you got." He shrugged.

"Damn, Tony, I never knew you to be so shallow."

"It's not called being shallow, it's called being realistic. Your track record with relationships isn't exactly stellar. They never last longer than a guiding job—one week—two at the most. Just long enough to sweat it out between the sheets, and then she's gone, never to hear from you again. Why should this time be any different?"

"Back off, Tony," Luke ground out.

Tony continued, seemingly oblivious to the storm brewing inside his friend. "She's just another piece of ass, right?"

"You son-of-a-bitch!" Luke shot to his feet, knocking his chair over and startling Sandy, who'd been sleeping beneath it.

He stalked across the kitchen away from his friend, fists clinched, afraid he'd punch Tony's lights out if he stood too close.

Tony hadn't moved an inch, even in response to Luke's outburst. His comment had elicited the desired effect. Luke's actions told him more than words ever could how his best friend felt about Lacey.

"Lacey's not just another . . ." Luke sputtered, unable to say the words, "she deserves to be treated with respect. Do you have any idea what she's been through? The hell she's witnessed?" *And been subjected to,* he thought. He raked his hands through his hair as he glanced back at Tony. "What the hell's the matter with you anyway?"

"Have you told her?" Tony asked quietly, as he fiddled with the salt shaker.

"Told her what?" Luke bit out.

"That you love her?"

CHAPTER TWENTY-EIGHT

Luke started the engine of his Piper Cherokee. The flight to the northern Caribbean coast would take him less than an hour. He'd hang out with the kids, help the volunteers pass out the shoes. Maybe the joy of the day would wipe away some of the funk from yesterday.

As he gained altitude, he thought about his conversation with Tony that morning. His outburst over Tony's comments had shocked the hell of out him. He loved Lacey. And it took his best friend's well-aimed remarks to make him realize it.

Since the day she'd provoked that crocodile, Luke had felt the desire, no, the need, to protect her. From vicious reptiles and seemingly runaway horses, from the memories and demons that powered her nightmares, from Tony's deceptively crude remarks. And now from herself.

He knew for a fact that she wouldn't be leaving Puerto Jimenez today. All the other charters were booked. That would at least give her the day to cool off. Then he'd go see her tonight. Apologize for being an ass. Ask her to stay. Hell, *beg* her to stay if that's what it took.

Pleased with his plan, even though he hadn't gotten past the begging her to stay part, he settled in for an easy flight. He'd be landing in the same field as before, where kids and their families would be waiting, and no doubt his friend, Akili.

Thirty minutes into the flight, a loud bang, like a loose wrench being sucked up by the engine, interrupted his musings. The engine began to run rough as smoke billowed from the engine compartment. "Well, shit." No sooner were the words out of his mouth that the engine locked-up and the prop froze. Then all he could hear was the wind passing over and under the wings.

The mountains were no place for an emergency landing. He needed to get over the central highlands first. He knew he could probably glide five, maybe ten miles, so he wouldn't make it to the planned landing spot.

"Holy hell." *Okay,* he told himself, *I can do this. I've trained for this.* He worked to keep the Piper in a glide, nose down, wings level.

He radioed Air Traffic Control, gave them his heading, and told them he'd had a catastrophic engine failure and was looking for a spot to land. So much for an easy flight.

Where was a nice environmentally irresponsible golf course when you needed one? He scanned the horizon. He just needed to find a field, a dirt road, crop land, anything flat and open. He checked his descent rate. Not bad. Scanning the horizon again for a break in the trees, he spotted a field of some sort off his left wing, narrow but doable. If he could reach it.

The trick was to land as slowly as possible without stalling. If he lost airflow over the wings, the plane would crash. Not a good scenario.

He only had one shot, so it better be good. He gripped

the yoke as the field came into view. "Easy does it." Sweat poured off him, making his hands slick. He had to keep the nosewheel off the ground as long as possible to prevent it from flipping the plane. He had to touch down close to the near end of the makeshift runway, leaving enough room to stop the plane and avoid crashing into the encroaching forest.

The plane touched. He kept the nose up until it came down on its own. So far so good, but he was running out of space. Then he saw it, a big hole, gouged in the middle of the field. Luke had no way to avoid it. He had no room on either side. The wings barely cleared the forest. He braced himself for impact as the nosewheel hit the hole, shearing it off with a grinding crunch.

The sudden halt of the forward momentum sent the nose plunging into the ground, before the plane cartwheeled. Luke lost his grip on the yoke. His head hit the doorframe with a sickening thud and pain shot through his arm as the plane tumbled to the edge of the woods.

Lacey's face was the last thing Luke saw before everything went black.

CHAPTER TWENTY-NINE

Lacey sat at the bar drinking a Café Rica and coffee, it being too early for tequila. Probably inappropriate to show up for her new assignment smashed, anyway. She'd been utterly miserable yesterday, and that New Year's Eve had sucked was a given.

Jill was kind enough to drive her to Puerto Jimenez for her flight to San José. It would have been so much easier if she could have left New Year's Day as planned. She tried, unsuccessfully, not to think about Luke. Not to wonder how his flight went. She also tried not to admit how much she missed seeing the kids, taking pictures, talking to them, witnessing their joy at receiving their new shoes.

She had a typed note in an envelope on the bar. It had all the information Luke would need to get his father's money, but no words of regret or even a goodbye.

Part of her had hoped that Luke would come by, tell her about his flight. But after their fight, who could blame him? She'd overreacted. She knew that now. She'd just been looking for an excuse to put some distance between them.

And she'd succeeded. Pouring a little more Café Rica in her coffee, she took a swig.

Jill came toward her, car keys in hand. Now it was too late. She'd never see Luke again.

"Ready?" Jill asked. Lacey stood and reached into her bag to pay for her coffee, but Jill waved her away and said, "On the house."

Before Lacey could thank her, Tony flew through the door as if his hair was on fire. "Lacey!" he called, out of breath. "Thank God I caught you." Before she could ask him what happened, he continued. "Luke never made it yesterday. We think . . . we think his plane went down."

Jill gasped, her hand to her mouth.

"What?" Lacey's knees felt weak and she could hear her pulse pounding in her ears. The room seemed to go dim. Tony and Jill grabbed her by the arms and drew her to a chair.

"You okay?" Tony asked as he chaffed her now-cold hands.

"Your color isn't good."

"Philippe, get Lacey some water," Jill instructed, "and a damp cloth."

"When?" Her own voice sounded so far away.

"Yesterday."

"Yesterday! And you're just now telling me?" She was frantic. Had they found the wreckage? Was he . . . she couldn't even think about that.

"Lace, it was chaos. Air traffic sent up a plane when they lost radio contact but they didn't find anything. We didn't learn about it until almost dark. By then it was too late to send up search planes. They're in the air now. Allie and I have been at the office all night with the other pilots planning the search and waiting for news."

Jill handed Lacey the water, then placed the cool cloth behind her neck. "Drink."

Lacey gulped down the water and almost immediately felt nauseous. This couldn't be happening. It had to be a mistake. Or maybe she was having a nightmare. That was it —a nightmare. She was used to those.

Tears filled her eyes as she thought about their last words to one another. She squeezed her eyes shut and tears ran down her cheeks. *Okay. This isn't helping.* She needed to get it together. She took a deep breath, brushed away the tears, and removed the cloth from her neck. "I'm okay." She looked at Tony. "What's being done? What's the plan?"

"We have planes in the air. Thankfully Luke filed a flight plan. That makes it a little easier, unless he veered off course." He muttered the last. "He was east of the mountains when he radioed, so odds are he found somewhere to land."

"Then why can't they find him? Why can't they radio him?"

"Lacey, the forest is thick. There are places he could land, fields, dirt roads, but sometimes they're not so easy to spot." He glanced at Jill. "It's possible his radio is busted."

Lacey knew what that might mean. That he hadn't managed a soft landing. That there might be damage to the plane. That he could be hurt, or worse, dead.

Tony knelt in front of Lacey, gazing into her tear-filled eyes. "Look, Luke is a seasoned pilot. He knows what to do in these situations. He's going to be fine. He *is* fine."

The way he said it, Lacey knew he was trying to convince himself too.

"I have to get back," Tony added.

"I'm coming with you."

"What about your assignment?" Tony asked, although he knew the answer.

"Fuck it."

———

Lacey paced the Environmental Expeditions office. She felt so helpless, just waiting, worrying. She wanted to be doing something. She wanted to be in one of those search and rescue planes, but before he'd left for the airport where search operations were set up, Tony'd said no.

They needed experienced eyes in those seats, Tony had explained, eyes trained to spot fields and roads suitable for landing. Eyes that could find debris fields. He'd left the last part unsaid, but Lacey knew that's what he meant.

"Lace, come sit down," Allie insisted. "We've got the area's best pilots up there. If anyone can find Luke, they can."

It was almost four p.m. How long could it take to find a plane in a country that would fit inside the State of Texas? And not even the whole country, but the northeast corner of it. Then she remembered the dense forest that covered that area. So remote, so isolated. She dropped into Luke's chair, exhausted, heavy with fear.

She looked across the desk at Allie. "What if . . . what if they can't find him today? What if he's hurt? What if he's . . .?" She broke down.

Allie came around the desk, then wrapped her arms around Lacey's shoulders. "Shh, *querida*."

The endearment only made her cry harder. "Oh God. I've been so stupid," she sobbed, "so stubborn. I love him. I love him. And I never told him."

Allie cupped Lacey's face, brushing the tears away with her thumb. "You will."

The phone rang, making them both jump. Allie made a grab for the phone. "*Hola.*" She paused to listen to the voice on the other end. "*Sí.*"

Then she began talking so fast, Lacey couldn't follow her. While Lacey's Spanish was decent, Allie's warp speed made it impossible to understand. She caught 'Tony', 'plane', 'San José', and 'hospital'.

God, she thought she would burst before Allie told her the news. Allie hung up the phone, grabbing her purse in the process.

"They found him."

Lacey's hand flew to her stomach. She'd been waiting for those words all day, but now she was afraid of what they'd found. "Is he . . .?" She was so breathless, she couldn't finish the question.

"I don't know what his condition is. They've flown him to a hospital in San José. Let's go. There's a helicopter at the airport waiting for us."

CHAPTER THIRTY

Lacey didn't recall the flight to San José taking so long. It seemed a lifetime. She fought to control her fears, focusing on her breathing. Then she wondered how she would ever breathe again if she lost Luke. Allie squeezed her hand.

Tony glanced back at the two of them from his seat next to the pilot, and reaching back, gave their clasped hands a gentle squeeze of his own.

When she and Allie had reached the Puerto Jimenez airport for the flight to San José, Lacey couldn't believe all the people milling around. Several small planes and two helicopters sat on the runway. It looked like a command station for a natural disaster.

Allie had hugged Lacey to her, explaining, "Luke is well-respected . . . and well loved. As soon as they heard, they volunteered to help."

Touched, Lacey vowed she would personally thank each and every one of them. No matter the outcome.

A car from one of Environmental Expeditions' competitors waited at the airport to whisk them away to the hospital. Lacey practically dove from the car when it reached the hospital's parking lot. Running inside, she stopped at the front desk. "Luke Hancock, *por favor.*"

The clerked flipped through a list. She just shook her head.

What the hell did that mean? That he didn't make it? Lacey worked to get her emotions under control before she started screaming at the clerk.

Tony and Allie walked up behind Lacey and Allie asked politely but firmly if they had a William Lucas Hancock.

The clerk told Allie he was being treated in the Emergency Room, and they would have to wait. Lacey's frustration rose. Allie gave her a look and then leaned over the desk to ask a question, blocking Lacey from view.

Lacey turned and dashed through the open doors leading to the treatment area, shoving curtains aside until she heard 'plane crash'.

She crossed to the other room, and froze outside the curtain, her hands pressed against her stomach. Now that she was there, she was afraid to move the curtain. Afraid of what she'd see. Afraid he wouldn't want to see her. It didn't matter. She had to assure herself he was okay. If he threw her out, then so be it.

She slipped behind the curtain. Machines beeped, lights flashed. A doctor stood in front of the bed, blocking Lacey's view. A nurse hovered on the other side, her gloves bloody.

Lacey gasped. The doctor and the nurse turned to look at her. The doctor frowned as the nurse tried to escort her from the room, soundly reprimanding her.

"Wait." The voice was hoarse, raspy, but she'd recognize it anywhere. "Let her stay."

Lacey's heart soared. He was alive! The doctor stepped aside and Lacey got her first look at Luke. He had a gash on his forehead, a black eye that was almost swollen shut. His left arm was in a sling, and he had an IV in the right arm. He had a busted lip and stitches on the back of his left hand. He'd never looked better.

"Lacey." Luke held out his good hand to her. She wasted no time getting to his side.

"Oh, Luke," she breathed. Her eyes filled with tears. "You're not going to go all mushy on me are you?"

"Yes. Yes, I am." And for the first time she didn't care who saw her cry. "Are you . . . all right?"

The doctor spoke in English as he studied Luke's chart. "Aside from the obvious injuries, he's got a concussion, some broken ribs, a dislocated shoulder, and he's dehydrated and mosquito-bitten from his overnight stay in the jungle. But other than that, he'll be fine."

"I'm much better now that you're here." He grasped her hand and squeezed. "I'm so sorry, Lace."

"Shh. Don't." She brushed a tear away. "I'm the one who should be sorry. I'm the one who acted like an idiot."

"No. It was me."

"Now that we've established you were both *idiotas*," the doctor interjected, "we need to get Mr. Hancock to his room."

"That's *Dr.* Hancock." She smiled at Luke through her tears.

"Fine. Dr. Hancock."

Two orderlies appeared at the curtain.

"Stay with me. Please," Luke whispered.

"I wouldn't leave your side even if you wanted me to."

Lacey moved alongside the gurney, her hand clasped tightly in Luke's. She gasped. "Tony and Allie! They must be worried sick." She was mortified that she'd been so selfish.

Luke spoke to one of the orderlies and asked if he would send his friends up to his room. After answering in the affirmative, the orderly walked in the direction of the waiting room.

Moments later, Luke was settled into his room amid much cursing and groaning as the orderly and a nurse shifted him to his bed.

As soon as she could, Lacey took Luke's hand in hers, concern for him written all over her face. "You okay?"

"I've been better. But I've also been worse." Especially when he thought he'd never see her again. He gazed into her eyes and gestured for her to lean down. Cupping her face in his hand, he murmured, "My brave, sweet, Lacey. My God how I love you."

Lacey laughed through her tears. She did get her chance to tell him. "I love you." She couldn't remember crying so much in her life as she had these last few weeks. But these were tears of joy, tears of relief.

"I can't get down on my knee at this moment, but I've waited too long and I don't want to wait anymore . . . marry me."

Lacey drew in a sharp breath, not expecting those words. Releasing her indrawn breath on sigh, she said the only thing she was capable of saying at that moment, "Yes."

"It's about damned time," Tony said as he strode into the room, Allie beaming by his side.

Allie crossed the room to give Lacey a hug. "Congratulations, *chica*." She left her arm around Lacey, gathering her close.

"God, you look like hell," Tony said, but the look on his

face belied his words. His eyes glittered with unshed tears, the worry of the last twenty-four hours carved into his face.

"You should see the other guy." Luke tried to smile but winced and touched his lip. "The plane's a wreck—wing's broken off at the root, nosewheel is gone, fuselage is . . .well, let's just say I got the better end of the stick."

Luke knew the plane was beyond repair. Their business would take a heavy hit without the flight services, and he couldn't afford a new plane right now.

But he had too many blessings to count. He'd survived, Lacey had come for him, and she'd agreed to marry him. A new year, a new life.

"What the hell happened? Was it the oil leak?" Tony asked as he perched on the foot of the bed.

"No. I think a cylinder blew a gasket. I'm just lucky I was on the eastern side of the mountains. God only knows where I would have landed otherwise." He squeezed Lacey's hand when she looked at him aghast.

"Doesn't matter now," he continued. "I'm safe, and I'm. . . I'm getting married." He laughed in disbelief at his own statement, then winced again, this time his hand going to his ribs.

Allie began making wedding plans. She knew the best shop in San José to get Lacey's dress, and hers too, of course. She had a friend in Puerto Jimenez with a floral shop, and Jill and Karl could handle the food.

As Allie chattered on about the wedding, Lacey looked around the room at her friends, and her new fiancée, and felt deep down that she belonged here. This was home.

A couple of months after all traces of Luke's injuries had vanished, she and Luke were married in a quiet barefoot ceremony on the beach surrounded by their friends and family.

Lacey couldn't believe her mother made the trip. Although horrified by her daughter's 'jungle wedding,' her mother had withstood the grueling journey and the hardship of living *sans* blow-dryer and curling iron because in her words, "I wouldn't believe Lacey was getting married until I saw it with my own two eyes."

Lilia and her husband and their two daughters also made the journey, arriving none-the-worse for wear.

Gregory Sommers considered it an adventure, relishing the opportunity to check out the real estate market in Costa Rica. Lacey's heart melted when her father put his hand out and Luke took it, giving her father a firm, welcoming handshake.

Even Luke's father, Mike, finally buried the proverbial hatchet. Luke claimed his father's settlement and placed it in a trust for him. The first thing his father did with the money was buy a small house not far from Luke's. The two had been practically inseparable ever since. In fact, his father would now handle the travel arrangements for Luke's clients, giving him a new purpose and meaning to his life.

Luke's mother and stepfather also joined the wedding party. His mother and father had remained friends after their divorce, thus alleviating the tension that so often accompanied mixed family gatherings.

Lacey thought Allie looked breathtaking, glowing from the inside out, her ever-growing baby bump the reason. Although she didn't know who glowed more, Allie or Tony. Tony clearly relished his father-to-be status, handing out cigars, despite Allie's reminder that one didn't do that until the child's birth.

Lacey had found a use for her own trust-fund money: pouring it into Luke's business by purchasing a new plane and upgrading their computer system. And not only did she not dive with the sharks, she gave up her pursuit of the next most dangerous assignment and quit her job altogether.

She'd taken Luke's advice, and her blog, *Good Vibrations*, increased its followers on a daily basis. Talks with a Central American news service about incorporating her blog into their website were ongoing.

In six months, her life had changed drastically—for the better. She'd come to Costa Rica to save her career, but she'd saved herself instead. Or had Luke rescued her, instead?

ABOUT THE AUTHOR

Rebecca Heflin is a bestselling, award-winning author who has dreamed of writing romantic fiction since she was fifteen and her older sister sneaked a copy of Kathleen Woodiwiss' Shanna to her and told her to read it.

Never quite sure what she wanted to be when she grew up, Rebecca didn't attend college until age 30, and earned her bachelor's in literature, before going on to complete her law degree.

Ever the late bloomer, Rebecca finally turned her attention to fulfilling her dream of writing, and published her first novel at age 48. When not passionately pursuing her dream, Rebecca is busy with her day-job at a major state university.

She and her husband are also co-founders of a non-profit organization, which raises money to help cancer patients and their families.

Rebecca's pen name is an abbreviated version of her great-great grandmother's name: Sarah Anne Rebecca Heflin Apple Smith. Whew! And you wonder why she shortened it.

Rebecca writes women's fiction and contemporary

romance, and she is a member of Romance Writers of America (RWA), Florida Romance Writers, RWA Contemporary Romance, and Florida Writers Association. Rebecca and her mountain-climbing husband live at sea level in sunny Florida.

Sign up for Rebecca's monthly newsletter, Rebecca's Readers, for all the latest news on upcoming releases, appearances, and contests.

facebook.com/RebeccaHeflinBooks

bookbub.com/authors/rebecca-heflin

goodreads.com/goodreadscomrebecca_heflin

pinterest.com/rheflinbooks

amazon.com/Rebecca-Heflin/e/B006RBM93C/ref=dp_byline_cont_pop_e-books_1

THE PROMISE OF CHANGE

DREAMS COME TRUE SERIES

DREAMS OF PERFECTION, BOOK 1

SHIP OF DREAMS, BOOK 2

DREAMS OF HER OWN, BOOK 3

STERLING UNIVERSITY SERIES

ROMANCING DR. LOVE, BOOK 1

WINNING DR. WENTWORTH, BOOK 2

EDUCATING DR. MAYFIELD, BOOK 3

SEASONS OF NORTHRIDGE SERIES

A SEASON TO DANCE, BOOK 1

A SEASON TO LOVE, BOOK 2

A SEASON TO REMEMBER, BOOK 3